Julie Wassmer is a professional television drama writer who has worked on various series including ITV's *London's Burning*, C5's *Family Affairs* and BBC's *Eastenders* – which she wrote for almost 20 years.

Her autobiography, *More Than Just Coincidence*, was Mumsnet Book of the Year

MURDER Fest

A Whitstable Pearl Mystery

JULIE WASSMER

CONSTABLE

CONSTABLE

First published in Great Britain in 2019 by Constable

Typeset in Caslon Pro by SX Composing DTP, Rayleigh, Essex
Printed and bound in Great Britain by CPI Group (UK) Ltd, Croydon CRO 4YY

Papers used by Constable are from well-managed forests
and other responsible sources.

Constable
An imprint of
Little, Brown Book Group
Carmelite House
50 Victoria Embankment
London EC4Y 0DZ

An Hachette UK Company
www.hachette.co.uk

www.littlebrown.co.uk

For the Annable family and the town of Borken

'Art is the lie that makes us realise truth.'

Pablo Picasso

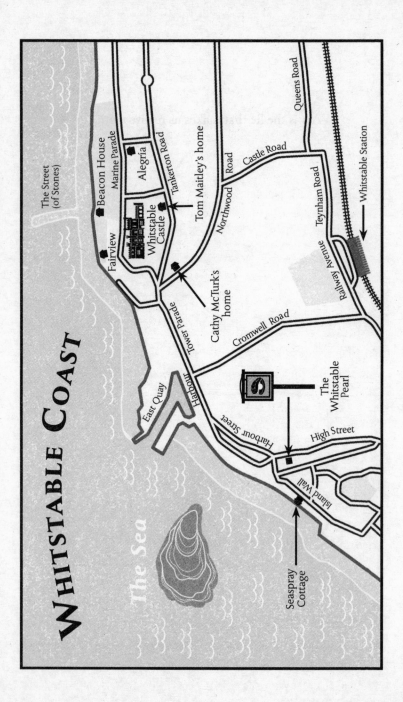

Prologue

Seaspray Cottage, Whitstable, June

It was early morning; the summer sun had barely risen. Pearl Nolan gazed up at Mike McGuire as he lay propped on one arm beside her, toying with a ringlet of her long gipsy-black hair that was spread across a white lace pillow. Outside Pearl's bedroom window, waves could be heard softly lapping upon the shoreline. The detective's ice-blue eyes scanned Pearl's features. 'Feels like I'm dreaming,' he said. 'After all this time?' He had been out of her life for several weeks. Nothing too unusual for the busy Canterbury police officer, except Pearl herself detected that something seemed to have shifted on his return, something indefinable, but it was there in his eyes and in his touch.

'You're here now,' she said.

McGuire nodded and his strong hand gently framed her cheek. For a moment Pearl thought he was about to kiss her, then he suddenly paused, as though struck by an idea. 'Look, I'm owed some leave,' he said. 'We should get away. Take a trip somewhere. Give things a chance.'

'Things?'

'Us.'

He allowed the word to sit there for a moment between them, before he finally leaned in again, his face lowering to fill her view. Pearl felt her body arching beneath him but in that same moment, the raw cries of a noisy seagull on the beach suddenly melded into another sound.

Opening her eyes, Pearl saw that her smartphone on the bedside table was buzzing her early-morning alarm. She reached out and silenced it. With the morning sunlight streaming into the room, McGuire had vanished, but a tabby cat by the name of Sprat was kneading a section of duvet on which his three-legged brother, Pilchard, had already made a comfortable bed for himself. On seeing Pearl awake, the cats gave a curious look, as though recognising the expression on their owner's face, a mixture of confusion and disappointment; the kind of look, in fact, that a cat might give on recognising its prey had somehow managed to escape . . .

Chapter One

Two weeks later

'I can't believe you volunteered me for this without asking.' Pearl Nolan was brandishing her smartphone in front of her friend and neighbour, Nathan Roscoe. On its screen was an e-mail she had received that morning. Nathan glanced at it then noted Pearl's frustration and the fact that her long dark curls were still glistening wet from her morning shower as she added: 'And you're not even going to be here.'

She waited impatiently for his response but Nathan took his time, carefully packing a pair of stylish shirts into an equally stylish suitcase on his bed, before he pointed out calmly, and in the relaxed mid-Atlantic accent he had acquired during the twenty or so years he had lived in Whitstable: 'I recommended you, Pearl. There's a difference.'

As Pearl watched Nathan close his suitcase she felt

conflicted, because Nathan had only just returned from a trip to Paris where he had been doing research for a travel article he had been commissioned to write. She had missed him, as she always did when he was away. He was her best friend, after all, and if he hadn't been gay, he could have been so much more to her; but now he was off to Glyndebourne for some opera and, instead of enjoying these last few moments with him, she was taking him to task for having saddled her with a commitment . . .

'Do you know how many people are meant to be coming to this event?' she asked.

Nathan remained unperturbed. 'Droves, I'd imagine,' he said casually. 'Your reputation goes before you. Who *wouldn't* want to sample food from The Whitstable Pearl?'

Having sweetened his compliment with a sugary smile, he saw she wasn't appeased. 'OK,' he sighed. 'So, just say no – stand aside and let some flashy restaurant on the beach take over and gain all the kudos from this event—'

'Kudos?' echoed Pearl, curious.

Nathan now gave her his full attention. 'This isn't any old bunfight, sweetie,' he explained. 'Whit Fest promises to be a comprehensive festival of our local arts, and its launch will be prestigious. Those representatives from that German twinning association will be taking back with them a full report of everything Whitstable has to offer: fine art, literature, music . . . *and* local cuisine.'

He pointed at her. 'The whole town is relying on you, my darling.' Then: 'As is poor Heather Fox. She's run herself ragged trying to get this off the ground – *and* take care of her sick father at the same time.' He allowed a moment for that thought to settle.

Pearl sighed. 'No pressure then.'

'Look, it really *is* your decision,' he continued. 'But, even at this late hour, you could still rise to the challenge? You always do. Besides,' he went on, 'as it's your restaurant, I'm sure you can invite a few special guests of your own.' He slipped his packed suitcase from the bed before offering two more words. 'Inspector McGee?'

'McGuire,' said Pearl, pointedly. Her eyes narrowed with suspicion. 'Why is it you can never get his name right?'

Nathan remained silent as he checked his appearance in one of the mirrored doors of his wardrobe, smoothing a hand through his chestnut-brown hair and examining a few silver strands at his temples. He wasn't the only person in Pearl's life who failed to give due respect to the Canterbury police detective by correctly remembering DCI Mike McGuire's name. Pearl's mother, Dolly, only ever used the pejorative term 'the Flat Foot' when referring to him – and that thought also now rankled for Pearl.

'Well?' she asked.

Nathan turned, and noted her peeved expression. He decided to make amends.

'All right. So, maybe I'm scared of losing you to him.'
Pearl's expression was pure shock. 'To McGuire?'

'Don't look so surprised! You make a beautiful couple.
You're all dark fury, like Cathy in *Wuthering Heights* and
he's . . .' Nathan paused. 'Well, he's tall, blond and . . . if
he ever leaves the police force, he could make a fortune
giving handsome lessons.' He raised a well-groomed
eyebrow. 'Isn't it about time you were more than just . . .
partners in crime?'

Pearl turned away from Nathan's knowing gaze and
confessed: 'Chance'd be a fine thing.' She slumped down
on the bed. 'If it's not his police work getting in the way,
it's my life.' As she began idly stroking Nathan's brand-
new taupe bedspread, he sat down beside her, concerned
both for Pearl and his bedspread. He took her hand.
'What is it, sweetie?'

She looked at him. 'We were planning to go away.
For a long weekend. A city break in Amsterdam. But
then—'

'Don't tell me,' Nathan broke in with a sense of fore-
boding. 'Someone got murdered?'

Pearl shook her head. 'Charlie got himself on a
summer course in animation and I ended up having to
drive him to Dorset.'

Nathan looked sidelong at her, convinced she was
teasing him. 'Sweetie, your son is twenty-one years old
and there *are* trains to Dorset.'

'But you didn't see what he took with him,' Pearl
protested. 'It barely fitted in my car.' She paused. 'When

I got back I found a text from McGuire explaining that he'd been assigned to some high-profile robbery case – *and* has a new DS.'

Nathan looked at her blankly. Pearl explained: 'Detective Sergeant Terry Bosley.' She gave a huff and went on: 'No doubt they'll be all buddied up by now. Racing around the county, chasing leads.'

Nathan looked decidedly unimpressed. 'That's what cops do on TV, sweetie, but I don't imagine it's half as much fun as you think.'

Nathan was well aware of Pearl's former ambitions to become a fully fledged police detective, and how an unplanned pregnancy had put paid to them. At the tender age of nineteen, and while showing real promise in putting her natural people skills to use with the CID, Pearl had given up on her police training and returned instead to her home town of Whitstable in order to bring up her beloved son, Charlie. Two decades on, and the unpretentious seafood restaurant that bore her name had become one of Whitstable's most popular eateries, with a selection of signature dishes that included squid encased in a light chilli tempura batter, marinated sashimi of tuna, mackerel and wild salmon, and a popular staple of sardines with garlic and chilli *ajillo*. One thing, however, always remained in popular demand, the single item that defined this little north Kent town which might have gone quite unnoticed without it: its native oyster. Over the course of twenty years, Pearl's dishes had come to satisfy the tastes of locals and visitors alike, but two years ago she had found herself at a crossroads when Charlie moved to Canterbury to begin a degree at Kent University, leaving his mother with an empty nest. Recognising the need for a new challenge in the next stage in her life, Pearl had started up her own detective agency – Nolan's – and Mike McGuire had entered her life.

'Well, I'm sure Inspector McGoo—' Nathan was suddenly silenced by Pearl's look. 'McGuire,' he then continued, 'will un-buddy himself before too long and find his way back here to regale you with stories about his case? But, until then, you have this *fabulous* event to cater – and I'm sure you'll exceed *all* expectations.' He smiled, rather too smugly for Pearl's liking, so she chose to remind him: 'I haven't actually agreed to do this.' She indicated the e-mail still on the screen of the smartphone in her hand. 'But I *have* replied to your friend, Heather, to say I'll pop round later for a chat.'

'Good,' said Nathan. He looked at his suitcase then at Pearl. 'And I only wish I could come along with you,' he added, torn.

'I don't,' said Pearl. 'Or you might end up volunteering me for something else.' She gave him a knowing smile and a peck on the cheek before turning for the door. Nathan called out to her. 'It's a wonderful thing, you know, to be called upon to support the arts?' He paused for a moment before adding: 'Could be lucrative, too, in the long run, though I know that would never be reason enough to persuade you.' He offered a wink which served to remind Pearl that, as usual, Nathan's flattery got him everywhere.

It was late afternoon before Pearl was able to get away from the restaurant. In the early summer months, before July came storming in, bringing fine weather and plenty of DFLs (the town's acronym for Down From Londoners), it was possible for Pearl to relax by taking a much-needed stroll along Whitstable's pebbled beach, before the restaurant's busy evening service began. She did so now on her way to meeting Heather Fox, heading east from The Whitstable Pearl towards her destination: a sea-facing cottage on the lower part of some grassy slopes. Fairview belonged to Heather Fox's father, Colin, and was situated between the Art Deco façade of the Continental Hotel and a municipal building which housed a café serving Mediterranean food. The cottage was aptly named, since it enjoyed an uninterrupted vista across the sea towards the Red Sands army fort that had been constructed eight miles offshore during the Second World War. On a clear morning, the fort sat squarely on the horizon, but this afternoon's heat haze concealed its steel supports so it appeared more like a phantom ship at sea.

Although Pearl had passed by Fairview many times, today she gave proper attention to its latticed windows and a neat front garden filled with flowering bushes of hebe, deutzia and philadelphus. A low boundary wall meant the property was as much on display to passers-by as Pearl's own home, Seaspray Cottage, which backed straight on to the beach. In the summer months, Pearl's sea-facing garden became the backdrop for numerous tourist 'selfies', as well as refuge for the odd holiday drunk seeking a few hours' snooze on her small square of lawn. Her own coastal view included the area known as West Beach, on which stood the famous white clap-boarded Old Neptune pub, and a stunning sunset vista which compensated for all intrusiveness from DFLs. As she walked up a sloping path to Fairview, she imagined the same was true for its owners, since the Fox family had lived there for decades.

Reaching the front door, Pearl noticed a movement behind the lace curtain at its bay window; before she had a chance to ring the bell, the door quickly opened to reveal Heather Fox, smiling warmly as she offered her hand.

'Thank you so much for coming,' she said brightly, beckoning Pearl quickly inside. Pearl reckoned she must be in her early thirties, tall and slim, with shoulder-length dark brown hair, streaked with chestnut highlights. Her outfit was fashionably nautical: a navy and white striped T-shirt, blue jeans and deck shoes, but her crimson fingernails and stylish silver earrings dis-counted any recent boating trips. She glanced quickly up the stairs before whispering: 'Dad's just taking a nap so I thought we could talk in the conservatory.'

The two women moved together through a hallway that was stacked with large cardboard boxes, into a dining room which appeared to be a curious mix of the traditional and 'on trend'; a fashionable display of poppies in a modern porcelain vase sat on a Victorian card table, while cushions bearing geometric designs were strewn over an antique chaise-longue. Heather explained. 'I'm sorry everything's so untidy but I gave up my flat in London recently. As storage is so expensive these days, I brought everything back here.'

Pearl nodded. 'Nathan mentioned your father has been unwell lately. I'm sorry to hear that.'

'Thanks,' said Heather, troubled. 'Dad's been seriously ill. He had to have a heart operation. To be honest, I'm not too sure how much longer he may need me.' Pearl noted that the comment was ambiguous, leaving Pearl in doubt as to whether Colin Fox was getting better – or worse. For a moment, Heather looked conflicted, but rallied quickly and led the way for Pearl to follow her into a small conservatory filled with cane furniture.

'Come in,' she said, taking some paperwork from the cushion of a chair so that Pearl could sit down. As Pearl did so, she took in the view of a carefully tended established cottage garden filled with colourful borders of foxgloves, delphinium, phlox and some hardy pink geranium. Heather went on: 'I was so relieved when Nathan suggested you might be able to help. I mean, it's one thing for me to organise this festival – I've worked in PR for almost ten years, so I'm used to promoting book launches, art exhibitions and concerts – but . . . well, I realised that what we really need for Whit Fest is a kind of . . . unifying event right at the very start, something to properly welcome the German committee members while showcasing the town at the same time? Oysters are the thing we're most famous for,' she continued, 'so your Whitstable Pearl restaurant would be the perfect venue.' She gave a smile which Pearl returned, warming to the young woman before her.

'Thanks,' said Pearl. 'But I'm not quite sure why you've decided to hold the festival right now – in June? Surely it would attract more interest, and visitors, in a month's time, during the Oyster Festival?'

Heather sat down to face Pearl. 'Perhaps,' she conceded, before adopting a softer tone. 'I'm not sure how much Nathan has told you, but my father has been chairman of the local twinning association for almost twenty years. He loves Borken and the whole community there, so keeping strong ties between the two towns has always been very important to him, especially as he's seen some of the other local twinning associations fade away due to lack of interest. Dad's a very strong European. He's always made regular trips to Borken but, well, since his last heart attack, he's been unable to travel, and though he doesn't complain much, I know how he hates not being able to see his old friends.' She looked pained once more then rallied again. 'But if he can't get to Borken, it occurred to me that a little bit of Borken might come to him.' She smiled. 'The German committee members told me they'd be more than happy to come, but they have to do so sooner rather than later, due to previous engagements. Unfortunately, some have had to drop out completely, but a lovely lady – Dad's old friend, Wibke Ruppert – and her brother, Laurent, who's a widower and a retired charity trustee, are still making the trip here as Borken's "ambassadors". They're both very cultured and adore Whitstable.' Her smile faded momentarily as she confided: 'I must admit, I was a bit worried about the cost of hotel bills, but then Marion, who owns Beacon House, came forward and kindly offered me her property for their stay. She's been wonderful, taken herself off to visit relatives in Italy, and isn't charging a penny.'

'Very kind of her,' said Pearl. The local landmark property had acquired its name from a signal which had once stood in its garden as a low-water warning to sailors. Although there were grander, more expensive seaside homes along the western coast, where a millionaire's row of 'new builds' jostled for the title of best design statement, Beacon House possessed a more distinctive style and arguably the best sea view in Whitstable, since it had looked out for over a hundred years at the mysterious 'Street', or Street of Stones, a stretch of shingle which became visible at low tide.

'Marion's a great supporter of the arts,' said Heather. 'She also runs the local book group.'

'Yes, I know,' Pearl smiled. 'My mother – Dolly – is a member. Mum's also visited Borken a few times, though I've yet to do so.'

'Oh yes, of course,' said Heather. 'I'm really pleased that we'll be showing some of Dolly's artwork in our exhibition at The Horsebridge on Friday.'

'Are you?' asked Pearl, trying to imagine her mother's eccentric efforts in the grand exhibition space at the local cultural centre.

'Of course,' Heather added with a fair degree of diplomacy, 'it's going to be a wonderfully eclectic exhibition. Something for everyone.'

In the silence that followed, the bells of St Alfred's Church suddenly rang out for the evening service, prompting Heather to add: 'Rev Pru is staging a candlelit concert on Saturday.' She turned to indicate a wall chart as she explained: 'And that will immediately follow a children's dance routine at the junior school.' She turned back to Pearl and explained: 'I'm still relying on this chart because the brochure's taken longer than expected to finalise – mainly due to a few hiccups . . .'

'Hiccups?'

'Nothing to worry about,' said Heather. 'But, well, let's just say it can be a challenge to manage "creative personalities"?' She looked up apologetically, as if having said too much, but a man's voice suddenly sounded from the hallway.

'Heather?'

'In here, Dad!'

In the next moment, Colin Fox followed his daughter's voice into the conservatory, brought up short to see she was not alone. He looked quizzically from Heather to

Pearl, his face drawn, its pallor making him appear like a waxwork. Heather gave him a warm smile and explained: 'This is Pearl Nolan, Dad.'

At this, Colin seemed to come to life with a genial smile. Stepping forward he took Pearl's hand. 'Of course it is. Good to see you,' he said. He pumped Pearl's hand before pointing a finger at her. 'You won't remember the last time we met, because you couldn't have been more than a young teenager. How's your mother?'

'She's well,' said Pearl, returning his smile.

'And looking forward to this festival, I shouldn't wonder. As are we all.' He looked back proudly at his daughter as he continued. 'Heather's been working so hard to get things off the ground. And I hear you might be tempted to help out with the food?'

Pearl took a deep breath, about to voice a few concerns. 'Well, I . . .' But she broke off as she saw Colin suddenly putting out a hand to steady himself.

'Dad?' Heather moved quickly to support him. 'Are you OK?'

Her father nodded, but glanced in some embarrassment towards Pearl. 'I . . . think I may have got up too quickly,' he said. 'Maybe I'll go and lie down again and leave you two alone.'

'Here, let me help you,' said Heather. But Colin gently pushed his daughter's hand away. 'I'm fine,' he insisted. 'No need to fuss.' Turning to Pearl, he managed a weak but sincere smile. 'Good to see you, Pearl. Please give my regards to your mum.'

He gave a gentle nod and turned for the door. Heather Fox watched him go and listened carefully for her father's footsteps climbing the stairs. Only with the sound of a door softly closing upstairs did she turn again to Pearl, concern still written on her pretty face as she asked: 'I'm sorry. Where were we?' It was clear the young woman's earlier enthusiasm had palled. Pearl reminded her: 'You were talking about the importance of having a welcoming event – at The Whitstable Pearl?'

'Oh, yes, of course,' said Heather, summoning enthusiasm. 'And it really would be wonderful if you felt you could possibly help but . . .' She broke off for a moment before admitting: 'I'm afraid I've not been able to attract any sponsorship from the high-profile businesses, but, nevertheless, I'm sure we could stretch to offering some of your finest oysters?'

Pearl studied the face of the young woman before her – it was clear from her earnest expression that there was much more at stake in Whit Fest than a series of cultural events. Pearl made a decision. 'I think we can do better than that,' she said finally. 'How about a full seafood buffet for your guests? A few drinks too – Prosecco; a light summery dessert and—'

'But . . . how? ' Heather had quickly broken in, and looked pained as she confided: 'My budget is barely shoestring.'

Pearl smiled. 'Let me worry about that.'

Chapter Two

Pearl's fruit and vegetable supplier, Marty Smith, the owner of the upmarket High Street store Cornucopia, stared down at the list in his hand, then back at Pearl as he asked: 'You want me to supply this lot at *cost*?'

He was looking at Pearl askance but she held her nerve. 'I've just explained,' she reminded him. 'This festival is for the benefit of the whole community, so it's actually a *privilege* to be invited to contribute.'

'Yeah, an expensive one,' said Marty, unimpressed. 'D'you know the price of asparagus right now?' He began to fiddle with an attractive display of choice asparagus spears as though it might have been a flower arrangement.

'Of course,' said Pearl. '*And* the cost of a truckle of Canterbury cheese, but nevertheless Nick's agreed to supply one.'

At this, Marty turned quickly back to Pearl. She saw his brow had furrowed. He was an attractive man in his early forties with dark good looks and a toned body gained from regular sessions lifting weights at the gym – and heavy crates in his shop. Nevertheless, over the years, Pearl had failed to find him any more than a casual friend, and vegetable supplier, though Marty never gave up hope of capturing Pearl's heart. Resenting competition, he now asked with suspicion: 'Nick? Him at the posh cheese shop, you mean?'

He was referring to Quel Fromage – a popular new Harbour Street store which, in spite of its French name, had been doing an excellent job of promoting local cheeses.

'I spoke to him this morning,' Pearl explained, 'and he said he's more than happy to help out,' adding: 'especially since he'll be getting a special thank you in the new festival brochure.'

At this, the corners of Marty's mouth set like a knitted buttonhole, but Pearl continued by throwing in another bargaining chip: 'He understands how important this festival is and that a mention in the brochure will provide very effective . . . free . . . advertising.'

'Oh, is that so?' said Marty, still sour.

'Of course,' Pearl went on. 'The festival's attracting a lot of local interest but, apart from that, I've discovered there are no fewer than forty thousand residents in Borken, and lots of them have already visited our town. With the German committee members reporting back about Whit Fest, there could be many more Borken visitors in Whitstable soon – perhaps in search of our . . . finest asparagus?'

At this, Marty's pinched expression relaxed. 'Forty thousand?'

Pearl nodded. 'Forty-one thousand, to be precise. And the Germans are *very* keen on their asparagus. I think they call it *"Edelgemüse".'* Seeing Marty looking blank, Pearl explained: 'The noble vegetable?'

Marty mused on this as he looked down again at the list in his hand then back at Pearl, who was waiting for an answer. If there was one thing that rivalled the place Pearl held in Marty's heart, it was making a good profit from selling his fruit and vegetables – and Pearl knew it.

'Right,' he said finally. 'When d'you want this lot?'

'First thing tomorrow morning?'

'Tomorrow!' said Marty, shocked. 'You could have given me a bit more notice.'

'Look, I know you can do this, Marty,' said Pearl. 'That's why you're my most trusted supplier.' As she smiled sweetly, the greengrocer's heart began to melt. He tucked Pearl's list manfully into his shirt pocket and declared: 'Never fear, Pearl. The . . . Eagle Mousse will be yours.'

'Edelgemüse,' said Pearl. Marty gave a nod and Pearl moved off to the door. She was almost safely out of it when Marty called to her: 'Any chance I could get a mention in this brochure *above* the cheese shop?'

Pearl turned and saw his expectant smile but said only: 'We'll see.'

After leaving Cornucopia, Pearl took a deep breath and basked in a warm glow of achievement, as she raised her face to the morning sun. It was still too early for the majority of tourists to be up and about, and the High Street was filled instead with early local shoppers: young mums with pushchairs and middle-aged women with shopping trolleys jostling for position on the narrow pavements. In an hour's time, the DFLs and overseas visitors would be ambling and dawdling in their place, investigating the pretty front windows of Whitstable's independent shops, which were a novelty compared to the cloned High Streets of so many other towns and cities. Pearl checked her watch and wondered if she had time for a coffee in town, but it was nearly 9.15 a.m. so she hurried on instead, towards Harbour Street.

Dolly Nolan's home was situated at the back of the small shop, Dolly's Pots, from which Pearl's mother sold her shabby-chic ceramics and other works of art. She wasn't in the shop that morning and an old friend was standing in for her, knitting what appeared to be an extremely unseasonable item of clothing, considering the sunny weather. Instead, Pearl found Dolly on her tiny overgrown back terrace, working on a canvas mounted on a rickety easel. Dolly's outdoor space was in stark contrast to Pearl's ordered garden, and almost crowded out by the extension she had built when she had sacrificed the rooms above her shop to create her little holiday flat, Dolly's Attic. The apartment remained popular for guests throughout the whole year, providing a source of customers for Dolly's handmade oyster platters, which Pearl also used in the restaurant. In Dolly's courtyard space, a number of terracotta pots housed various flowering plants – peonies, Busy Lizzies, and Brown-Eyed Susans – but a batch of bamboo had proved to be a bedding error since it had spread inexorably across the entire area, giving what little garden there was a distinctly jungle feel. Set against this backdrop, Dolly suddenly became visible to Pearl like Captain Kurtz in *Apocalypse Now* – but in colourful drag which consisted of a paint-splattered paisley smock and a primrose-yellow turban, from which a flash of magenta fringe protruded. Dolly's hair needed as much taming as her bamboo, and though she was usually full of boundless energy, this morning she looked somewhat defeated.

'I do so wish Charlie was here,' she opined as she saw Pearl approaching.

'So do I,' Pearl admitted in all honesty. 'But he'll be back soon.' She now offered a smile to reassure herself as much as Dolly, then noticed how the bark of one of her mother's old pear trees had almost totally grown over what remained of an old piece of washing line left tied to the tree.

'Not soon enough for me,' Dolly sighed. 'I could have done with his help on my frames. This canvas is as baggy as a granny's knickers.' Pained, she picked up her brush from the paint-splattered stool on which she'd left it, while Pearl peered over her mother's shoulder to see what it was she was creating.

'What do you think?' Dolly paused to chew on her lower lip, attracting a smear of bright fuchsia-coloured lipstick to her teeth as she did so. 'Come on. Be honest!'

Pearl tried hard to summon a tactful response. The painting was a departure from Dolly's usual style of work, which consisted mainly of small seascapes dotted with various *objets trouvés* acquired from her regular beachcombing sessions – pretty shells and various dried beach plants. Pearl usually found room for her mother's work on the walls of The Whitstable Pearl and had agreed to do so with this canvas, as a special preview before it was exhibited for the festival. However, her new painting was a distinct contrast to the rest, being so much larger and with a dramatic dark tone – an abstract spiral in which trailing seaweed had been caught up – while giving off a strong sulphurous smell. Pearl found herself almost lost for words. 'It's certainly a . . . Dolly Nolan,' she said finally, nodding confidently to assuage any performance anxiety on her mother's part.

''Think so?' asked Dolly, unsure and a little confused by Pearl's comment as she pointed out: 'I've used a totally different palette. None of my usual ochre or—'

'But it works,' Pearl insisted brightly, doing her best to offer encouragement while knowing her mother's work was an acquired taste, her canvases appreciated more by friends and fellow artists than the owners of the trendy galleries of Harbour Street.

'Perhaps,' Dolly conceded, slightly bolstered, though knowing, for her own part, that her daughter's opinion wasn't to be wholly relied upon since Pearl's creativity lay in cookery, not painting. Taking a rag to wipe her brush, she turned to face her. 'You don't need my help at the restaurant today, do you?' she asked anxiously. 'Because I really do have to get on, or I'll never finish this in time for the exhibition. On top of that I'm going to have to find something to wear for the Private View. Everything in my wardrobe seems to have shrunk.'

Pearl noted her mother's helpless expression but chose not to comment on the constant losing battle Dolly fought with her weight, a battle the two women failed to share since Dolly was as short and broad as Pearl was tall and willowy. Dolly was from old Whitstable stock, but her late husband, Tommy, had been an oysterman of Irish heritage, able to trace his own roots back to Galway. Pearl had inherited her mother's spirit but had been blessed with her father's dark good looks.

On most days Pearl would tie up her long dark curls and seldom wore jewellery, certainly no rings on her fingers that could become lost in restaurant dishes during their preparation. The restaurant was often used as an excuse for Pearl's simple style, but her modest wardrobe of clothes – bought, for the most part, for comfort and practicality – included many beautiful vintage items, and represented a personal rejection of

Dolly's flamboyant fashion choices. What was clear to everyone was that Pearl looked striking whatever she wore and whatever she did to herself. With gipsy-black hair and grey eyes the colour of moonstone, some said she had the look of the 'black Irish', descendants of the Spanish Armada sailors who had escaped death on the beaches of the west coast of Ireland to serve under rebel chiefs such as Sorley Boy McDonnell and Hugh O'Neill. Unlike Dolly, Pearl had never experienced her clothes mysteriously shrinking.

'The restaurant's fine,' she said in an effort to quell her mother's anxiety. In fact, The Whitstable Pearl was more than fine because hiring a new young chef, Dean Samson, had taken considerable pressure off Pearl, which she had hoped would give her the time she needed to promote Nolan's Detective Agency, though Whit Fest threatened to provide a further delay to that.

'I just thought you'd like to know I had a meeting with Heather Fox,' said Pearl, as Dolly continued work on her painting.

'Heather . . .?' Dolly looked momentarily confused.

'Colin Fox's daughter,' Pearl explained. 'He says he knows you so I've agreed to put on an event for the festival – to welcome members of the German twinning association.'

'Oh excellent!' Dolly exclaimed. 'I've been trying to brush up my schoolgirl German for this festival.' She frowned before adding, 'Not the easiest of languages, I must admit. Too many rules for my liking . . .'

Dolly wasn't a fan of rules of any kind, having managed to remain a rebel at heart, even at sixty-two years of age. She continued to question all authority, including that of the police, so twenty years ago she had been sorely disappointed by Pearl's decision to join the force, and equally relieved when Pearl had left. Dolly made no secret of her view of Pearl's relationship with DCI McGuire, and worried that Nolan's Detective Agency brought her daughter into jeopardy . . .

At that moment, Pearl's smartphone trilled an incoming e-mail and she checked it to find it was from Heather Fox, offering thanks to Pearl for all she had promised at the meeting. Pearl slipped on her reading glasses and opened an attachment. Curious, Dolly leaned in closer. 'What's that?' she asked.

Pearl began scrolling through a list of the names that had been confirmed for the gastro evening at The Whitstable Pearl. They included Colin Fox, the Borken representatives, musicians from a samba band, a dance troupe, teachers from the local junior school and a group of six artists, which included Dolly. 'It's a definitive guest list.'

'Let me see,' said Dolly, quickly grabbing the phone from Pearl's hand. She peered at the smartphone screen and smiled to herself. 'Ah,' she exclaimed, 'look at that! I see I'm actually *heading* the Fine Art section.' She preened at this but Pearl explained: 'That's because the artists are all listed in alphabetical order. Look – Nolan, Peisley, Phillips, Taylor, Williams . . . You're lucky there wasn't a Butterworth there.'

Dolly frowned at this. 'So . . . who's confirmed for the other events?'

Pearl looked pointedly at her mother. 'I haven't had a chance to look yet,' she said, motioning quickly for her phone, but Dolly was refusing to relinquish it and instead suddenly reacted to something else she had just seen. 'My goodness,' she gasped. '*That's* a bit of a coup.'

'What is?'

'Blake Cain.' Dolly was clearly impressed, though the name meant nothing to Pearl. Dolly elaborated. 'B. J. Cain. The author?'

Pearl's memory was suitably jogged as she remembered this to be the pen name of a novelist who had once filled the entertainment supplements of local newspapers.

'But I thought he moved abroad . . .'

'He did,' said Dolly, 'for a while.' She began scrolling down a short biography as she explained. 'He disappeared off to California with a new publishing deal then came back a couple of years ago when the book failed to sell . . . He was trying something new, of course, and it didn't work out but . . .' She broke off suddenly, her jaw dropping open. Pearl looked at her in frustration. 'What is it now?'

'Heather's only gone and matched him with Cathy McTurk. His *ex-wife*.'

Pearl took this in for a moment then shrugged. 'Lots of divorced couples have good relationships—'

'Not Blake and Cathy,' said Dolly determinedly. 'They're a stormy pair – the Richard Burton and Liz

Taylor of our local literary world . . .' She gave a final gasp as she stared down again at the phone again.

'And they're on with Vesta!'

'Vesta?' echoed Pearl, increasingly confused.

'You really *must* catch up with your reading, Pearl. Come to one of Marion's book club meetings—'

Pearl persisted. '*Who* . . . is Vesta?'

'Why, Vesta Korbyn, of course. The Queen of Gothic Noir?' Seeing Pearl was none the wiser, she went on: 'Surely you've seen her around town? Wraith-like figure . . . Long black hair, pale complexion – looks like she's on her way to a Halloween party? She drives a vintage black sedan car, like a hearse.'

'Oh yes,' said Pearl. 'I think I've seen it parked on Ham Shades Lane.'

'That's where she lives,' said Dolly. 'Big old house – like the Bates Motel?' She gave a knowing look. 'Her books are very popular, you know. Edgar Allan Poe meets *Fifty Shades of Grey*? A winning formula, it seems. Not only that . . .' She paused for effect before finally whispering, 'I believe she's sunk her talons into Blake Cain.'

'Really?' asked Pearl, intrigued.

'Really,' said Dolly knowingly.

Pearl glanced down at the phone still in her mother's hand. 'And . . . Heather's put them together for this . . . "Take Three Writers" event?'

'Looks like it.' Dolly gave a nod, then handed the phone back to her daughter. 'Make sure you get us some tickets, Pearl,' she ordered. 'Because I wouldn't miss that one for the world.' And with that, she picked up her brush once more and resumed painting her seascape.

Much later, after a busy day at the restaurant, Pearl left the evening service in the capable hands of Dean the chef and headed home, taking a scenic route across the beach. With an incoming tide, the air always felt fresher, and she paused for a while to sit down on a bench at a spot called Cushing's View to watch the sun set. The bench bore a metal plate explaining that it was in memory of Peter Cushing, the actor well known for his roles in horror movies, who had once lived only a stone's throw from Pearl's cottage on Island Wall. That thought prompted Pearl to consider all that Dolly had told her about the Queen of Gothic Noir, Vesta Korbyn, and the curious mix of writers that Heather Fox had put together for the festival's literary event. Considering Dolly's reaction, it now seemed to Pearl that this could well be Heather Fox's way of guaranteeing some free fireworks for her festival – especially since any other pyrotechnics were beyond her meagre budget.

Pearl took her notebook from her bag and checked her own progress with the gastro event at The Whitstable Pearl. She had managed to attract quite a few local suppliers: a local artisan baker had agreed to supply sourdough bread, and a shop called the Whitstable Produce Store had found a Kent stockist to donate cider and Prosecco. A local brewery was laying on some oyster stout, and Marty had come up trumps with a generous supply of asparagus, samphire and salad items, together with the raspberries that would form the basis of Pearl's homemade sorbet. All would be followed by a selection of Kent cheeses from Quel Fromage. Pearl closed her notebook, satisfied she had successfully rustled up everything she needed for a great evening – apart from one final element.

Taking out her phone, she sought one name from her contact list – McGuire – then tapped it to make a call. As she'd suspected, it went straight to voicemail, but still she relished hearing the sound of the detective's voice on the line.

'This is DCI Mike McGuire. I'm otherwise engaged right now so please leave a message after the tone and I'll get back to you.' A beep sounded. Pearl quickly responded. 'Hi. It's me. I know you're busy working and I hope all's going well with the case and . . . Terry Bosley.' She broke off for a moment, realising how easy it would be to tell him how much she missed him, and how she wished he was here with her right now to watch the sunset, but her pride was too great and instead she said only: 'Call me when you can. There's a new festival coming up in town. And a special event I want to tell you about.'

Ending the call, Pearl got to her feet and moved on along the beach to Seaspray Cottage, while wondering what exactly it was that McGuire was otherwise engaged in. Questioning a suspect? Making an arrest? Addressing his DCs in a police incident room – or perhaps writing a report for his loathed superintendent, Maurice Welch, the man who had never fully accepted McGuire, a DFL, on his local force? Welch was the reason McGuire had to work doubly hard at his job, never giving any cause for his boss to find fault. As a London detective, McGuire had arrived in Whitstable on a temporary transfer, but a murder case, and meeting Pearl, had proved reason enough for him to stay on. He had made his home in Canterbury, just a few miles from Whitstable, though it seemed sometimes to Pearl that he could have been a million miles away, especially on a beautiful evening like this, when all she had for company were the two cats who welcomed her as she approached her cottage gate. She sat down on her garden wall and, as twilight began to fall, she looked out to sea where the navigation lights of freighters had already begun twinkling on the horizon like a string of precious stones – rubies, emeralds and diamonds.

Nathan was right; with a million things to do before the Whit Fest launch, Pearl knew she had plenty to fill her time – until, that is, McGuire was no longer 'otherwise engaged'.

Chapter Three

Over the next few days, news spread across town about Whitstable's inspiring new arts festival; even those who weren't remotely interested in music, literature or fine art began buying tickets to events in order to see family members performing in concerts or poetry readings – and a few writers coming to verbal blows at a literary event at the cultural centre. Hoardings appeared bearing the message, in bold lettering: 'Whit Fest - Celebrating 30 years of Twinning with Borken', and a banner went up across the harbour. Pearl had been given a smaller version to string across the ceiling of The Whitstable Pearl restaurant, and she did so prior to the festival's welcoming event, climbing a stepladder which her young waitress, Ruby, steadied for her.

'Sure you don't want to wait for Dean?' asked the young girl anxiously. But characteristically Pearl insisted on remaining independent. 'We can manage, Ruby,' she replied, knowing full well that her assistant chef would have enough to do preparing much of the buffet menu for the evening's event. Nevertheless, Pearl recognised another instance where her son Charlie's presence would have come in useful – if he hadn't disappeared off to Dorset on his animation course.

Having pinned the banner successfully in place, it was only as Pearl was stuffing the stepladder back into a kitchen cupboard that she recognised a familiar voice echoing from the radio, responding to a question from a local breakfast-show host. 'You're right,' said Heather Fox. 'I'm not sure Whitstable has ever done anything quite like this before. The town has its Oyster Festival, of course, and an annual carnival – but a truly comprehensive arts festival, featuring food, fine art, music, literature? No, it's totally new, but we're *very* lucky to have so much local creative talent in Whitstable, as well as support from across the whole town to honour our historic twinning with Borken.'

'Sounds like it's not to be missed!' said the presenter, his smile almost audible across the airwaves. 'So if you haven't yet got your tickets for the upcoming events, visit the Whit Fest website today because you're in for a treat. Thank you, Heather.'

'No,' she replied. 'Thank *you*, for inviting me on the show.'

As the interview segued into a 1970s pop hit, Pearl reflected for a moment on how professionally Heather

Fox had come across in the few brief comments she had caught, before remembering that Heather had previously worked in PR in London. She certainly had a professional knack of knowing what was required to attract maximum attention for the festival, including putting together a controversial mix of writers.

The kitchen doors swung open and Ruby called over, 'Someone to see you, Pearl.'

Ruby quickly ducked out again and, before Pearl could follow her, another figure appeared in her wake.

'Heather,' said Pearl, taken aback. 'I just heard you on the radio . . .'

'Ah yes,' smiled Heather Fox. 'The interview was pre-recorded. I did it last night. But I've had so much to do today, I forgot to listen. Did I sound OK?'

'Perfect,' smiled Pearl.

'Oh good,' Heather smiled again, visibly relieved. 'And I'm sorry to barge in like this. I promise I won't take up too much of your time, but I really would like you to meet two very special people . . .' She gestured back towards the restaurant floor.

Curious, Pearl followed after her, to see two silhouettes framed by the sunlight streaming in through the windows. Heather's guests were leaning forward, as though investigating one of Dolly's paintings on the wall but, as the kitchen doors swung shut after Pearl, both figures looked up expectantly. Heather turned back to her. 'Pearl, I'd like you to meet Borken committee members, Wibke and Laurent Ruppert.'

Wibke moved forward first, a short woman who looked to Pearl to be in her late fifties, with iron-grey hair cut into a stylish bob. She wore a beige linen trouser suit and a slash of pale coral lipstick, which perfectly complemented the shade of her long silk scarf and flat leather shoes. 'What a wonderful restaurant you have here,' she said in perfect English, turning now to Laurent beside her. An attractive man in his early sixties, Laurent sported a loose teal-coloured cotton shirt over white jeans, his casual outfit perfectly matching his relaxed charm. 'Indeed,' he said, in agreement with Wibke. 'My sister and I have just been admiring your choice of artwork,' he continued. 'Highly original,' he added, looking back at the gallery of paintings on the wall.

Pearl smiled. 'My mother will be very pleased,' she said. 'Because those are all hers.'

Laurent set a pair of bifocal glasses on his nose as he leaned forward again to examine the largest canvas, comprising a familiar dark spiral of oil paint, now studded with a variety of broken shells: mussel, oyster and clam.

'*Undertow*,' he read, using a German pronunciation. 'By Dolly Nolan?'

Pearl smiled. 'That's right. It was inspired by an area of quite dangerous currents, just east of our harbour.'

Laurent took this in, nodding as he surveyed Dolly's work. 'Indeed,' he said. 'I like this painting very much.'

'I'll let her know,' smiled Pearl.

'Or you could tell her yourself,' said Heather brightly.

'Because you're bound to meet Dolly during the festival, Laurent. This canvas goes up in The Horsebridge art gallery tomorrow.'

'Good,' he nodded. 'Then I will look forward to it.' He turned now to Pearl. 'And Heather tells us you are kindly inviting us all for a welcome meal this evening?'

'That's right,' said Pearl. 'We'll be ready for you later tonight.'

'And . . . some of the festival participants?' asked Wibke keenly, before adding: 'I have to confess I am a special fan of BJ's.' Looking suddenly embarrassed, she quickly corrected herself: 'I mean, the work of Mr B. J. Cain.' Giving a sidelong glance to Heather, she asked: 'He *is* still taking part in the festival?'

'He most certainly is,' said Heather, proudly. 'And he'll be here tonight at our launch party.'

Wibke gave a short exhalation of air, as though she had been physically winded by the news. 'Oh,' she gasped, 'I can hardly wait.'

Pearl was just considering how news of Blake Cain's attendance at The Whitstable Pearl had managed to transform a middle-aged woman into a breathless teenager when Laurent quickly clarified: 'My sister and I are very pleased to be here at this time – especially to meet our old friend, Colin, again.'

'And he'll be very happy to see you too,' said Heather. 'But I know you've been travelling all morning and I really should get you both to Beacon House so you can settle in.' She turned to Pearl. 'I hope we didn't disturb you too much, Pearl, but I couldn't possibly drive past without introducing you.'

Pearl smiled. 'No problem,' then she turned to the German visitors. 'Welcome to Whitstable. I hope you have a wonderful stay.'

'Oh, we will,' said Wibke. 'It's wonderful that we'll be staying in the property that overlooks . . . the Street, you call it? The stones that stretch out to sea? I hear no one quite knows how they got to be there.'

'That's right,' said Heather. 'Some say it's the remains of a Roman road built on land that was later lost to the sea. Others believe it was an ancient landing stage for vessels of some kind, but no one can be sure, so I guess it's what you'd call . . . a Whitstable mystery?' She smiled. 'And maybe one for Pearl to solve one day.' She saw her German guests were looking slightly confused and so explained. 'Pearl has a detective agency as well as this restaurant.'

Wibke and Laurent turned to study Pearl, unsure if they were being treated to a private joke.

'It's true,' Pearl confirmed. 'A one-woman operation. And I haven't had a case in a few months now, which is no real tragedy as the restaurant keeps me busy enough.'

'Interesting,' mused Laurent. 'I would presume these days it's never been easier to set up as a private detective?'

'With access to the internet, you mean?' Pearl asked.

'But of course,' he replied. 'So much information is now available online.'

'That's true,' Pearl agreed, 'but you'd be surprised at

how much detective work still relies on old-fashioned methods.'

Laurent raised an eyebrow. 'Such as?'

'Dogged perseverance, for one thing,' Pearl smiled. 'I may not have access to police forensic results, for instance, but working as a member of the police can actually be a hindrance at times – arriving on a crime scene with flashing lights, badges and sirens. Private detectives work in a much more . . . subtle way – especially when we have some local knowledge.'

Wibke frowned. 'But . . . why a detective?'

Pearl explained: 'Because, many years ago, I began training as a police officer. I had to give it up. You could say . . . life took me in a different direction.'

'But still you need to solve crimes?' said Laurent.

Pearl was about to reply when she saw Ruby moving across from the window, pointing towards the street where a traffic warden was visible outside on the pavement. 'Is that your car?' she asked.

'I'm afraid it is,' said Heather. She quickly began steering Wibke and Laurent towards the door. '*Es tut mir leid*,' she said in a perfect German accent. '*Wir müssen uns beeilen . . .*'

Ushering her guests off like a pair of ducklings, she looked back at Pearl. 'Thank you so much, Pearl,' she exclaimed. 'See you later.' And with that, they were gone.

From the restaurant window, Pearl watched as Heather appeared to charm the traffic warden outside, while steering her guests back into the vehicle. Once they were all in the car, and the warden suitably appeased, Heather offered a last wave to Pearl before driving off.

'Nice and friendly, considering.'

At Ruby's remark, Pearl turned to see the girl had joined her and was staring out of the window.

'Considering what?' Pearl asked, curious.

'Well, we did a project on Borken at school,' the young waitress explained. 'Didn't you know we flattened the whole town during the war?'

Pearl frowned. 'No, I didn't,' she said, perturbed. 'Are you sure about that?'

Ruby nodded dolefully.

'Well,' Pearl decided. 'Let's make sure we do our very best to keep everyone happy this evening, shall we?'

Chapter Four

By seven o'clock that same evening, The Whitstable Pearl restaurant was packed with almost all the specially chosen guests who had been invited to enjoy the private launch party. A large buffet table groaned beneath platters of gravadlax with caraway and coriander; an *insalata di mare* of squid and octopus, drenched in lime and fresh herbs; a fine scallop ceviche with jalapeño and avocado, and a magnificent fresh poached salmon lying on a bed of samphire. Both Pearl and Ruby wore smart black and white outfits for the evening: Pearl was in a black 1940s-style crushed velvet dress, with a white bandeau taming her long dark curls, while Ruby had changed into black trousers and a cardigan with a white pixie collar, her long fair hair scooped up into a ponytail. They circulated with iced trays of Pearl's finest oysters, served with a classic mignonette sauce, but it was Pearl who kept a keen eye on her guests – and not simply due to the food on offer. It seemed clear that a few local councillors had managed to infiltrate the guest list, keen to expand their contacts prior to an upcoming election, while photo-bombing any possible publicity shots that might appear in the local press. Among the gate-crashing local politicians, Councillor Peter Radcliffe, more commonly known as 'Ratty' to his constituents, was most conspicuous due to the dark brown toupee he always insisted on wearing.

Pearl noted that Ratty had been holding court to Colin Fox, who, along with Wibke and Laurent Ruppert, appeared hypnotised by the councillor's hairpiece, which had seemed to take on a life of its own, expanding in the evening's humidity to resemble something worthy of the councillor's rodent nickname. Members of the local samba band had gravitated towards the Fish Slappers – an eccentric dance troupe featuring a number of women, of all ages, dressed in aquatic costumes that included oyster-shaped bras and cod headdresses. The Slappers had been known to perform at the Whitstable Oyster Festival over the years, and Dolly, having been one of their original members, would have joined the group this evening were it not for the fact that her old costume scarcely went near her these days, even though gusseted – so, instead, she had arrived independently and in a billowing, colourful smock. Pearl was grateful that Whitstable's mini-skirted vicar, the Reverend Prudence Lawson, informally known to all as Rev Pru, was busy chatting to a group of choir members; in doing so, she had managed to put a helpful distance between guests Pearl assumed would be best kept apart.

Blake Cain's former wife, Cathy McTurk, had taken up a position close to the seafood bar – a tall, beautiful woman in her early fifties, with platinum-blonde hair styled into an elegant chignon, she wore a white satin shift dress and a matching box jacket, adorned very simply with a silver Art Deco brooch in the shape of a ballerina. Cathy had arrived precisely on time accompanied by a beautiful young woman with skin the colour of carob, her hair hidden beneath an elaborate cerise turban. Heather Fox had hastily explained to Pearl that the younger woman was Mila Anton, but it was Dolly who now clarified for Pearl that Mila was Cathy's daughter. 'Well,' she said, helping Pearl place flutes of Prosecco on a tray. 'I say "daughter", but Cathy and B. J. Cain fostered quite a few young children when they were married – and Mila was one of them. The others all moved on, but Mila and Cathy remained very close. I believe she lives in Canterbury now, where she's started up a poetry workshop. Lovely-looking girl, isn't she?'

Pearl looked across the room and had to admit Dolly was right. There was something majestic about the young woman, emphasised by the clothing she wore; a long silk coat over a colourful kaftan gave her a regal bearing, and her dark eyes, highlighted in kohl, were like those of an Egyptian princess. High cheekbones, and a smile that flashed brightly at something Cathy chose to confide, formed only part of her exotic beauty. Before Pearl could ask Dolly more about her, Laurent appeared, having escaped a long tirade from Councillor Radcliffe.

'Mrs Dolly Nolan?' he asked. 'The artist?'

Dolly visibly softened at this, though whether due to the title he had just bestowed upon her or the charming smile he now offered, Pearl couldn't be sure.

'Laurent was admiring one of your paintings the other day,' Pearl explained to her mother, bracing herself for the reply to come back in German – which it did.

'Oh – *wunderbar!*' Dolly exclaimed.

'Yes,' Laurent agreed. 'I think it *is* quite wonderful – your oil canvas, *Undertow*. I wonder if you could tell me a little more about it?'

Dolly primped her magenta fringe and offered her sweetest smile to Laurent. 'Why, of course,' she said sweetly, 'exactly what is it you'd like to know?'

Pearl smiled to herself as she watched her mother moving off with Laurent, then she glanced across the room towards a pretty young woman who was avidly scribbling in a reporter's notebook. The girl was tall with short-cropped fair hair, but it was the dress she wore that had caught Pearl's attention. White, with mother-of-pearl buttons down its front, Pearl suspected it was an original vintage frock from the 1950s, since it was a style she often wore herself. It gave the girl an almost angelic appearance, especially in contrast to Vesta Korbyn beside her, who, as Dolly had aptly described, looked as though she was in

Halloween fancy dress. The Queen of Gothic Noir made for an imposing figure in a batwing purple dress, her black fingernails studded with astrological symbols, and though her tall, slender frame gave her a youthful look, Pearl assumed the writer to be somewhere in her late forties, since it was impossible to hide the parchment-like skin on the back of her hands and the thin spidery lines at the corner of her bright green eyes. Vesta's thick, jet-black hair was worn long and straight, and streaked with a single stripe of grey, and as Pearl moved across and offered both women some Prosecco, she noted a striking necklace – a silver web – lay at the author's throat, while two matching earrings featured dangling tarantulas. The heavy perfume that the writer wore was unmistakably patchouli-based, and seemed to hang in the air like a thick miasma as she accepted a flute from Pearl's tray. 'Thank you,' Vesta said in a low voice, her emerald-green eyes holding Pearl's gaze. She pursed her thin lips, which were painted a deep burgundy colour, and sipped her drink. The young journalist at her side, however, declined Pearl's Prosecco, and continued with her questions to Vesta. 'So, your next book,' she said keenly. 'Can you tell me more about it?'

Vesta Korbyn opened her mouth to reply but, at that very moment, a laugh went up, diverting Pearl's attention towards a group of young artists who were chatting together at the buffet table. Pearl now noticed Marty, wearing a sharp suit and his usual overpowering musky aftershave, moving closer to Wibke, leaning in towards her as he introduced himself, before saying: 'I hear you've quite an appetite for it.'

'I'm sorry?' said Wibke, taken aback.

Pearl moved in quickly, indicating her buffet table as she explained: 'I was telling Marty the other day how popular asparagus is in Germany.'

The greengrocer pointed to some spears on Pearl's buffet table and nudged Wibke as he smiled, knowingly: 'The noble vegetable?'

Wibke looked somewhat relieved. 'Ah yes, of course,' she said. 'Though traditionally in my country our own *Spargel* is served with melted butter and potatoes, or with ham, or hollandaise sauce? We Germans are *so* crazy for it that in some places these days it's even presented as part of a dessert.'

Marty looked impressed. 'You don't say.'

'Oh yes,' Wibke went on. 'We have several asparagus-growing regions and the city of Schwetzingen claims to be the "Asparagus Capital of the World". It holds an annual *Spargelfest* – rather like your own Oyster Festival – and attracts visitors from all over. In North Rhine-Westphalia, where our town of Borken is situated, there are over a hundred farms that make up a special culinary route they call the "*Spargelstrasse*".'

Marty looked mystified so Wibke explained: '"The Asparagus Road".'

'Oh,' said Marty. 'Plenty of demand, then?'

'Oh *ja*,' said Wibke. 'And that's why we have such a shortage.'

Marty had just been about to take a sip of his drink, but he hesitated now as his interest was further piqued. 'Shortage?'

Wibke nodded. 'I read somewhere that we consume something like seventy thousand tons of asparagus every year, but we only produce sixty.'

Marty's jaw dropped open. 'You mean . . . you're . . . *ten thousand tons* short?'

Wibke nodded again. 'I believe so. It's a short season, harvested from mid-April to the end of June. And during that time we enjoy asparagus at *least* once a day. *Every* day. So we have to import it to meet the high demand.' She shrugged and sipped her drink but Marty looked at Pearl, lost for words. Before she could offer an opinion, a voice sounded close by to distract her.

'Pearl Nolan?'

Turning, Pearl saw the young fair-haired reporter before her. 'Sorry, I was just trying to finish an interview with Vesta back there,' she explained. Her notebook was still in one hand while the other was outstretched towards her. 'I'm Lucy Walker. Covering the festival for the local *Chronicle*?' She smiled as Pearl shook her hand then she gestured towards the buffet table. 'And this is an amazing spread. But I suppose I shouldn't be too surprised by that because I hear The Whitstable Pearl is something of a local institution?'

'We've been here quite a while,' said Pearl, returning the girl's smile. She was just about to circulate with her tray of drinks when Lucy quickly added: 'And I hear it's

45

not just food you provide?' The girl paused before adding: 'You have a detective agency, too. Nolan's?'

'That's right.' Watching Lucy sip her Prosecco, Pearl added: 'That's a very beautiful dress you're wearing.'

Lucy looked down at it, slightly disarmed by the comment. 'Thanks. It's not high fashion just . . . a little vintage number from a shop in Canterbury.'

'It really suits you,' said Pearl before she smiled again, warmly this time, as she recognised something of her younger self in the girl, particularly in her inquisitive look as Lucy glanced around the room before turning back to Pearl with another question. 'Tell me,' she said. 'Why would a chef and restaurateur be interested in solving crimes?' She set her glass down on the buffet table and opened her notebook as she waited for Pearl's response. 'Well,' said Pearl, gazing down at her buffet table as she continued. 'I always say clues to a crime are rather like ingredients for a meal. Put them together in the right order, and the results can be very satisfying.' She helped herself to a sprig of Marty's samphire.

'Trailing cheating spouses?' said the young reporter, doubtfully.

'So far I've taken on more interesting cases.'

'Like?'

Pearl paused for a moment. 'Murder,' she said starkly.

Lucy looked up from her reporter's notebook. 'Surely that's a job for the police?'

Pearl nodded. 'But the police can't do their job without help from the public.'

'And private detectives?' asked Lucy knowingly.

'Sometimes,' said Pearl, offering the girl an enigmatic smile, knowing McGuire wouldn't thank her for a story in the local press about how a private detective helped the Canterbury Police Force with its murder cases.

Lucy Walker nodded as she made a final note for herself. 'Fascinating! Maybe we can talk about this again some time?' Pearl was about to give an answer when she noticed Heather Fox across the room, beckoning to her. 'I'm sorry, Lucy, will you excuse me?'

Moving across to Heather, Pearl saw that the festival director was checking her watch and looking concerned.

'Something wrong?'

Heather frowned. 'I'd hoped to start my speech by now, but he's still not here.'

'He?'

'Blake,' said Heather, edgily. 'I called his assistant, James, as soon as I got here, and he assured me they were on their way, but they must have got caught up. I'm afraid Blake's never been very good at arriving anywhere on time.' She looked away anxiously.

'I didn't know you knew him so well?'

Heather turned back to Pearl and explained. 'I worked with him a while back. When I was in London? So I know what he can be like and I suppose I've no one to blame but myself if things go awry.' She exhaled wearily and Pearl suspected another source of anxiety, as Heather glanced across the room towards Cathy McTurk standing with her back to Vesta Korbyn.

'You've . . . matched Blake for the festival event with those two writers,' said Pearl.

'Yes,' said Heather thoughtfully, almost to herself. 'And I'm probably tempting fate by doing so. It's a literary coup,' she added. 'But as I'm sure you've heard, Cathy is Blake's ex-wife, and Vesta? Well, she's . . . just "good friends" with Blake, as they say.' She gave a knowing look. 'To be perfectly honest, I'm sure he's behaved abominably with them both. Cathy had a nice, secure life with her barrister husband, Tom Maitley. Then she met Blake and fell for him . . . No,' she said, revising her train of thought. 'They fell for each other – a *coup de foudre* – and Blake lured her away.'

'But it didn't last,' said Pearl.

'Of course not,' said Heather. 'Thunderstorms rarely do.' She looked knowingly at Pearl. 'I'm sure Cathy put up with more than most women would bear – Blake's giant ego and everything emanating from it. But I do believe she'd still be with him now had she not committed the one sin for which Blake could never forgive her.'

'She had an affair?' asked Pearl, shocked.

'No,' said Heather. 'She wrote a book and it sold more copies than his.'

Pearl's mouth dropped open. Heather moved in closer and added: 'He swears she also stole his research, but you know what they say: good ideas go round in the ether? While Blake may not be able to write a bestseller these days, he's still sufficiently entertaining to draw in the crowds – *if* I can only get him there tomorrow night.'

She looked back at Pearl but Wibke suddenly appeared between them and gave a warm smile to Pearl as she said: 'I think I've just enjoyed the most delicious raspberry sorbet ever! Thank you so much – for everything.'

'A pleasure,' Pearl replied.

Wibke now turned her attention to Heather and tentatively asked: 'I'm . . . wondering when Mr Cain might arrive?'

'Yes,' sighed Heather. 'You and me both.'

For a second, Wibke looked a little confused, but the door to the restaurant suddenly swung open and a young man with sandy-blond shoulder-length hair entered, holding it ajar for the person who followed him. Recognisable from his photograph in the festival brochure, B. J. Cain now stepped into the door frame, where he remained for a moment until he was sure he held the attention of everyone in the room. Standing over two metres tall, he made for an imposing figure, dressed in a peacock-blue silk shirt worn loose over a pair of white jeans. A topaz, set in a silver disc hanging from a leather string around his bull neck, perfectly matched the colour of his eyes, which were set widely in a strong, handsome face. His black straight hair was thick but peppered with silver. A sudden hush spread from the doorway to the bar, a wave of respectful silence in honour of an important new guest. Only then did Blake Cain finally announce: 'I see you've all started without me?' As a few smiles dissolved into guilty expressions, Blake began to laugh, loudly, at everyone else's expense.

'Go on, boy,' he said, pushing the young man at his side forward. 'Looks like we've got some catching up to do!'

The young man accepted two flutes of Prosecco from the tray Ruby offered, and gave one to Blake, who promptly downed it before taking the other from his hand and downing that too. A smile finally spread slowly across his face. 'That's better,' he said.

Heather quickly moved across. 'Good evening, Blake. I'm glad you could finally make it.' Her tone was barbed, though she smiled through it, and allowed Blake to lean forward and kiss her cheek.

He eyed her. 'I bet you are,' he said. 'I can see I'm your pigeon, set among the cats?' He glanced between Cathy and Vesta, but Heather continued in a restrained tone for the benefit of all the guests. 'You're a respected author, nominated for a Booker—'

Another voice broke in. 'But never won.' It was Cathy McTurk who had interrupted, and Blake now turned towards her. 'True,' he said, casually. 'But not to worry, my darling.' He sauntered towards her. 'Because there's always the next book, isn't there?' He held her gaze for a moment then smiled. 'How are you, Cathy?' Taking her hand in his own, he kissed it, his generous lips lingering on her slender fingers; then he turned to Mila, who hugged him politely and appeared to whisper something in his ear. Blake reacted immediately and stared at her. 'Make a scene?' he said. 'Me? Never!' He looked at her in mock innocence and Mila, in turn, looked helplessly at Cathy, who placed her hand on the young woman's arm to reassure her. Blake was already moving on towards someone else. 'And the lovely Vesta,' he smiled. 'What have you been cooking up in your cauldron lately?'

'Good evening, Blake.' she said, controlled, but with a certain vulnerability that seemed wholly incongruous to her sorcerous image. Blake scanned her face then turned back to Heather. 'Amazingly beautiful women,' he said, 'and so talented too. How lucky I am to find myself *squeezed* between them for the event – the filling in this festival sandwich!' He leaned forward and plucked an oyster from the buffet table but, before he could put it to his lips, someone else quickly stepped in and introduced herself. 'Lucy Walker,' smiled the young reporter. 'I wonder if I could possibly speak to you this evening, Mr Cain?' She handed him a business card. Blake stared at it for a moment then appraised the girl. 'The local *Chronicle*?' He looked distinctly underwhelmed. 'Is this what it's come to?'

'We do go out all over Kent.' Lucy smiled but Blake heaved a weary sigh. 'Then I s'pose I should be grateful.' He tipped the oyster into his mouth, gave a wet crunch and swallowed. 'Now, what is it you want to talk about? My great past – or an uncertain future?'

The girl frowned. 'I . . . don't quite understand?'

Blake smiled at her confusion. 'Don't worry, my dear. I'm only teasing you. I've been working on something new.'

'Excellent!' she exclaimed.

'Yes,' said Blake. 'Tell them what it is, James.'

His young companion went to speak but then faltered as his eyes met Lucy's. It was clear to Pearl that she was witnessing a moment of instant attraction between two young people, but James appeared to remember himself and explained quickly: 'Mr Cain is writing an autobiography.'

A murmur went around the room but Blake quickly added: 'And it's no misery memoir either! It's a full-blooded, brutally honest, blow-by-blow account of the life, loves and losses of B. J. Cain . . .' He glanced over towards Vesta, Cathy and Mila, as Lucy began scribbling in her reporter's notebook. 'And . . . do you have a publisher for this new book, Mr Cain?'

'Not yet. But I will,' he said confidently, taking a sip of his drink. 'They'll be fighting over this manuscript once I'm done.' He cast a look around the entire room. 'I do hope you'll all be coming to the event tomorrow night, to hear more about it?' He turned to Heather. 'You did suggest we might each give a reading from a new work?'

'That's right,' said Heather, looking vaguely uncomfortable as she glanced towards Cathy and Vesta Korbyn.

'Good!' said Blake. 'Then I'm sure we will have ourselves a night to remember.'

Pearl noted enthusiasm written on so many faces in the room. Heather put down her drink to step forward and gain attention by raising her voice.

'Now that Blake is finally here,' she began, 'I just want to say how pleased I am that you could all come along here tonight to The Whitstable Pearl. This festival promises to be a superb testament to the creative talents of so many people: to Blake, Cathy and Vesta, and to all our artists, musicians and dancers, but also to those who kindly agreed to support this event, like Pearl, and her wonderful suppliers. I say thank you to you all – and to Wibke and Laurent from our twin town of Borken, I say welcome.'

Heather raised her glass and Colin Fox did the same, but to Pearl's deep embarrassment, and everyone else's amusement, it was Dolly's voice that suddenly called out: '*Willkommen!*'

All the assembled guests now followed in unison, with the toast: '*Willkommen!*' before they took a sip of Prosecco – all, that is, but one. Pearl noted that Cathy McTurk had failed to join in the toast and, instead, was looking across at her former husband as though she had been turned to stone.

Chapter Five

A few hours later, Pearl's buffet table was finally cleared and almost all the invited guests had left, though a few stragglers remained, taking advantage of the last of the Prosecco. Councillor Radcliffe was one. Acting as a barometer of the alcohol he had consumed, his toupee had slipped to one side of his head, where it remained perched precariously above his right ear. Taking a hefty sip from his glass he pointed a finger at Dolly as he remembered something. 'You know . . . I have a friend.'

'Really?' said Dolly, with feigned innocence.

Radcliffe missed Dolly's sarcasm and nodded sagely. 'He wants to buy a property in Harbour Street and hasn't yet found what he's looking for – right price, if you know what I mean?' He offered her a wink, then: 'It's been some time since your place had a makeover,

Mrs Nolan, and it just occurred to me that you might be open to offers. After all, Harbour Street is very desirable these days. Is there any real need for you to be there?' He sidled closer to Dolly as he confided: 'You could make quite a tidy profit for yourself if you sold up now and settled into a little bungalow somewhere. Pensioner's dream home? So, how about I leave my card and you give me a call tomorrow?' As the councillor fumbled in his wallet, Pearl chewed her lip as she waited for her mother's reaction. It came swiftly and abruptly. 'Don't bother,' Dolly snapped. 'I'm not quite sure where I'd put it.'

Radcliffe looked up, confused. 'What?'

'Your card,' said Dolly. 'Though I know what I have to say to your suggestion. I may be a "pensioner" but I have no desire for a "dream home" and no appetite for "tidy profits". I have quite enough to live on and I wish for no more. In fact, my maxim in life has always chimed with that of the Cree Indians: "Only when the last tree is cut, the last fish is caught, and the last river polluted, will you realise . . ."' she paused for effect, but it was another voice that completed Dolly's sentence.

'. . . "You cannot eat money."'

Dolly turned to see Laurent approaching. 'Precisely!' She beamed at Laurent who gallantly offered his arm to her.

'May I walk you home, Mrs Nolan?'

'Oh, thank you,' she smiled. 'Or . . . should I say, *Danke*?' She took his arm. Laurent turned now to Pearl.

'Thank you for a wonderful evening and delicious food. If this evening is an indication of what Whit Fest has in store for us, I cannot wait.' Then he looked back at Dolly, gave her a warm smile and escorted her to the door.

Once they had left the restaurant, Ratty scowled at Pearl. 'Your mother is a hopeless hippy, you know that?' He had just begun to drain the last of his Prosecco when Pearl replied: 'Yes, I do. And *you* . . . were not invited.' She looked down pointedly at the empty glass in his hand. Reluctantly, Radcliffe relinquished it before setting off and weaving a circuitous route across the restaurant floor. As he opened the door, a stiffening sea breeze whistled in and caught his toupee, which flopped straight to the ground like a shot grouse. Ratty was forced to turn back to pick it up, his eyes narrowing as they met Pearl's. He stuffed the hairpiece into his jacket pocket and exited smartly, while Pearl managed to stifle her amusement until the door of The Whitstable Pearl had finally closed after him. Then she smiled, looked down at the empty glass in her hand, and headed with it to the kitchen where she found Ruby busily putting away some platters.

As Pearl prepared to load up her dishwasher with the last of her glasses, she noticed that the one in her hand was not in fact the last, because Marty Smith was still sipping from his own as he stood by the refrigerator, musing.

'Seventy thousand tons of asparagus, eh?' He shook his head slowly at the thought. 'That's some market.'

56

Downing his drink, he was just preparing to reward himself with a refill when Pearl took his glass from him and promptly stacked it in the dishwasher. 'Sorry, Marty,' she said. 'Party's over.' She moved efficiently back into the restaurant and began setting chairs on tables. Marty followed her quickly, offering her a hand as he went on: 'I would, of course, consider cutting you in.'

'On what?'

'The deal, of course. I'm beginning to think this festival could be more than just a beano for the local arty crowd.' He pointed at Pearl as he continued: 'You know when you toss a pebble into a lake and the waves all ripple out? Whit Fest could be like that for the whole town.'

Pearl considered what he had just said as she upended the last of her chairs. 'Yes,' she said, thoughtfully. 'I have a feeling you may be right.'

Marty took a pen from his jacket pocket and picked up a paper napkin on which he began to do a few calculations. 'And who'd imagine they'd be so hot for it, eh?'

'Sorry?' said Pearl, distracted.

Marty eyed her. 'Asparagus, of course. You heard what the German lady said, Vibky . . .?'

'Wibke,' said Pearl.

'There's a gap in the supply chain and, with my connections, *I'm* the man to plug it.' He looked up from his calculations, cash registers almost visible in his eyes.

'With *Spargel*?' asked Pearl.

'That's right,' mumbled Marty, still working on his figures.

'I . . . don't think so, Marty.'

At this, he looked up quizzically, and Pearl explained. 'It's a . . . different kind of asparagus.'

'Eh?'

'*Spargel* is white . . .'

Marty's nose wrinkled. '*White?*'

Pearl nodded. 'Didn't Wibke mention this?'

His silence spoke volumes. 'Well,' said Pearl. 'I thought you would have known. Or . . . did the prospect of a "gap in the market" cause you to forget?' Marty looked down at his calculations, his lips setting tightly shut as he screwed up the paper napkin in his hand and shoved it into his pocket.

'Never mind,' said Pearl, 'as I pointed out to you in the shop, I'm sure Wibke *will* return home with a glowing report about your own *green* spears. And you must admit,' she went on, 'it *was* a privilege to be invited to contribute tonight?' She gave him a wink and Marty took a deep breath before issuing a small sigh at the sight of her warm smile.

'I suppose so,' he finally agreed.

Pearl planted her hands on his strong shoulders and leaned in towards him. 'Thanks, Marty,' she said, rewarding him with a chaste peck on the cheek. Buoyed by this, the greengrocer suddenly beamed. Pearl handed him his jacket and he headed to the door where he suddenly paused to look back at her, recognising that she was the only woman who could dash his spirits – then raise them again – in such a short space of time. 'G'night, Pearl,' he said.

As he exited, Pearl stared after him until Ruby appeared at her side.

'It was a great night,' she said brightly.

Pearl turned to see her waitress getting into a little black jacket, flipping her long fair hair out from under its collar. 'Everyone seemed to have a good time?'

Pearl nodded. 'Yes,' she said, adding softly to herself. '*Almost* everyone.'

Half an hour later, back home at Seaspray Cottage, Pearl was about to relax with a large vodka and tonic when her phone rang. She answered it to find Nathan on the line.

'So how d'it go?' he asked.

'Very well,' said Pearl. 'Though you were sorely missed.'

'Always good to hear,' he said. 'Did your detective make it?'

Pearl paused for a moment before admitting: 'No. But it wouldn't have been his kind of thing.' She covered some disappointment with a question: 'What about the opera?'

'Spectacular performance!' Nathan said. '*Pelléas et Mélisande.*'

'I'm . . . afraid I don't know it.'

'Debussy, darling. Based on a love triangle.'

'A little like Heather's literary event then – Blake Cain, Cathy McTurk and Vesta Korbyn?'

'Not quite,' said Nathan. 'The opera's triangle features one woman and two men. And how's Dolly?'

'Helping the *entente cordiale*,' smiled Pearl. 'Or the German equivalent – because she's entertaining one of the Borken "ambassadors" as I speak.'

Nathan was taken aback. 'What?'

'Laurent Ruppert from the Borken committee,' said Pearl. 'He escorted her home tonight so he's probably getting a peek at some of Mum's masterpieces right now . . . Her artwork, that is,' she added quickly before she smiled and sipped her vodka.

'And you?'

Pearl stared down at her glass. 'Well, I've . . . just poured myself a well-earned drink.'

A pause followed before Nathan spoke again. 'It's a mystery.'

'What is?'

'Why an attractive woman like you should be sitting all on your own at the end of the evening with only two cats for company.' He paused then added softly: 'Or maybe there's no mystery at all. Maybe you just prefer it that way.'

'And maybe you're right,' Pearl said, considering this for a moment as she took another sip of her drink.

'What're you thinking?' asked Nathan.

'Something Marty said tonight . . .'

'Ah, Mr Turnip!'

'Don't be so mean.'

'I'm not. He'd take that as a compliment. The man talks of nothing else *but* vegetables. He really needs to get himself a life – aside from tubers and rhizomes. So what piece of wisdom did he have to impart?'

'He happened to say how Whit Fest could have an important impact on our town. A bit like . . . ripples spreading out after a pebble's been tossed into a lake?'

'Well, he's right there,' said Nathan. 'It's getting a lot of publicity already. Aren't you pleased I got you involved?'

'Yes, I am,' she admitted with a smile, pausing for only a moment before adding: 'But you will be back in time for the opening event tomorrow?'

'Just try keeping me away, sweetie. Come to me at six and we'll head off together, OK? Now I must fly. Nighty night.'

A moment later and the line went dead.

Pearl reflected for a moment on her conversation with Nathan, then moved to the kitchen door and stepped outside into the garden. In spite of the sea breeze, the night was still warm and the sky streaked with a golden glow, promising another good day tomorrow. Waves could be heard lapping on to the shore as she strolled on towards her office in the garden. Unlocking the door she stepped inside and switched on the light. Checking the answerphone, she found no calls, but noted a tiny money spider was busy weaving a web across the phone receiver and its cradle. She sat down at her desk and watched the spider for a few moments, reminded of Vesta Korbyn's extraordinary earrings, then she brought up the Take Three Writers event on the festival website on her laptop.

The page featured a series of extremely flattering photos of Cain, McTurk and Korbyn. Cathy's beautifully benign smile stared straight out from the screen while Vesta glared menacingly and Blake gave a look that conveyed all of his natural swagger and charm. Information followed about the authors' novels and accolades, while the festival blurb, written by Heather, promised an 'entertaining' event from a 'panel of writers at the top of their game' who would be 'talking frankly' about their novels and the inspiration for them. Pearl reflected on the writers, intrigued by them all, by their individual success and the fact that they were all so distinct and yet connected . . .

Taking another sip of her drink, she mused on the question that the young journalist, Lucy Walker, had asked her tonight: 'Why would a chef and restaurateur be interested in solving crimes?' In fact, it had been some considerable time since Pearl had received an enquiry for the detective agency. Perhaps she would never get another case. Perhaps she should just stick to running The Whitstable Pearl, as Dolly and McGuire never tired of telling her. And yet something in her refused to give up and leave it all behind. She picked up one of her Nolan's Detective Agency business cards and read the words on it: 'Sole proprietor Pearl Nolan', and tried to convince herself of her own talent and significance beyond cookery. Surely, in time, another case would come along – something to exercise the natural skills she possessed; skills that she knew easily rivalled McGuire's, with all his formal training. Another mystery would surely be along for her to solve. Maybe sooner rather than later.

Chapter Six

The next morning, Pearl arrived at The Whitstable Pearl to find Ruby humming to herself as she set bud vases of pale pink antique roses on to the restaurant's freshly laundered table linen, while Dolly sat hunched in a corner near the kitchen, nursing an espresso. As soon as she looked up and saw Pearl, Dolly groaned.

'Don't tell me,' said Pearl. 'Too much Prosecco?'

'If only,' sighed Dolly. 'But I'm afraid we went on to something stronger.'

'We?' Pearl asked pointedly.

'Laurent wanted to see my paintings and I happened to find that leftover bottle of corn schnapps Charlie brought back from Berlin. Remember when he went over to design those T-shirts?'

'How could I forget?' But with a wry smile Pearl added: 'To be honest, I'm surprised you ever have a bottle of anything left over.' She sat down with Dolly, who put a hand to her head and said proudly: 'I have a fine history of being able to resist schnapps – that is, until a German happens to visit. Then it would be churlish not to join them in a little.'

'Have you had something to eat?'

Dolly grimaced. 'I really don't think I could face anything . . . yet,' she said. 'I had to come out to get some paracetamol.' She produced a bottle from her pocket, shook it and winced at the resulting sound. Not for the first time, Pearl considered her mother with a curious mixture of frustration, compassion and good humour. In spite of being in her sixties, it seemed that Dolly was determined to behave more like an adolescent daughter than Pearl's mother.

'So you had a good time?' asked Pearl.

Dolly managed a weak smile. 'Wonderful,' she said. 'Laurent is such a cultured man. He knows an awful lot about art and I did try to practise my German, but it really is such a complex language with all the grammar and pronunciation.' She now leaned forward to confide: 'But he loves my work, Pearl. He said my vision was . . . "truly authentic". So, I think I might gift him *Undertow*.'

'But you're meant to be selling—'

'I know,' said Dolly quickly. 'But it would be so nice to see the painting go to the right person?'

'Yes, it would,' Pearl agreed finally, recognising that Dolly viewed the results of her creative endeavours as work to be enjoyed rather than valued materially. 'And it's lovely to have someone be so appreciative of your paintings,' Pearl added, before she paused to reflect on how nice it would be if McGuire ever fully appreciated her own talents in crime detection, rather than betraying irritation at what he all too often considered to be interference in his police work.

'Sure I can't rustle up some scrambled eggs for you?'

Dolly grimaced at the suggestion and got to her feet. 'No, thanks. I'm going to head home before the paracetamol wears off and try for a nap – or as the Germans would say, *eine Nickerchen* – or is it *ein*?' She frowned, unsure, then shrugged and said, 'I'll have to ask Laurent.'

'So . . . you're seeing him again?' asked Pearl. Dolly paused as she headed to the door. 'But of course!' she said, offering a wink. '*Auf Wiedersehen*, Pearl.' And with that she was gone.

Pearl had barely had time to pick up Dolly's empty coffee mug when Ruby appeared with a white envelope in her hand. 'I just found this near the till,' she said. 'It's from the cleaner. Seems a guest left something behind last night?'

Taking the envelope from Ruby, Pearl read the note inside then took out the contents. Dangling a single earring between her fingers, she considered the silver spider suspended from a delicate thread – aware that there was only one guest it could possibly belong to. Taking her mobile phone from her bag, she quickly dialled the number for Heather Fox. When the call went straight to Heather's voicemail, she decided against leaving a message and rang off.

'Something wrong?' asked Ruby, noting Pearl's thoughtful look as she continued to consider the spider earring. Pearl checked her watch. It was 9.40 and the restaurant didn't open for another hour. 'No, Ruby, it's fine,' said Pearl. 'Just hold the fort and I'll be right back.'

It took less than ten minutes to drive to Ham Shades Lane where Pearl managed to park directly outside Vesta Korbyn's home. The street had gained its poetic name in the mid-1940s and Vesta's imposing gabled house sat near its southern end. It lay close to an area of open land on which, more than a hundred and fifty years ago, a stationary winding engine had once been installed to help the Invicta railway engine cope with a steep incline on the historic line running between Whitstable and Canterbury. Over a century later, this green space had also offered room for campsite accommodation to serve the overspill of visitors during the town's Oyster Festival, and staged numerous charity boot fairs. The area's mature trees and dense scrub and hedgerows also provided a foraging habitat for bats and a home to many birds, including the carrion crow. That last fact struck Pearl as particularly appropriate as she approached the home of the Queen of Gothic Noir, on a visit Pearl knew she was making more to satisfy her own curiosity than a real need to return a customer's item of jewellery in person.

A wooden fence separated Vesta's home from the road, and on a large driveway sat the conspicuous black sedan car which Pearl now identified as a vintage Cadillac. The house itself looked as forbidding as Pearl's Seaspray Cottage was welcoming. There was no evidence of any flowerbeds in the front garden, just a rash of Virginia Creeper clinging to dark brickwork. Approaching a sombre front door, Pearl hesitated as she saw that the heavy cast-iron doorknocker was in the form of a large black rat but, at that very moment, Pearl heard voices coming from beyond a wooden gate to the garden and she moved towards them, certain she had just heard the stentorian tones of Blake Cain.

'So what are you going to do about it?' he asked.

Silence.

Pearl moved closer to the gate, hearing Vesta offering a reply in a soft, low tone. 'You haven't exactly left me much choice, have you?'

'And would you do, dear Vesta, if you were in my position?'

'I'm not,' she said flatly. 'And I never would be, because I'd never do this to you.' She heaved a sigh. 'Look, what's done is done, Blake. *The moving finger writes and, having writ, moves on*, remember?'

'Indeed,' Blake agreed.

'So why dredge up the past?'

'Because all I care about now . . . is the present.'

A pause before Vesta spoke again. 'And yourself, of course,' she said. 'Nothing's changed there, has it?'

A silence fell before Blake spoke again. 'I'm a writer, Vesta, as are you. Haven't you understood by now that we are all rather like . . . pedigree dogs? In the same way that a retriever retrieves or a scent hound picks up a trail, we writers simply write. It's what we do. It makes us who we are. So I'm writing this book whether you like it or not. As to the "moving finger", you'd do well to remember: *Nor all your piety nor wit shall lure it back to cancel half a line. Nor all your tears wash out a word of it.*'

A silence fell and, for a tense moment, Pearl suspected the garden gate might suddenly open to reveal her eavesdropping on the other side. She quickly called out. 'Hello? Anyone there?'

Footsteps sounded on the other side. The gate opened and Vesta Korbyn peered from behind it. In spite of the fact that it was still morning, she was wearing a long black dress with a low neckline studded with sequins that reflected the sunlight. Her emerald-green eyes were filled with surprise – and a little fear – so Pearl explained quickly, 'I'm so sorry to bother you, but I believe this is yours?' She handed the earring to Vesta, who studied the silver spider for a moment before meeting Pearl's gaze. 'Yes,' she said, confused. 'Yes, of course. I . . . realised last night that I'd lost it.' Looking awkward, she glanced back quickly towards her garden before offering an explanation. 'I wasn't sure if it had fallen off in the car but I . . . haven't had time to check properly.'

Before she could say another word, Blake Cain appeared behind her, puffing on a cheroot in his hand.

'Ah, The Whitstable Pearl!' he exclaimed. 'What a fine party you threw for us last night.' He offered an amiable smile.

'I'm glad you enjoyed it,' said Pearl. 'But I always find it's the guests who make a good party.'

'Indeed it is.' He smiled again and appraised Pearl unashamedly as he sucked on his cheroot. Vesta exchanged a quick glance with him then turned her attention again to Pearl. 'Well, thank you for returning this,' she said, pocketing her earring. 'It was careless of me to lose something so precious.' She looked pointedly at Blake now.

'Not lost my dear,' he said. 'Merely mislaid. Whitstable's Pearl here found it for you.' As he offered another smile for Pearl, Vesta looked decidedly uncomfortable. 'I really should be getting on with some work now,' she said.

'Ditto!' Blake decided. 'A few more pages and I should be at my glossary!'

Vesta glanced sharply at him, but Blake kept his eyes on Pearl for a moment before asking. 'Don't suppose you fancy giving me a lift back into town?'

On the spot, Pearl replied: 'I don't see why not.'

Vesta frowned. 'Blake?'

He looked back at her, unconcerned. 'What is it, Vesta?'

Looking between Pearl and Blake for a moment, she then shook her head. 'Nothing.'

'Good,' said Blake. 'Then I'll see you this evening, for what should be a very enjoyable – and enlightening – evening.' He gave a slow smile before adding: 'For the audience at least.' He leaned forward to kiss her, but Vesta turned her face to one side so that his lips merely brushed her long, raven-coloured hair. Taking another drag on his cheroot, Blake stepped out of the garden. 'Onwards then, Whitstable Pearl!'

Once they had reached Pearl's Fiat, Blake looked back only once to see Vesta's garden gate closing. Pearl could see he was musing for a moment, then he opened the passenger door to her car before suddenly remembering the cheroot still in his hand. Taking a final suck on it, he dropped it down the drain beneath Pearl's front wheel. 'Evil things, those cheroots,' he said. 'But fortunately I'll be back on my hand-rolled Havanas soon.' He took his place beside Pearl. 'Ready?'

'As I'll ever be,' said Pearl, as she started up the ignition.

Pearl drove back towards town, passing the old railway station with its white wooden canopy shining brightly in the sunshine. A train had just arrived from which passengers had alighted, most of them wheeling luggage for a weekend stay in town – some guests destined, perhaps, for Dolly's Attic, thought Pearl.

'And where would you like to be dropped?' she asked, realising she had just taken on the role of B. J. Cain's chauffeur.

'As near to Marine Parade as you'd like to take me, my darling.' He winked at her.

'You mean . . . you'd like me to deliver you to your front door,' Pearl said knowingly.

'Nice of you to offer,' he said charmingly. 'Or else I'll have to walk. I've no car these days – lost my licence due to speeding – and James doesn't drive.'

'James?'

'My assistant – you met him last night.'

Pearl nodded. 'It's not a bad day for a walk,' she suggested, but Blake shook his head. 'I'll pass on that, if you don't mind. I find most exercise to be highly overrated. Everyone I know who indulges in it has plastic knees – at least, everyone of my age, that is. And all the old reprobates I once knew who gave up booze and baccy seem now to have given up on life too.' He looked at Pearl. 'What's so precious about a few more years if they're spent clogging up a geriatric home, eh?' He shrugged. 'The Scandinavians have a saying, you know: "When the devil grows old, he goes to live in a monastery." Not for me. I'd rather go out with a bang than a whimper.'

Pearl said nothing to this but Blake noted her wry smile and said: 'You think I'm an amusing old fool, don't you, Whitstable Pearl?'

'Amusing, perhaps,' she said. 'But hardly old – and certainly no fool.'

Blake fixed her with a steely gaze. 'And you,' he said, 'are a beautiful woman. But you'll know that – being no fool yourself.' He looked out of the window as Pearl drove on, past the harbour and towards the old almshouses before the castle gatehouse came into view, where she took a left turning and climbed the slope on old Tower Hill, past her favourite summer tea gardens that looked out over the coastline directly above Colin Fox's cottage, Fairview. Not a single wave seemed to stir the sea as they headed on to Marine Parade. The clear sky had turned the waters a deep blue, unblemished by anything other than the Street of Stones, which was becoming visible with the lowering tide like a sharp golden arrow pointing out towards the horizon. 'Our German visitors are staying at Beacon House down there,' said Pearl. 'The house overlooking the Street.'

'So I hear,' said Blake, impassive. 'The woman, Wibke, has invited me there for tea. She seems to know that I use my summer house as a writing studio, and so she asked if she can come and have a photo taken with me there.' He looked at Pearl and smiled. 'Whatever others may think of me, I've still managed to keep at least one fan.'

'I'm sure you have many more than that.'

'Including you, Whitstable Pearl?'

'I'm . . . afraid I haven't read any of your books.'

'Yet,' said Blake. 'But you will,' he said confidently. 'I guarantee everyone will be reading my new book. Even you. In fact, I shall give you a signed copy on publication. How's that?'

'Are you really close to finishing it?'

He nodded. 'I am indeed. Just a matter of days, I reckon. And I can't tell you how pleased I am about that. If there's one thing I enjoy more than writing, it's finishing writing.' He gave a smile which seemed to freeze as he went on. 'I've given up on worthy fiction and taken a leaf out of my wife's books – forgive the pun. And I should say my "former" wife, of course. Cathy's always known what readers want: sex, scandal and—' He was just about to add something more when he broke off suddenly. 'You can drop me here!' he said quickly, tapping the windscreen with his newspaper like a driving instructor signalling for an emergency stop. Pearl braked and looked up at the large house outside which she had just drawn up. She had passed it many times before and always gave it more than a casual glance, since it was so striking – painted white, with a distinctive wooden balustrade across the whole of its first floor in the style of a cricket pavilion.

'I didn't realise you lived here,' she said. 'Didn't this used to belong to Stanley Reeves?'

Blake looked blank. 'Stanley who?'

'Reeves. I think the family came to Whitstable some time in the sixteenth century. Reeves Beach is named after them and I read somewhere that Stanley built this house in the 1920s?'

'The date's certainly right,' said Blake, looking out of the passenger window towards his home. 'It was an old care home for a while but I got it for a song and redeveloped it.' Taking a deep breath he became reflective as he stared away from the house and out towards the sea. 'I wasn't expecting to be back here ever again, so close to the cold North Sea. Out in Malibu I'd got rather used to a view of the Pacific Ocean, but I must admit that with the work I've done on this place, it now has a certain California feel, don't you think?' Pearl noted the tall yucca plants in large terracotta urns on the front patio. 'I named it Alegría,' he said. 'Spanish for "joy".' He summoned a smile and leaned in close to her. 'And once my new book is published, I expect to be moving to somewhere where the sun *always* shines.' He paused and turned to her. 'Thank you, Whitstable Pearl,' he said. 'See you tonight?'

'Of course,' said Pearl. 'I wouldn't miss your event for the world.'

'And neither would I,' said Blake Cain. 'Neither would I.'

His eyes met Pearl's once more and for a second she felt trapped in his piercing gaze, all part of the physical magnetism he still possessed. Then he appeared to look beyond her to the house. 'Ah, there's the boy,' he said. 'Solicitous as ever. A good arrangement,' he added. 'James seems to need very little apart from a roof over his head, and in return he keeps me in check, or, at least, he does his best to.' He looked away towards James and said wistfully: 'Oh to be that age once more, eh? Tell me, Whitstable Pearl, would you do things differently if you could?' Before Pearl had a chance to reply, he quickly added: 'No. You really don't have to answer that. Writers are far too nosy.' With that, he gave a wink and pushed his thick black hair back from his forehead. 'Thanks for the lift.'

He stepped out of the car and Pearl watched him as he moved on towards the house. James Moore stood on the threshold of Alegría to welcome his employer home. Blake moved directly inside, leaving his young assistant to offer Pearl a polite wave of thanks from the door, before he too re-entered the house. She then started up her Fiat, before pausing for a moment to reflect on Blake's last question, allowing it to resonate as she stared away towards the beach below the slopes. As a young woman with a bright future clearly marked out before her, like the exposed shingle on the Street of Stones below, Pearl had found herself suddenly presented with a dilemma. It was true she could have continued on the path she had chosen – a promising career in the police force which might have set her at McGuire's rank by now – but instead she had followed her heart and stayed in Whitstable to bring up her son. As Blake Cain's words echoed in her mind, Pearl considered whether it would have been possible for her to have done things differently. But the answer coming back to her was a resounding no.

Having raced back to town, Pearl discovered that her staff had already opened The Whitstable Pearl in her absence. Chef Dean was pan-frying a mackerel fillet, and the pungent aroma of garlic, cumin and ginger filled the kitchen air from a Moroccan fish tagine cooking in the oven. Ruby was busy assembling a *salade Niçoise*. Pearl took off her jacket and quickly pinned up her long hair as she apologised to her staff for being late.

'No problem,' smiled Ruby. 'But someone's asked for you at table five.'

Curious, Pearl moved on to the restaurant floor to see Cathy McTurk seated at a window table beside a tall man with receding dark hair. 'They just had brunch,' Pearl's young waitress explained. 'The man's paid, but Mrs McTurk said she wanted to wait to see you.'

'Thanks, Ruby.'

As the girl returned to her salad-making duties, Pearl studied Cathy McTurk's companion for a second or two more. In spite of being dressed casually in a short-sleeved shirt and Chino trousers, he had an oddly formal bearing about him, sitting with a rod-straight back and the expressionless features of a good poker player as he listened intently to Cathy, who broke off at the sight of Pearl approaching.

'Ah, there she is!' Cathy's eyes met Pearl's. 'I'm so glad I caught you. I didn't want to leave last night without thanking you properly for that wonderful buffet – but you had your hands rather full at the time.' She smiled. 'Heather told me how you'd stepped into the breach. That was so very good of you.' As she looked at Pearl, her head tilted, bird-like, to one side. Her expression seemed as warm and open as her companion's was inscrutable. 'Sorry,' she said quickly. 'Let me introduce you – Tom Maitley, meet Pearl Nolan.'

The man gave a polite nod but Cathy continued brightly, as though she was accustomed to filling a natural gap in their conversation: 'I thought I'd bring Tom here for a treat. And to say thank you to him too.' She smiled at him and explained to Pearl: 'Tom's my guru for all things legal.'

At this, Tom Maitley's expression softened as he finally returned Cathy's smile. 'My pleasure,' he said. For a moment he seemed lost in her gaze, then appeared to remember himself and looked away.

'Can I get you some complimentary drinks?' Pearl asked. 'Coffee? Juice? A liqueur?'

'No,' said Cathy quickly. 'We've just had the most wonderful brunch here and I really should be getting back to prepare for the event this evening.' Her face seemed to cloud at the thought but, as she picked up her handbag, she asked: 'Will we be seeing you this evening at The Horsebridge?'

'Of course,' Pearl smiled. 'I'll be coming along with my mother and an old friend, Nathan.'

'Nathan Roscoe?' asked Cathy tentatively. 'The travel writer?'

Pearl nodded. 'That's right.'

'How lovely,' said Cathy. 'I enjoy his articles so much, I've always wanted to meet him. Perhaps tonight I shall.' She got to her feet while Tom Maitley solicitously pulled aside her chair and then wrapped a pale blue pashmina about her shoulders. For a moment, as Cathy tucked her bag under her arm, Pearl thought she detected her cheerful mask slipping, but Tom Maitley attentively placed his hand on her shoulder and steered her towards the door. After they had exited the restaurant, Pearl waited a moment then took out her mobile phone and dialled a number.

'What is it, Pearl?' asked Dolly sleepily.

'Sorry to wake you,' she said. 'But I'm sure Heather mentioned the name Tom Maitley last night?'

'Yes,' Dolly yawned. 'That'll be Cathy McTurk's ex-husband. The man she left for Blake Cain? He's a lawyer of some sort. Why?'

'Nothing important,' said Pearl. 'Enjoy your nap.'

Later that afternoon, after ensuring adequate cover at the restaurant, Pearl headed home to Seaspray Cottage and took a cool shower before searching through her wardrobe for something suitable to wear for Whit Fest's opening event. The dry heat of the day had become muggy with the vanishing tide, and the salt smell of seaweed clung to the air entering Pearl's bedroom window as she looked through her summer dresses. Since Dean had joined her staff, Pearl had been looking forward to spending a little less time at The Whitstable Pearl, so she had recently splashed out on a few more items. Though her tall, slim figure was the perfect frame for most fashions, vintage styles were her favourite. She was a romantic at heart – one reason why she had failed to compromise over the years and settle for second best – and she couldn't help thinking that the white cotton dress worn by the young reporter, Lucy Walker, the previous evening, with its pretty mother-of-pearl buttons, would have been the perfect outfit for tonight's event, if only Pearl had seen it first. It would also match the beautiful freshwater pearl earrings that McGuire had given her last summer . . .

79

She took them from her jewellery box and put them on, noting how well they always matched her moonstone grey eyes; but without a suitable occasion on which to wear them lately, and having been stashed away too long, the pearls had seemed to have lost their lustre. Pearl decided that wearing them for tonight's event would enliven them – and the wearer . . .

She slipped into a bright red shift dress and matching espadrilles and shook out her long dark curls. Adding a slick of scarlet lipstick and a puff of Italian perfume she had bought on a holiday in Sorrento, she judged herself ready and was halfway down the stairs when her doorbell rang. She smiled to herself, assuming that Nathan, impatient as ever, had decided to come to her rather than waiting, as planned, for Pearl. But on opening her front door she found somebody else on her doorstep.

'You . . .'

'I'm sorry,' said McGuire quickly, 'I know I should have called first, but it's been difficult . . .' He broke off, suddenly silenced as he properly took in the sight of Pearl standing in the doorway. Over the last few weeks he had often summoned up an image of her in his mind, during the long hours spent on surveillance operations, writing up reports and preparing evidence for the CPS, but as he looked at her now, he realised his memory didn't do Pearl justice.

'The case, you mean?' she murmured, confused.

McGuire gave a quick nod then leaned back to cast a look down Island Wall.

'What is it?' Pearl asked, noting his concern.

'Can I come in?' He took a step forward, which forced Pearl to explain quickly: 'I'm . . . just about to go out. There's a festival on.'

Seeing her torn expression, McGuire became even more tense. 'I know and . . . that's what I want to talk to you about.'

'Good,' said Pearl. 'I left a message for you the other night but I wasn't sure if you'd got it. Would you like to come along?' She looked at him expectantly, and McGuire noted she was wearing the pearl earrings he had bought for her. He looked pained. 'I can't,' he said. 'I'm heading back to the station with . . .' Before he could utter another word, a woman came up and stood at his side. She was tall and slender and wore a beige linen jacket and blue jeans; her long blonde hair was clipped back efficiently from her beautiful face. She cocked her head sideways and said: 'Call from the station. We really should go, sir.' She looked back in the direction from which she'd just appeared, and Pearl leaned forward to see McGuire's car parked nearby. He stiffly replied to the attractive blonde: 'In a second. I need to talk to Miss Nolan about the message.'

Pearl frowned at the formal title he had used for her. 'What message?'

For a moment the blonde looked as though she might argue with McGuire, but instead she glanced back at Pearl and then returned to the car. Pearl watched her go before turning to McGuire as she asked, pointedly: '"Sir"?'

'My new DS,' he explained.

Pearl's mouth dropped open. 'That . . . is Terry Bosley?'

McGuire gave a nod. 'Terri with an "i".'

Pearl glanced down the street to see DS Terri Bosley in the passenger seat of McGuire's car, indicating her mobile phone to him.

Pearl frowned. A million thoughts entered her head, along with a million questions about the beautiful blonde, but all she could verbalise in that moment was: 'Looks like she needs you.' She closed the front door firmly behind her. McGuire stepped forward, concerned. 'Look, if you'd just let me explain . . .'

But Pearl felt an instinctive urge to escape. 'I'm sorry,' she said quickly. 'I'm late. I . . . really have to go.'

Stepping out on to the pavement, she headed off briskly down the street towards Nathan's cottage, while McGuire stared after her, wanting to pursue her. But, instead, he looked back at DS Bosley, who offered him a sweet smile. After all these weeks away from Pearl, McGuire could have kicked himself for handling this reunion so badly. Although he lived for his work, there were times he wished he'd never joined the force. This was one of them. He took a deep breath and trudged back to his car.

Chapter Seven

Five minutes after Pearl had left McGuire on the doorstep of Seaspray Cottage, Nathan turned to her from the passenger seat in her Fiat, and asked: 'Can you tell me why we're *driving* to The Horsebridge?'

Pearl's eyes remained fixed on the road. 'Because the event begins at six thirty and I promised Heather I'd be there way before. It's already gone six now, so we're late.'

'And we're late because of McGee?'

Pearl glanced at Nathan, who raised his hands to surrender as he commented, 'OK. So his new cop buddy turns out to be a woman. He didn't actually lie to you about it, did he?'

'He omitted to tell me.'

'And so you assumed this new person had to be a guy?'

Pearl looked at him but said nothing. Nathan continued: 'Wasn't that a little sexist of you? I mean, I assume you wouldn't be so upset if "DS Terri" was ten years older and had a face only a mother could love?' He waited patiently for Pearl's reply.

'Maybe not,' she admitted. 'And if you must know, I'm not "upset". I'm just . . . angry with myself. Can you believe I was actually feeling *sorry* for him for missing out on our trip away and having to bed in a new partner?'

Nathan's eyebrows rose at this, but Pearl quickly ordered, 'Don't say a word! And yes, I *did* imagine Bosley to be male, pale and stale, and not a ringer for Cameron Diaz.'

Nathan's eyes widened with interest. 'Cameron—?'

'Can we drop this now?' said Pearl quickly, in a tone that gave Nathan little choice.

'Sure.'

'Good.'

Five minutes later they had managed to find a parking space in an area known as Keam's Yard, close to the beach and the evening's venue at The Horsebridge centre. The Horsebridge actually referred to a strip of land that had once served as an approach route for horses to unload at sea. But, in time, Europe's first passenger and freight steam railway, the Crab and Winkle Line, had taken over transportation, and for years the site had remained ramshackle, even more so after a bomb had dropped nearby during the last war. It seemed these days that only a few people remembered the nearby disused bus garage, which had been taken over and run by local artists, Johnny's Art House having served as a space for exhibitions and local events. Dolly had once rehearsed there with the Fish Slappers, when her costume still fitted, but the council had finally torn down the old building to make way for a new development – and The Horsebridge centre was now the town's cultural hub.

With its roof shaped like the upturned hull of a timber ship, the new building staged art exhibitions, concerts and classes ranging from yoga to flamenco. It overlooked a historic pub, the Pearson's Arms, and a spacious beachfront restaurant which had gained a good reputation with the London press – though this caused no professional anxiety for Pearl. Entering the bar at The Horsebridge with Nathan, Pearl found several familiar figures gathered near the balcony. Heather and her father, Colin, were standing near to Cathy and her former husband, Tom Maitley, while the young journalist, Lucy Walker, this time dressed in a smart blue trouser suit, was chatting to Mila Anton. Vesta Korbyn was seated at a distance from the others, wearing striking make-up and a stunning black dress with a pointed hem, looking every inch the Queen of Darkness, as well as Gothic Noir, as she chatted to a group of tattooed teenage fans.

'You go ahead and say hi to the others while I get us a drink,' said Nathan. As he moved off to the bar, Pearl did as he suggested and headed out on to the balcony, across which a welcome breeze blew in from the sea. Mila Anton ended her conversation with Lucy Walker and came over immediately to offer her hand to Pearl. 'Thank you so much for hosting the party last night,' she said warmly. Close up, and in sharp focus, Mila's beauty was simply breathtaking. Again she wore a bright turban, this time of gold silk, from which a silver pendant hung, lying flat against her forehead. Her sensuous lips drew back into a smile as Pearl shook her hand.

'My pleasure,' said Pearl finally. 'The festival's turning into quite a phenomenon,' she added, looking around the room. 'So much local talent.' She looked back at Mila as she added: 'And I hear you write poetry?'

Before Mila could respond, a loud, familiar laugh went up at a table on which sat Wibke and her brother, Laurent, with Dolly braying like a donkey over something Laurent had just said. Cathy sidled up to Pearl, having heard her question.

'Mila's very modest about her work,' she said. 'But she does indeed have real talent, not only in expressing herself but in encouraging others.' She smiled proudly at the beautiful young woman who explained: 'I run a workshop, with some arts funding.'

'In Canterbury?' asked Pearl.

Mila nodded. 'Are you interested in poetry?'

Pearl smiled. 'Yes, though I can't say I'm up on many contemporary poets.'

Mila reached into her bag and produced a flyer. 'Then you must come along to our festival event this week.'

Pearl considered the event's title. 'A Way with Words . . .'

'It seemed a good description,' said Mila. 'I found my own way, my identity, through words. And now I try to help others to do the same. I also read for those who haven't quite got up their confidence to do so.'

Cathy spoke now. 'It'll be held at my home in Northwood Road, near the castle? The children always loved playing out in the orangery, but now it serves as an excellent functions room.' She shared a smile with Mila and put her arm around the young woman's shoulder. Pearl succumbed to their charm. 'Thanks. I'd love to come.'

Cathy now glanced at the bar and put on her glasses. 'Is that Nathan Roscoe?'

Pearl followed Cathy's gaze to see Nathan waiting impatiently for service at the crowded bar. 'It is indeed,' said Pearl.

'Then I shall go and introduce myself. Coming Mila?' Cathy slipped off her glasses again and the two women set off for the bar, while Pearl leaned against the rail of the balcony to gaze out across the small piazza it overlooked. It seemed to be filled with tourists, either studying maps or glancing up curiously at The Horsebridge building in a way that few locals would ever have cause to do. Pearl raised her face to the cool breeze and, a moment later, caught sight of Tom Maitley nearby. He seemed to Pearl to be in need of some air, or a welcome break from conversation, or both. As his eyes met Pearl's, she smiled. 'Must be very handy to have legal advice always close to hand.'

He took Pearl's gaze to Cathy talking to Mila and Nathan at the bar, then he looked back again at Pearl.

'The same with culinary skills, I'd imagine,' he said. 'Of which I have none.' He sipped from the glass of red wine in his hand. 'I'm not an expert in publishing contracts,' he continued. 'But I've always helped Cathy as much as I can. Creative people need protecting,' he said. 'Or they're liable to be taken advantage of.' His expression set with this thought and, as though uncomfortable at meeting Pearl's gaze, he stared down into his glass before knocking back the rest of his wine. Having done so, he realised he had lost another aid to making small talk and he toyed now with the empty glass.

'Yes,' Pearl agreed. 'I'm sure that's true.' She could tell Tom Maitley was a man who was as grey as Blake Cain was colourful, and who clearly found social occasions to be something of an ordeal. So why, she now wondered, would he possibly be putting himself through this evening's event, if not to support a woman he still loved? In the next instant, she noticed Nathan beckoning her to the bar; with no further response from Tom Maitley, she felt grateful to escape his taciturn company. Making her excuses, Pearl headed over to Nathan, who indicated Heather Fox, concern written on her face.

'What's wrong?' Pearl whispered.

'Heather's worried because Blake isn't yet here,' Nathan told her. He turned to Heather who explained: 'I didn't want him arriving late again like he did last night, so I took great pains to remind James to make sure he was here by quarter to six.' She tapped her watch. 'It's now almost quarter past. And I don't want to make a fuss because Dad will become involved but . . . this really is the limit. Bad time management is nothing less than a form of arrogance and, quite honestly, Blake is one of the most arrogant people I have ever met. Making everyone else wait around for him like this? Somehow creatives get away with it – as though it's almost to be expected. But now he has James working for him, there's really no excuse . . .' She broke off suddenly, and looked instantly relieved. 'Oh, thank goodness!' She closed her eyes for a moment, as though thankful all had been resolved. 'There he is now.'

Pearl and Nathan turned to see James Moore entering, dressed casually in a light cotton blazer over a T-shirt and black jeans, and with the straps of a small backpack slung across one shoulder. Heather moved directly to him, looking all the while beyond him to the door. 'Where's Blake?'

'Sorry?' The young man looked confused.

'Isn't he with you?' She stared around as Pearl and Nathan joined her to see only festival guests entering the bar for a pre-event drink. James Moore threw a look around the balcony. 'I-I don't know,' he stammered. 'It was my afternoon off so I've just come straight from Canterbury . . .'

'And Blake?' asked Heather tersely.

'Well, he . . . was writing when I left, but . . . I ordered a car for him.' He sprang into professional mode. 'Let me check with the firm.' Moving quickly to a table, James took the backpack from his shoulder to find his mobile.

'Something wrong?' asked Cathy McTurk, approaching with Mila.

Heather Fox heaved an impatient sigh. 'Ten minutes until the doors open and Blake's still not here.'

'Oh, my goodness,' said Cathy. 'How infuriating.'

Overhearing the comment, Colin Fox now came across. 'Are you OK, Heather?'

'Yes, Dad,' she lied. At that moment, James returned, slipping his mobile phone into his blazer pocket.

'Well?' asked Heather.

The young man looked uncomfortable as he explained: 'The car firm says their cab arrived on time but . . . no one answered the door.'

Heather exploded. 'I don't believe this!' she cried in exasperation. 'Call him, James, will you?'

'I just did,' said the young man. 'But I'm afraid he's not picking up.'

Before Heather had a chance to process this, Wibke appeared. 'I wonder,' she said, 'whether Mr Cain might be able to sign my books before the event rather than after?' She indicated a selection of novels by B. J. Cain in her shoulder bag.

As though this was the very last straw, Heather turned to Nathan to whisper: 'What am I going to do?'

Before he could respond, Pearl made a decision and took control. 'Don't worry,' she said. 'I have my car here. I'll give James a lift back to Alegría and we'll call you from there. If you hear from Blake in the meantime, let me know.'

Heather's face was a picture of relief. 'Thank you!'

As Pearl began to head off with James, Nathan quickly followed and asked, 'Want me to come with you?'

'No,' said Pearl firmly. Lowering her voice she added, 'Stay and take care of things here. *And* Heather.'

A few moments later, Pearl and James hurried down the staircase from the bar, battling their way past a long queue that was forming for entry into the main auditorium. It consisted of an eclectic mix of people: distinguished-looking couples, groups of middle-aged women, and a younger crowd of Goths wearing a uniform of white make-up, dyed black hair and various piercings – all of whom would no doubt be disappointed if the chemistry behind Take Three Writers was diluted by the event turning into a duo.

Pearl unlocked her car and James quickly took a seat beside her. Fastening her seat belt, she asked: 'Is he used to taking things to the wire like this?'

'I'm afraid he can't help it,' said James. 'Blake's what's known as a classic Type B personality – lots of writers are the same. They're laid-back and more interested in concepts and issues than—'

'Arriving on time?' asked Pearl pointedly.

'I . . . think Blake just experiences time differently to most of us.'

'And I think you could be making excuses for him,' said Pearl knowingly.

At this, James looked troubled, his expression a mixture of concern and frustration, but his response was nevertheless diplomatic. 'It's my job to make sure he gets to appointments on time.'

'No excuses, James, he's a grown man.'

As James looked at Pearl, she registered now that he was probably little more than Charlie's age, though he seemed burdened with the responsibilities of taking care of B. J. Cain and his gigantic ego. She sighed. 'He really should be able to take responsibility for arriving at an important event like this.'

'But it's more complicated than that,' James insisted. 'Blake's so engrossed in his work, it's like he's on another planet. I told the cab firm they should call him as soon as they arrived outside the house, but I should have asked them to phone me too so that I could call him myself.'

'From Canterbury?'

James nodded. 'Yes, like I told Heather, it was my afternoon off. I needed to go to the library at the Beaney Museum, then I dropped in on Mila – just for a coffee.' He frowned. 'But I should've called Blake to make sure he hadn't fallen asleep. He's been working late most nights.'

'On his new book?'

James nodded, then looked out of the passenger window, as if for some distraction, but a Whit Fest banner was strung across the road and the clock on Pearl's dashboard reminded them both that the event was due to start in only five minutes. Pearl sped on beyond the castle and Beacon House, as James began nervously tapping the set of keys in his hand. Finally, Pearl parked up outside the white balconied house facing the sea, and turned to the young man beside her.

'Come on,' she said. 'Let's go and get him.'

Exiting the car first, James hurried up the path to the front door and opened it with the keys in his hand before leading the way for Pearl into a grand hallway. An antique hallstand was littered with promotional material: estate agent's flyers and business cards from gardening companies, while the stale smell of cigar tobacco hung in the warm air. James was about to head straight on towards the rear of the house when a soft thud was heard upstairs. He gazed up towards the source of the sound and called, 'Blake? Is that you?'

Another gentle thud, slightly softer this time. The young man looked relieved. 'Sounds like he's getting ready upstairs. Will you excuse me?' He gave a smile and pushed his hand through his sandy fair hair before he headed quickly up the carpeted staircase, leaving Pearl alone in the empty hallway. For a second or two she merely glanced around at the walls, which were studded with a few grand seascape paintings, then she heard the soft tinkling of what sounded like wind chimes from beyond the hallway. Moving on, out of the hall, towards the back of the house, Pearl found herself in a spacious dining room with a bank of windows facing out on to a large garden. One of them had been left slightly open, allowing the soft southerly breeze to pass through a set of wind chimes. Moving on to some French windows, Pearl took in the view of the garden: broad flowerbeds surrounding a vast, square-shaped lawn that was dominated by a large cylindrical wooden structure which she took to be Blake Cain's studio. Pearl gazed towards it but a bright light suddenly blinded her, like a brilliant torch being shone in her direction. As it quickly passed, she realised it was a beam of sunlight reflecting off a series of CDs that were hanging from some tall evergreen oaks in the garden. She suddenly remembered that this was a method Dolly had once used in her own small back garden to deter jays from disturbing nesting sparrows.

Finding the French windows unlocked, Pearl stepped outside on to the lawn from where she could now hear the sound of music travelling softly on the warm air – a familiar melody – soothing, plaintive . . .

For a moment Pearl wondered if it could possibly be the choir of St Alfred's practising for their candlelit concert. Looking back at the upper windows of the house, she could see no sign of James or Blake, so she strolled out across the well-kept lawn, recognising as she approached the studio that the music was in fact coming from a source within it. The melody became ever more familiar – pizzicato strings, a humming chorus – and through the open doors of the structure on the lawn, banks of shelves became visible, lined with various tomes and reference books. A low table housed an ashtray and a box of cigars. Beside it, a comfortable armchair was covered with a Peruvian rug near to an untidy stack of newspapers and magazines. An ice bucket stood on a coffee table beside several bottles of amber liquid and a cut-glass tumbler. The open doors of the summer house swung gently on their hinges as the chorus continued within. Pearl climbed some shallow steps to the entrance. One. Two. Three. Then called: 'Hello? Anyone there?' With no reply, she tapped on one of the doors. Silence – but for the music still playing – so she entered . . .

Blake Cain was seated in a comfortable antique revolving captain's chair before a sturdy mahogany desk facing a large window. Pearl could see that the writer's elbows were spread wide on the green leather desktop, and his head was lowered as though concentrating on his work. The music continued softly in the background but the pizzicato strings seemed suddenly to drift out of time with another sound, like rain tapping against a window pane, though outside the studio the sun still shone brightly straight into the window. Pearl took a step forward, stopping in her tracks as soon as she saw the red pool on the floorboards. It extended beyond the captain's chair, formed from the drops that were falling slowly but insistently from above. One. Two. Three. Bracing herself, Pearl spun the chair around to face her and with it came Blake Cain.

The writer's head fell back like the wooden skull of a ventriloquist's dummy and his right hand dropped down as though pointing to the red stain on the floor. His eyes stared up glassily at the ceiling and a crimson stripe encircled his bull neck like a liquid scarf, the source of which was a single entry wound from a dagger plunged to the hilt into the author's throat, with such force it protruded to one side of his spinal column. The handle featured the delicate oriental design of a lion's head and was thrust upwards towards Pearl as though inviting her to withdraw it. Blood continued to drip, like a metronome beating out its own slow staccato rhythm on the floor.

'He's not there . . .' The words were uttered before James Moore broke off abruptly, as though suddenly winded by the sight that confronted him. The young man was standing beside her, his mouth gaping open like the wound at Blake Cain's throat.

'No . . .' The word trailed off as James began panting, as though he was struggling to breathe. In the next instant he rushed from the studio and began retching on the manicured lawn outside. Only then did Pearl's gaze lower to see the rope that was tied securely around Blake Cain's thighs. At the very same moment she recognised that the music playing from a record revolving on an old deck in the studio was the Humming Chorus from the opera, *Madam Butterfly*, its final notes sounding like a beautiful lullaby – but one from which B. J. Cain would never wake.

Chapter Eight

Soon after Pearl made a call to notify the emergency services of Blake Cain's murder, a swarm of SOCOs, or Scenes of Crime Officers, arrived to transform Alegría into a temporary police incident room. As the first people to discover the body, Pearl and James were asked to give voluntary witness statements, after being separated to ensure their respective recollections of events could not be influenced by each other's accounts. An ambulance was re-routed from a road traffic accident in order to record formally that all life was extinct, and the area surrounding the summer house was sealed off by an inflatable forensics tent. Pearl knew from her police training that Blake Cain's body and the entire crime scene at Alegría would be photographed and videoed while officers pored over every inch of his studio for whatever clues might link to his killer.

After giving her witness statement to a detective constable by the name of Sarah McDonald, Pearl was handed a cup of sweet tea before being left for a short period during which she mentally revisited the events leading up to her discovery of Blake Cain's body. She saw again a blinding flash of light in the tall trees in the garden, heard once more the tinkling sound of wind chimes blending with voices floating across a manicured lawn – not the choir of St Alfred's Church practising for a candlelit concert, but the soft humming of a familiar plaintive melody. Calming and reassuring, it had drifted across on the warm summer air, inviting her to investigate the intriguing summer house.

She saw again the banks of shelves lined with tomes and reference books, a low table housing an ashtray and a box of cigars. A comfortable armchair covered by a Peruvian rug near to a stack of newspapers and magazines. An ice bucket standing on a low table beside several bottles of amber liquid, and a cut-glass tumbler on a tray. Finally, the figure of Blake Cain came into view, working at his desk as a percussive dripping noise drifted out of sync with the tempo of a record spinning on an old deck. A creak from a revolving captain's chair and Pearl had come face-to-face with Cain's glassy stare, the ornate handle of a dagger thrust upwards towards her as his hand fell to his side, as though pointing to the crimson stain of his own blood spreading out on the timber floor, growing larger with every second . . . Drip . . . Drip . . .

'Would you like to come this way?'

The woman's voice snapped Pearl instantly back to the present, and she looked up to see the tall blonde before her and began wondering if she might be imagining this too. The woman continued: 'I know we haven't been formally introduced, but I'm Detective Sergeant Bosley.' She offered the mere ghost of a smile then indicated the way for Pearl to follow. As Pearl did so, stepping back into Blake Cain's dining room, she saw McGuire already seated at the table on which coffee cups and papers were spread before him. His eyes held Pearl's before he glanced to Bosley, who indicated a chair to Pearl before she took her own seat beside McGuire, whose tone was now brisk efficiency.

'I know this has been an ordeal,' said McGuire. 'But there are a few things we need to go over from your statement.'

Looking between McGuire and Bosley, Pearl reflected on the collective 'we' that he had just used, which made Pearl feel like an outsider. Picking up his pen, McGuire began tapping it on the notepad before him, reminding Pearl of a young man nervously toying with a set of keys in the passenger seat of her car just a few hours before.

'This could be done at the station,' he continued. 'But time's of the essence and . . .' He paused for only a moment – long enough for Pearl to interrupt. 'I know,' she said. 'It's important to gain as much information as possible while recollections are still fresh and the murderer has had little time to plot an alibi or make an escape. In short,' she continued, 'the more time that passes, the colder the trail gets.' At this, Bosley looked up from her notes and gave a sidelong glance at McGuire, but Pearl explained for Bosley's benefit: 'I trained as a police officer,' she said. 'It may have been many years ago but some things never change.' She looked back at McGuire. 'What is it you want to know?'

The inspector looked down at the statement in front of him, but it was Bosley who spoke. 'As Deputy SIO I'll lead this, Pearl, since you and DCI McGuire are known to one another.' She glanced at McGuire then continued: 'You mentioned to DC McDonald that you found the body first,' she said, 'before being joined by Mr Cain's assistant, James Moore?'

Pearl nodded. 'We came back together from The Horsebridge centre after Blake Cain failed to show. We heard a noise upstairs, like someone moving around? James went upstairs to see if it was Blake getting ready.' She frowned. 'Clearly it wasn't.' She looked to McGuire for an answer. After a pause, he gave it.

'Mr Moore says he found an unlatched window. It was banging upstairs in the breeze.'

As Pearl took this in, Bosley spoke once more. 'And why did you go to the summer house when Mr Moore had asked you to wait in the hall?'

Pearl looked back at her and shrugged. 'Curiosity.' Then: 'I heard chimes.'

Bosley gave a blank look. Pearl explained: 'Wind

chimes. That suggested to me that a door or window on the ground floor was open somewhere, so I stepped into this room and found the French windows to the garden were unlocked. Then I heard music.'

'From the record playing in the summer house?' said McGuire.

Pearl nodded. 'It came to an end just as I found Blake's body. The Humming Chorus from *Madam Butterfly*.' She paused for a moment, considering this, then remembered. 'It was shortly after that, that James followed me into the studio . . .'

'But he didn't touch the body?' asked Bosley.

'No,' said Pearl. 'He took one look and . . . then he went outside.'

'And you didn't touch the body either?' asked Bosley with a hint of suspicion. 'Not even to check if the victim was actually dead?' She eyed Pearl, waiting for a response.

'There hardly seemed need,' Pearl said finally, 'with a dagger wedged in his windpipe?' She held Bosley's gaze but McGuire quickly intervened. 'The studio,' he said. 'Did you notice if the window was pointing west, in the direction of the castle?'

Pearl frowned. 'What kind of a question is that?'

Without looking up from her notes, Bosley spoke quickly. 'You're a private detective, aren't you? With powers of observation?' Her tone was provocative but McGuire explained calmly: 'The structure revolves.'

'It does what?' asked Pearl.

'It's built on a revolving pivot,' McGuire continued. 'Operated by an electrical system.' He paused for a moment and Bosley added: 'It seems Blake Cain liked to write in longhand, facing daylight.'

McGuire checked his notes. 'When the first police officers arrived, the main studio window was facing due west, towards the rear of Whitstable Castle.'

Pearl took some time to assimilate this, but Bosley broke in, interrupting her train of thought: 'We're trying to establish if you could have changed its orientation.'

'And why would I do that,' Pearl asked quickly, 'when I didn't even know any of this in the first place?' She looked to McGuire. 'How did Blake Cain operate this . . . electrical system?'

McGuire shared a look with Bosley. 'That's not important right now.'

'But I'd like to know,' said Pearl, testily.

'Can we just deal with these final points?' Bosley's patience was wearing thin.

'What points?'

McGuire spoke now: 'When I came to see you yesterday it was to ask if the words . . . "Murder Fest" meant anything to you?'

'That's the reason you came to see me?' asked Pearl, betraying some disappointment.

'If you could answer the question . . .' said Bosley.

'But I don't understand . . .'

McGuire explained. 'Yesterday a call came in to Canterbury Police giving only a short message. The words "Murder Fest" were used – in a voice that was said to be very clearly disguised.'

Pearl took this in. 'Were you able to trace the number?'

'You don't need to know . . .' Bosley began, but McGuire said quickly: 'Seems it was made from a public callbox near the beach in Whitstable.'

Pearl mused. 'Close to Windy Corner Stores,' she said softly, thinking about the small local café and grocery store near the tennis courts at West Beach. She looked back again at McGuire. 'It's the only public callbox left in town . . . So, you . . . think this may have been a warning?' she asked. 'Of Blake's murder?'

McGuire held her look but Bosley replied quickly and dismissively. 'Or more likely a crank call,' she said. 'If you'd continued with your police training, you'd know we get enough of those as it is.' Bosley leaned back in her chair and observed Pearl. McGuire took a deep breath and framed a question carefully.

'You're a Whitstable local, Pearl. You know practically everyone in town and you're also connected to this festival. Does this message mean anything to you?'

Pearl took a moment to observe McGuire, sitting with his new DS beside him, and was suddenly struck by their physical similarities. Both were tall, blond and attractive, with golden suntans that gave them the look of a Scandinavian couple having just arrived back from a skiing trip. Pearl and McGuire, however, were as opposite as yin and yang – in temperament as well as appearance. Pearl always trusted to her instincts, while

McGuire relied only on the certainties of procedure. He was a sociable loner while Pearl excelled as a 'people person'. McGuire would always be a DFL while Pearl remained firmly rooted to her home town. One thing had brought them together – murder – and, yet again, it had done the same, only now McGuire appeared to have found a female clone to work closely with in the role Pearl had always wanted for herself. She took a moment to centre herself, aware that every reaction she made during this interview would be duly noted by McGuire's new DS. 'I've told you everything I know,' she said calmly. 'So unless you'd like to arrest me for something, I'd like to go home?'

Bosley opened her mouth to protest but McGuire said quickly. 'We'll arrange a car.'

Pearl argued: 'I can drive myself.'

Bosley piped up. 'You won't be able to use your car until Forensics have finished with it.'

'Then I'll walk.' Pearl got up and began moving to the door. Both detectives moved quickly after her but McGuire reached Pearl first and held her look as he opened the door for her. As they stepped into the hallway, Bosley was stopped by a forensics officer, which allowed McGuire to move on with Pearl, his strong hand upon her arm, steering her past a whole host of police officers as he said: 'There's a murderer out there somewhere, Pearl, and I want you to stay safe.'

Looking up at him she saw concern written on his face, but as a pair of uniformed PCs moved past, efficiency took over once more. 'We'll need to interview you again so—'

'Don't worry,' she said. 'I won't be going anywhere.' She looked, beyond McGuire, to see Bosley still distracted with the forensics team and asked, 'Is James still here?'

McGuire shook his head but before he could explain, Bosley called across. 'Sir?'

He looked back at her and she tipped her head towards the white-suited officers she had been talking to, indicating he was needed. Torn, McGuire looked back at Pearl before giving instruction to a uniformed PC at the door. 'Take Miss Nolan back to Island Wall, will you?'

In that moment, as Pearl's eyes connected with McGuire's, she wanted nothing more than for him to lean forward and hold her in his arms, but instead the moment was broken by the PC gesturing towards her. Pearl moved off down the path with the constable while McGuire stared after her, waiting until he saw that she was safely in the police car before he turned back to face Alegría.

Meanwhile, inside the police car, a few splatters of light rain splashed across the passenger window, concealing the fading image of Blake Cain's front door closing on McGuire as he joined his new detective sergeant. Murder had brought Pearl and McGuire together once more – but it was also keeping them apart . . .

*

Ten minutes later, as soon as Pearl stepped through the door to Seaspray Cottage, she heard her telephone ringing. It was Dolly. 'Pearl, are you all right?'

'I'm fine,' Pearl lied.

'Why don't I come over and get you? I could be there in minutes . . .'

'I know,' said Pearl quickly, 'but I'm OK. I just need time to process what's happened.'

'What a terrible thing,' said Dolly. 'Stabbed to death? And why on earth would anyone tie his legs together like that?'

Pearl frowned at this. 'How do you know about that?'

'Everyone knows,' said Dolly. 'I called Colin Fox and he told me the police released that poor young man, James, after questioning him? He's up at Cathy's house right now, apparently.'

'Cathy McTurk?'

'Yes. He's staying the night there – at least until all those men in white suits have finished their work.'

Pearl took this in but said nothing, so Dolly continued. 'Let me come over, Pearl. Please?'

'No,' said Pearl firmly. 'I need to sleep.'

'But you'll have nightmares surely . . .'

'I'll be fine,' Pearl insisted.

Dolly heaved a sigh on the line. 'All right,' she said finally, knowing better than to argue with her daughter when Pearl's mind was made up. 'But call me if you need me.'

She rang off and Pearl's thoughts immediately strayed to Charlie, wishing she'd had the forethought to warn Dolly not to tell him about the murder. She decided to do so now and moved to pick up the phone when it sounded again. This time, Pearl heard McGuire's voice: 'I can't talk much right now.'

'So why call?' she asked wearily.

McGuire whispered. 'Because I care.' A pause, then: 'I'm still at the house . . .'

Pearl put a hand to her head. 'I'm sorry. I'm cranky. I need some sleep.'

'I understand,' said McGuire gently. 'So let's talk tomorrow. I need to explain.'

'Explain?'

'About Bosley.'

'What about her?'

Waiting for his response, Pearl could now hear only muffled voices on the line before McGuire spoke again. 'Tomorrow, Pearl,' he said. 'I'll explain everything tomorrow.'

'McGuire?'

But the line was dead in her hand and in the next instant all she heard were waves lapping on the shore outside.

Chapter Nine

'I can't believe something so awful has happened,' said Heather Fox. 'Right here, on our doorstep, in Whitstable of all places.' She had been pacing anxiously in the living room of her father's cottage but now paused at the window, where she stared out for a moment as if trying to console herself with the beauty of the view. The tide was rolling up on to the beach and the sun still shone despite Blake Cain's brutal murder. After a moment more, she turned back to face Pearl. 'I'm sorry,' she said. 'It must be even worse for you having found his body.'

'And James,' Pearl reminded her, before venturing: 'He went to stay with Cathy McTurk last night. Did you know?'

Heather nodded. 'Yes. He was in a terrible state of shock, apparently. I know Blake Cain was not the easiest man to work for, but James had been with him for some time – almost a year, I think – and I honestly believe he thought the world of Blake.'

'How do you know that?' Pearl's question forced Heather to reassess her statement.

'Well . . . he was very loyal to him,' she said, 'always making excuses for his bad behaviour – even yesterday with his timekeeping?'

'Except now we know there was a good reason for Blake not turning up to the event.'

Heather looked away and said quickly: 'Of course.' She bit her lower lip and then admitted: 'I feel so awful having arranged everything.'

Pearl frowned at this. 'Why? Do you think Blake's death could possibly be connected to Whit Fest?'

Heather looked confused. 'I don't know,' she admitted. 'Maybe if I hadn't drawn attention to him with this event . . .' She trailed off helplessly for a moment then gathered her thoughts and looked at Pearl, 'perhaps this lunatic wouldn't have wanted to gain notoriety by murdering him.'

'But if it's notoriety they're after,' said Pearl, 'they'd have to make themselves known.'

Heather took a moment to absorb this. 'Yes, I suppose that's true. But . . . if it wasn't a random psychopath, who on earth would have wanted to murder him? And in such a vicious way?'

Pearl said nothing, causing Heather to prompt her. 'Pearl?'

'Most murders aren't committed by "random psychopaths",' said Pearl finally, 'but by close members of the victim's family – or friends.'

Heather nodded. 'Yes, I've heard that too . . . But Blake no longer had any family and—'

'He did once.'

At this, Heather frowned once more. 'You're not suggesting that Cathy or Mila could have—'

Pearl broke in quickly. 'I'm not suggesting anything,' she said clearly. 'Only stating what I know.'

Heather looked back at her. 'Of course. And you know far more than any of us. You're a detective yourself. So . . . you *will* try to find out the truth?'

'There's an ongoing police investigation doing that . . .' Pearl began.

'I know,' said Heather firmly. 'But *you* found the body. You were there. You met Blake; whatever his failings, he certainly didn't deserve to die like this.'

Pearl saw Heather Fox fighting strong emotions within herself, and decided to change tack. 'What will you do,' Pearl asked, 'about the festival?'

Heather's face clouded in consternation. 'I really don't know, Pearl, I . . .' She had just begun to falter when another voice suddenly answered for her. 'We'll carry on.'

It was Colin Fox. Pearl turned to see he was standing in the doorway, still looking physically frail, though he seemed emboldened in spirit as he took a step forward to stand at his daughter's side. 'This murder is a tragedy,' he said. 'But our festival is in honour of something extremely important – the relationship between the people of two countries. The sharing of values, culture and common humanity is far more important than any one person. I'm a strong European, and I firmly believe that all those things have helped us to preserve peace over the past seventy years – but now they must abide. If ever our town should come together to show strength against evil, it's now.' He looked at Heather, who took a moment to compose herself before she gave a determined nod. 'Yes,' she said. 'Dad's right. We'll cancel the literary event, of course, but . . . we'll dedicate this whole festival to Blake Cain – and we'll carry on. Whit Fest *will* continue.' Confirmed now in this view, she nodded to Pearl as Colin Fox placed his arm around his daughter's shoulder, presenting a united front.

Two hours later, Pearl sat with Nathan in The Whitstable Pearl, a bowl of plump green Sicilian olives before him as he sipped a glass of Rioja. He had popped in to the restaurant on his way home from town and Pearl was doing her best to tempt him to stay. 'Are you sure you won't have a bite of lunch?' she asked. 'I was hoping we could talk.'

'Me too,' said Nathan, 'but I've still got that deadline to meet – the Paris travel piece?'

Pearl nodded. 'How about later – this evening?'

'Can't,' Nathan told her. 'Engagement party to go to. Down near the east quay – but we could always walk and talk if you care to join me on a saunter?'

'Thanks,' said Pearl. 'That would be good.'

Nathan saw her concern and looked pained himself for a moment before he laid a hand upon hers. 'Pearl, I'm so sorry I got you involved in all this.'

'The festival, you mean?'

'Murder,' he said darkly.

Pearl paused for a moment before commenting, 'Do you know Heather's decided to continue with the festival?'

'Can't say I'm surprised,' he said, sipping the last of his wine. 'I hear ticket sales have gone through the roof since yesterday – the festival equivalent of rubbernecking at a road accident?' He gave Pearl a knowing look. 'Have you . . . been able to discover anything from your police contacts – Bosley and McGuire?' He managed a wry smile and added, 'Sounds like a TV cop series, doesn't it?'

'Yes,' said Pearl, unamused. 'A bad one.'

Nathan's smile faded as he saw Pearl was now looking beyond him to the door. McGuire had just entered. Nathan set his wine glass back down on the table and got up from his seat. 'I sense my presence is superfluous.'

'Nathan?'

But he ignored her as he continued on to the door where he came face to face with McGuire. 'Don't worry, Inspector,' he said, 'she's all yours.' Throwing a glance back at Pearl he added: 'See you later, sweetie, for that walk on the beach?' Then he blew her a kiss. As he exited, McGuire looked back at Pearl.

'Not a good time for questions,' she said flatly, picking up Nathan's empty glass. 'I have my hands rather full.' McGuire glanced around the busy restaurant.

'So I see, but I'm actually here for some lunch.' He offered her a charming smile, took off his jacket and sat down at the table. Disarmed, Pearl hesitated for a moment, then slipped into professional mode and handed him the menu. McGuire barely glanced at it, his eyes still fixed on Pearl. 'What do you recommend, Ms Nolan?'

Pearl pointed to the menu in his hand and took out her notebook. 'Our Day Boat special. And perhaps a little more consideration?' She quickly wrote down an order and handed it to Ruby, who was passing on her way to the kitchen.

McGuire met Pearl's look. 'If you mean Bosley – it's not what you think.'

'And what do I think?'

'Why don't you tell me?'

Pearl paused and braced herself before sitting down beside him. 'All right. I "think" you hide behind your work,' she began. 'And you only come out when it suits you. You're not always straight with me either, are you? Terry, with an "i"?'

McGuire took his time before replying. 'I'm not the only one who hides behind their work, Pearl. You juggle this place with a detective agency,' he said. 'Even though you don't need to.'

She frowned. 'How do you know what I need? You're hardly ever here—'

'You were the one who cancelled our trip to Amsterdam. And I know you don't need to split yourself in two with this place and the detective agency – just for the money.'

'The money helps Charlie,' said Pearl defensively. 'One day he might want to move back here to Whitstable . . .'

'True,' said McGuire. 'But at the moment he seems quite happy living in Canterbury.'

'It's not the same as being home.'

'For him? Or for you?'

As Pearl looked away, McGuire took a deep breath and tried again. 'Look, it seems to me that Charlie's making his own way,' he said gently, 'the same way you did at his age, with this place, and I did too, on the force. But the detective agency is about something more than money, isn't it?'

'You're not really here for lunch, are you?' Pearl said knowingly. 'Why don't you admit that you find yourself in the middle of a local murder investigation and you need my help?'

McGuire shrugged, but his ice-blue eyes twinkled with mischief. 'As a witness, you're obliged to help with my investigation.'

'And I have. I've given a statement – and supplementary answers to your Deputy SIO, Terri Bosley.' She paused, her fingers tracing the vase of antique roses on the table as she asked: 'Did you . . . select her yourself?'

McGuire continued in a low tone. 'If you must know,

she was assigned to me by Welch. And for a very good reason.' He left a pause before continuing: 'She's a trap.'

Pearl looked at him askance but at that moment Ruby reappeared at the table with a serving of Pearl's Moroccan fish tagine. McGuire thanked her and Ruby moved off while Pearl continued to eye him.

'Are you serious?'

McGuire looked at her unmoved then picked up a fork.

'How do you know?' She looked on as McGuire took a bite of his food and took his time to reply as he savoured the fish. 'This is good,' he said finally.

'Of course it is,' said Pearl. 'That's why I ordered it for you. Now tell me about Bosley,' she said impatiently.

'I had my suspicions about her right from the start,' he said. 'Which is why I've kept my distance.'

'From me?'

'You're a private detective, Pearl. I'm a police officer. My relationship with you is the one weak link in the chain.'

'What chain?'

McGuire set down his fork and explained. 'I've never declared you as an informant, Pearl. But you know as well as I do, there are strict rules governing the relationships between a police officer and . . .' He paused and looked at her before giving up on his formal explanation and instead he leaned in close to her. 'In any case,' he said. 'You're *more* than just an informant.'

Pearl smiled slowly. 'Am I?'

He nodded. 'You know you are,' he said softly.

'And *you're* entitled to a private life.'

'With a witness in a murder investigation?'

Pearl frowned, but McGuire continued. 'You found Blake Cain's body so you're a potential suspect.'

'But you don't seriously believe I could have murdered Blake . . .'

'No,' he admitted. 'But if you listen to me, I'll explain. If there's one thing I am, it's a good police officer. But Welch is inefficient. Inadequate. And I'm still a thorn in his side. I was only ever meant to be here on temporary secondment, remember? But I stayed. And I also out-stayed my welcome.'

'With Welch maybe,' said Pearl wryly.

McGuire softened with her smile. 'Since we closed the last case, Bosley's been watching my every move,' he explained. 'I'm pretty sure she's keeping tabs on me and reporting back. But I had a good enough police reason to stop by and see you yesterday.'

'The phone message?'

He nodded. 'Which happened to precede a murder.'

'Have Forensics come up with anything?'

He went back to his lunch. 'Not yet.'

Pearl mused. 'Method. Motive. Opportunity.' She paused for a moment to consider this as McGuire continued with his meal.

'Method,' she said. 'No need to wait for autopsy results to know the cause of death. A dagger through the throat is pretty lethal.'

'And the weapon belonged to Cain.'

Pearl looked at him. McGuire explained: 'He used it as a paper knife, apparently.'

Pearl frowned. 'Did James Moore tell you that?'

'Corroborated by his ex-wife, Catherine McTurk, who reckons Cain bought the dagger from an antique shop in Harbour Street years ago. But there's also this . . .' He took out his smartphone and brought up an image which he showed to Pearl. It was a photo of Blake Cain looking considerably younger, and seated at the same desk, with the paper knife clearly visible on the desktop beside him. 'A publicity shot,' McGuire explained. 'It's been circulating since 2010.'

'OK,' said Pearl, handing him back the phone. 'So . . . back to basics: we know the method used to kill Cain.'

'And motive?' asked McGuire, waiting for her view.

Pearl shrugged. 'He was a charming but difficult man,' she said. 'And he'd upset at least two women: his former wife, Cathy McTurk, and the writer Vesta Korbyn – though I'd imagine there are at least two other people who could be added to that list.'

McGuire frowned. 'Who?'

'Cathy's former husband, Tom Maitley. She left him for Blake but I don't need to be a detective to know he's still in love with her.'

McGuire's eyebrows rose at this. 'An assumption?'

'They were sitting right here only yesterday – and I saw the way he looked at her. She said he'd been helping her with a legal matter and I'd hazard a guess that might well have involved him offering some advice to her about Blake's new book.'

McGuire took a pause from his meal and put a napkin to his lips before he asked: 'James Moore mentioned an autobiography but said it wasn't finished?'

Pearl nodded. 'That's right. Blake bragged at the party that he was writing a "warts and all" memoir. And I'm sure there are things a former wife would prefer to be kept secret.'

McGuire continued with his lunch. 'Who else?'

'Sorry?' asked Pearl, suddenly lost in thought.

'You mentioned a fourth person.'

'Oh, Mila Anton.'

McGuire looked up from his meal. Pearl explained. 'Cathy was desperate for a family with Blake but, after discovering she couldn't have children, they fostered. Mila remains like a daughter to Cathy. She lives in Canterbury and runs a poetry workshop that's featured in the festival. I'd say she's more than a little protective of Cathy.' She thought for a moment before asking: 'Where's Bosley now?'

'Interviewing Blake Cain's neighbours.'

'Any luck?'

'No one heard a thing.'

She frowned. 'Not even the music? I told you, the record was playing when I found him.'

'But you said it was low volume.'

'Yes,' said Pearl. 'And there's something about it that bothers me.'

'Like what?

Pearl shook her head. 'I'm not sure. Yet.'

As McGuire finished the last of his lunch, Pearl stole a glance at him, taking in the fair shadow of stubble on his strong jaw. He looked back at her and his eyes suddenly locked with hers, the pupils of his bright blue eyes darkening.

'I hear James spent last night at Cathy McTurk's,' said Pearl.

'He'll be allowed back home later today.'

'Though it may not be "home" for very much longer,' said Pearl thoughtfully. 'The accommodation went with the job.'

'I plan to talk to him again later.'

'About?'

'This book, for one thing.'

'Yes,' mused Pearl. 'It may very well help with our investigation.'

'*Whose* investigation?' McGuire stared at her but, before Pearl could respond, his phone sounded. Answering it, he gave his attention to the caller but continued to look at Pearl.

'No,' he said finally to the person on the line. 'I'm just grabbing a bite to eat. I'll see you there.' He rang off and slipped the phone into his pocket.

'Bosley?' asked Pearl knowingly.

McGuire nodded. 'Autopsy results are through and we've got a Forensics report. I have to go.' Getting to his feet, he gave her an apologetic look and opened his wallet, but Pearl said quickly, 'On the house.'

'Pearl . . .'

But she put up a hand to silence him. He frowned for a moment then said: 'You mentioned Blake Cain having "upset" Vesta Korbyn? How can you be so sure?'

Pearl smiled. 'Ask her what Blake was doing at her home yesterday morning because, when I arrived there, you could have cut the atmosphere with a knife – or do I mean a dagger?'

McGuire considered her and smiled slowly. 'You really *do* get everywhere, don't you?'

'Which is why I make such a good informant.' She returned his smile, then laid her hand on his as she said with all sincerity: 'I do understand. About your problems with Welch? He may have given you no choice with Bosley – but you *can* still work with me. Solve this murder and he'll have nothing to use against you – especially if you manage to resist DS Terri's charms?' She held his gaze.

'That should be easy enough,' said McGuire.

'Good. Sure you don't have time for some humble pie?' She smiled and glanced around her busy restaurant. 'If not, I really do have to get back to work.'

'Me too,' said McGuire. He leaned forward, his lips brushing her cheek. He knew there would be a day when nothing would come between them but, for now, he gave her all he could: the smile he reserved only for her – and left.

120

Chapter Ten

The view from the wraparound timber verandah of Beacon House was always truly spectacular, especially when the tide was fully out, as it was right now, but an early morning haze gave the lone figure walking on the Street of Stones a spectral appearance, and Dolly sighed at the sight. 'Is Wibke all right?'

She looked to Laurent beside her for a response as he watched his sister turning back in the direction of the house. Pearl noted that his usual charming smile had vanished and instead there was only concern written on his face. He shook his head. 'Poor Wibke,' he said. 'She took the news of Mr Cain's death so badly. She had been so looking forward to inviting him here. She had it all planned – afternoon tea. Very English. Right here on this verandah.' He raked long fingers through his grey hair and cast a look around the deck on which they were sitting at a wooden table. Comfortable steamer chairs lay empty in the bright morning sun.

'Had she always been a fan of Blake's work?' asked Pearl.

Laurent nodded solemnly. 'Oh yes. I'd go even further to say she was more than a little smitten with Mr Cain himself.'

Pearl frowned. 'I . . . didn't know she'd ever met him – before the other evening.'

'She hadn't,' said Laurent, 'not properly anyway,' he added. 'She once spoke to him at a book signing event in Berlin, I believe. His first work was published in German, as were others later on. I understand Mr Cain could be very charismatic – especially with women.'

Pearl reflected on this for a moment. 'Well,' she began, 'he certainly knew how to flirt. But for all his glamour and literary success, a happy relationship seemed to have escaped him.' She accepted the glass of homemade lemonade that Laurent offered, but before she had time to take a sip, a voice sounded.

'Armer Mann,' sighed Wibke, almost to herself, as she mounted the wooden steps to the deck. Dolly proudly translated for Pearl, whispering: '"Poor man".'

Wibke went on: 'It's hardly surprising his relationships were blighted when you consider his childhood.' She stood for a while at the top of the wooden steps, then took off the straw boater she wore and came forward, tossing the hat on to a steamer chair, before she joined them at the table. Laurent poured her a glass of lemonade and Wibke took it from him, managing a sip before she continued. 'Everyone thinks of B. J. Cain as a cultured intellectual . . . And he was,' she added. 'He had an Oxford University education, but in fact he wasn't able to take up his place until he was almost twenty-two years old.'

'Why not?' asked Dolly.

'Because Barry Collins came from a poor and dysfunctional background. That was his real name,' she explained. 'His father was a gambler and his mother an alcoholic. They separated; his sister developed anorexia as a teenager and it was down to the young Barry to support the family as best he could. He left school at sixteen and went to work in a car factory, but with such a bright and enquiring mind he must have known he was underachieving.' She looked pained. 'It must have been so very difficult . . . Then his sister Marie died of her eating disorder and his mother took her own life.'

'Dreadful,' said Dolly

'How?' asked Pearl.

'Pills, I believe,' said Wibke. 'From that moment on, he was on his own in the world, but ironically he was also free of the demons that had plagued his family. He went abroad, hitchhiking, spent time working on boats in the south of France. He always had . . . magnetism and charm, but he must also have had a great curiosity about the world beyond his limited experience at that time. He picked up the French language very well and then some Spanish, followed by Italian . . . He became inspired to study by the people he met. He took his exams and his grades were good enough for Oxford – where he finally came into his own, with his writing. He assumed the pen name of Blake Cain. And the rest is history, as they say.' She sipped her lemonade.

'Fascinating,' said Dolly.

'Yes,' Pearl agreed. 'And I presume that will make a fine opening sequence to his autobiography . . . featuring the relationships that went awry along the way.'

'I'm sorry?' asked Wibke, confused.

Pearl reminded her: 'The book he told us he was writing?'

'Oh yes,' said Wibke, frowning as though pained. 'Except . . . now I suppose we shall never get to read it.' She stared gloomily down into the bottom of the glass then added: 'And I shall also never get to thank him properly.'

Pearl looked up. 'For?'

Wibke looked blank for a moment before she said, 'What else? For all his wonderful books, of course.' She heaved another sigh. 'I promised our committee in Borken that I would write a full account of the festival, and return with signed books and a photograph taken of me with the author himself in his special writing studio. We were going to auction off the whole package for charity.'

Pearl turned to her, picking up on what she had said. 'Oh, that's right. Blake mentioned to me that you wanted a photo. So you . . . knew his writing studio was "special"?'

'Yes, of course,' said Wibke. 'Any fan of his would know. He wrote a blog about it a few years ago, just before it was built.'

'I'm sorry,' said Dolly, confused. 'I don't follow.'

Pearl explained. 'Blake Cain had a writing studio built that revolved so he could always be facing the sun.'

Wibke offered a smile. 'Inspired by your great George Bernard Shaw, who did the same,' she said. 'Though I believe Mr Shaw's was far less sophisticated.' She shook her head, bereft. 'I so wish I could have seen that studio,' she said. 'And the desk at which he created so much wonderful work.' She took a handkerchief from her sleeve and blew her nose. Laurent looked concerned for her. '*Bist du in Ordnung?*' he asked.

'*Ja,*' Wibke nodded. 'I'm fine.' She managed a brave smile for him and patted his hand to reassure him.

'Wibke,' said Pearl, 'knowing so much about the man and his work . . . did you not find it odd that Heather had organised the Take Three Writers event to include Cathy McTurk and Vesta Korbyn? Blake Cain's name alone would surely have filled The Horsebridge venue?'

'Oh yes,' Wibke nodded. 'But Cathy is a very successful author in her own right – as is Vesta, though her books are not to my personal taste. Too grotesque and *unheilvoll* . . . Sinister.' She wrinkled her nose, then looked back at Pearl. 'Nevertheless, they are both local authors and connected to Blake Cain.' She paused. 'At least, I . . . believe there was a connection to Vesta.' She looked modestly away but Dolly piped up unabashed.

'They were certainly seen around town together in that car of hers – or should I say the "hearse"?' She pursed her lips as she commented: 'Sadly appropriate, considering the poor man's demise.' She sipped her lemonade.

Pearl reminded herself of Vesta Korbyn's shocked expression as she had opened the garden gate of her home on Ham Shades Lane to discover Pearl on the other side of it.

'Well,' said Laurent. 'No doubt the police will do their job and find out who killed Mr Cain.'

'Yes,' said Pearl thoughtfully, as she raised her lemonade glass to her lips. 'I'm sure they will.'

Ten minutes later, Pearl sat beside Dolly in her convertible Morris Minor car. With its roof down, and at the mercy of her mother's driving, Pearl always felt somewhat vulnerable in the passenger seat – and today was no exception. Dolly scraped the gears as she accelerated towards the castle and the town.

'I'm glad I didn't hear you say to Laurent that you'd take on the job of finding B. J. Cain's killer.' She glanced at Pearl for a response.

'Are you?' Pearl offered innocently.

'You know I am,' said Dolly. 'You have quite enough on your plate running the restaurant in the height of summer.'

Pearl considered this before reminding her: 'There are still a few more weeks to go before the DFLs descend for the Oyster Festival.'

'Nevertheless,' said Dolly, 'I want you to leave it to the Flat Foot.' She looked at Pearl once more as she asked: 'I presume he's in charge of this case?'

'He is,' sighed Pearl. 'And, as you well know by now, his name is DCI Mike McGuire.' She looked pointedly at her mother.

'His name is trouble,' said Dolly darkly. 'Because whenever he's on the scene you begin pining about a career in the police force.'

'Too late for that.'

'Good,' said Dolly abruptly. 'And you also know my thoughts about private detectives – hired busybodies.'

'I am *not* a busybody,' Pearl insisted. 'I offer a professional and confidential service . . .'

'Maybe,' said Dolly quickly. 'But not in this instance, because no one is hiring you. So it's *not* your case.' Peeved, Dolly continued to frown as she drove past the harbour where tourists milled, eating chips and seafood on the hoof. 'I don't know why,' she went on, 'but for some reason, murder seems to stalk you – even in a little town like this.' She turned to Pearl. 'And perhaps that's no accident.'

'What do you mean?'

'I mean,' said Dolly, 'everyone in The Horsebridge bar on the night of the murder must have been well aware that you run a restaurant *and* a private detective agency.'

'So?'

'So perhaps it wasn't such a coincidence that you happened to find the body.' She paused before adding:

'Perhaps you were *meant* to find the body. Have you considered that?'

Pearl mused on this for just a moment before deciding, 'That's not possible. It was *my* idea to drive James to Alegría.' She paused as she recalled: 'And the only reason I had the car with me that night was because I happened to be late leaving home.'

'Why?'

'Why what?'

'Why were you late?'

Pearl paused for a moment before deciding to own up. 'If you must know, I had a visit from the police.'

'The Flat Foot?'

'I haven't seen him for weeks. He's been on a case.'

Dolly considered this. 'And now he's on another,' she said. 'A *murder* case. So leave this to him.'

'But—'

'*No*, Pearl,' said Dolly emphatically. 'I don't want you to end up the same way as Blake Cain so . . . *Achtung!*' She screeched to a halt as she noticed a parking space outside Seaspray Cottage. Reversing into it, she connected with the bumper of the car parked behind her, before she translated her warning for Pearl. 'Beware!'

Pearl gave her mother a rueful look. 'Thanks.'

'You're welcome,' said Dolly.

Walking up to her front door, Pearl heard a familiar shriek of tyres as Dolly sped off again towards Harbour Street.

*

Later that evening, as arranged, Nathan arrived to take a walk with Pearl along the beach to the east quay of the harbour. He was dressed for the humid weather in a loose lilac-coloured shirt over a pair of cornflower blue trousers that he had brought back from a holiday in Morocco. He also carried a gift for the engaged couple that he had bought following a sortie to the more expensive shops in Harbour Street: a stylish wooden container in which was planted a young pomegranate tree – said to be the Tree of Love.

'So . . . you really think it's appropriate to carry on with the festival?' Pearl asked him.

'But of course,' said Nathan. 'What possible good could it do to cancel it all?' he asked in return. 'Surely we should all be showing some . . . solidarity against Blake's murder? I think Heather and her father are right.'

'Even in the light of the message the police received the day before?'

'Hardly a message, was it?' he said dismissively. 'Just a couple of words – and pretty vague at that too, don't you think? "Murder Fest"?' He shrugged with indifference.

Pearl reflected on this. 'Well, it was enough for McGuire to make a link with the festival here – in Whitstable.'

Nathan eyed her. 'Or maybe he just used that as an excuse to get back in touch with you. He'd been away on that case, you said.'

'True,' Pearl replied. 'But Blake was scheduled to

take part in the very first Whit Fest event, so I think it's worth noting.'

'If you say so,' Nathan said casually. He paused before asking: 'So you've forgiven him?'

'McGuire?' asked Pearl. She paused and confided: 'He seems to think his new DS is working with the enemy.'

'Enemy?' echoed Nathan, confused.

'McGuire's superintendent. McGuire thinks Bosley's spying on him – and that she's been assigned to him as . . . temptation – put deliberately in his way.'

'You're not serious,' said Nathan. 'A honey trap? They're surely only for spies and politicians . . .'

'This is political too,' Pearl said quickly. 'Police politics. His superintendent would love to see the back of him. McGuire's a DFL, after all.'

'As am I, sweetie,' said Nathan proudly.

'But you're not in the police force.'

'Thank goodness,' he said, 'it's far too cloak and dagger for me.' He looked at her. 'Still, if he loses his job he can always come and work with you at your agency.'

'Work *for* me perhaps.' She smiled. Nathan observed her as he commented: 'Dolly's right, you know, what she said to you? Murder does seem to stalk you. But it also puts you back together with McGuire every time, doesn't it? If he was sent back to London I . . . guess that would be it between you two.'

Pearl looked thoughtful at this. Nathan asked softly: 'Don't tell me you haven't thought about that?'

'I have,' Pearl admitted. 'But to be perfectly honest I've never been too sure of where we stand.' She looked at him helplessly, but Nathan merely replied: 'And I'm sure that's half the attraction, sweetie.' He gave her a knowing look and went on. 'You could have married and settled down long before now, and with half the men in this town, but you chose not to. Why?'

Pearl smiled. 'Isn't it a little sexist of you to expect that all women might want to get married?'

'Touché!' he exclaimed. 'But I know you, Pearl Nolan, you've been holding out for Mr Right, even if it meant turning down the offer of a comfortable life with Mr Turnip himself – Marty Smith.' He smiled. 'I do understand, sweetie,' he went on. 'Which is why I'm still alone – but not lonely. I think you could safely say we're *both* looking for Mr Right. The difference is: you may have found him and you're just too scared to admit it.'

Pearl protested. 'I'm not scared—'

'Of most things – no,' Nathan said quickly. 'But I do think you're worried about losing your safety net.'

'My what?'

'The restaurant and everything you have here, including your status and your family. If your Mr Right was transferred back to London, do you think you'd ever consider moving *with* him?'

Pearl remained silent for a moment then piped up determinedly: 'I've never said he's "Mr Right". And he's *not* going to be transferred – because *I* am going to help him with this case.'

Nathan considered Pearl's determined expression. 'I'll get the truth out of you one day.' He reached out and tapped her nose affectionately with his finger, then headed off towards his party venue as Pearl watched him go. A banner was strung across the entrance, congratulating two people on their engagement – Sophie and Bruce; two strangers to Pearl, but the sight of their names, and the beautiful gift Nathan had bought for them, caused her to reflect for a moment on what he had just said to her.

In truth, she realised Nathan could well be right. Perhaps it wasn't McGuire who was scared of commitment, but Pearl herself. Certainly it was true that – over the years – she had wrapped herself in layers of responsibility, principally to the love of her life, Charlie, but also to Dolly and to all those she held close to her heart, including members of her staff like young Ruby who, in the recent past, had looked to Pearl not only for financial support but for guidance and protection too. But time had moved on. Charlie was grown and set out upon his own path, while Dolly had now settled into the life of a 'merry widow' – passionate about her art, and fearless in her own relationships with the opposite sex. In fact, it now seemed ironic to Pearl that it was Dolly who had captured the attention of attractive Laurent Ruppert, and not her daughter at twenty years her junior.

Perhaps Nathan was precisely right, and Pearl had been using all her emotional ties, even to her home town, as an excuse not to commit to any man. At one time those ties might have acted as a comfortable but necessary buffer, allowing Pearl to build up her restaurant and create financial security for her family, but now, having achieved all this, she began to see that she was perhaps trapped, like the smallest Russian doll, hidden away inside so many others. The agency had been one way of trying to find herself, but instinctively she knew McGuire was another – the only man in twenty years who had managed to hold her attention, and the only man to have inspired her jealousy. In fact, her reaction to DS Terri Bosley had clearly served to demonstrate just how much McGuire meant to her. At this moment in time, it also prompted her to think about Cathy McTurk and how much she must have loved Blake Cain to have endured the humiliation of his affairs and his recent liaison with Vesta Korbyn – right on Cathy's doorstep. But could it possibly have driven Cathy to murder – and in such a brutal way?

As Pearl moved back along the coast in the direction of the harbour, she gazed out to where surf rushed up on to the pebbled shore and a long path of marker buoys defined a safe area for various water sports. The beach was empty of sunbathing holidaymakers, who preferred the open expanse of coastline beneath Tankerton Slopes to the more industrialised area of the east quay which was also home to an aggregates company. As Pearl looked out to sea, a lone figure became visible, negotiating the waves, not aboard one of the noisy jet skis or power boats that were so prevalent in the summer, but on something far less sophisticated.

SUP was the term for Stand Up Paddle boarding, a relatively new sport that had become increasingly popular in Whitstable, especially among photographers who wanted to gain a higher vantage point than the surface of the water. Using a surf-style board and a long paddle, SUP looked to Pearl to be a cross between canoeing and surfing, and something she had promised herself she might try, though she had yet to find time to do so. The figure at sea made for a compelling image, gliding effortlessly – as though walking on water – before heading in towards the shore and dismounting from the board to steer it into the shallows. Having clambered up on to the beach, the figure then left both board and paddle propped against a timber groyne and shook out his sandy-blonde shoulder-length hair, pushing it back from his face as he gazed up towards the sunny sky, allowing Pearl to recognise finally that the boarder was in fact James Moore.

Chapter Eleven

Pearl moved down onto the beach and called to the young man. He lowered his head – as though trying to hide some shame.

'What's wrong?' she asked.

'I . . . know it might look like I was out there enjoying myself,' James Moore began awkwardly, 'but it's really just my way of trying to escape.' He said nothing more but looked up to see Pearl was actually gazing beyond him to where the blue waters disappeared into a heat haze on the horizon. 'I understand,' she said. Looking back at him now with a smile, she explained. 'I have a dinghy and I often take it out when I need some space or time to think.'

James gave a nod and managed a smile for her. 'I've been coming out here most days at high tide, when Blake doesn't need me . . .' He stopped and corrected himself. 'Didn't need me.' He frowned now and admitted: 'It's going to be impossible for me to think of him in the past tense. He was so full of life.'

'Yes,' Pearl nodded. 'In good health too.'

'In spite of his drinking and smoking,' said James. 'In fact, I'd never seen him happier than he was lately.'

Pearl considered this. 'Must be very satisfying for an author to finish writing a book.'

'I'd imagine so,' said James. 'But I only write poems, and to be honest it's difficult to know when they're finished. I'm always tempted to keep working and reworking them. Mila's been great though – encouraging me. She even invited me to write something special for the festival poetry event.'

'And have you?' asked Pearl.

'I'm not sure I'm capable of writing anything worth reciting,' James told her.

Pearl smiled. 'Why don't you let the audience be the judge of that?'

James stared away to where a number of parasols sat high up on the east quay itself at the entrance to the harbour. 'Can I buy you a drink?' he asked.

Pearl nodded. 'That would be very nice.'

Together they took their places at a table at a little café near the edge of the quay, where a heavy metal chain fell in low scallops as a safety measure. Pearl stared across it towards the mouth of the harbour through which all vessels entered. A long cargo ship was moored on the east quay itself, but a pleasure cruiser passed by, taking a starboard turn into the harbour, before heading to the point on the south quay from which an old Thames sailing barge, the *Greta*, made charter day-trips around the bay, including to the Red Sands Fort. A waiter came across and took their orders, after which Pearl observed James toying with one of the coasters set before them.

'How long had you been working for Blake?' she asked.

James shrugged. 'Just over a year.' He set the coaster back down on the table and took on a pained expression. 'Who would want to kill him like that?'

Pearl took a deep breath. 'I was rather hoping that was something you might be able to tell me.'

James looked quickly back at her. 'No way,' he said. 'Blake had a reputation for upsetting people, but still everyone loved him.'

'Everyone?'

'Everyone I knew,' he said firmly. 'He and Cathy may have been divorced but she still cared about him. She was distraught at the news.'

'And you stayed there on the night of the murder – at her home on Northwood Road?'

James nodded. 'She called the police and they explained that I couldn't go back to Alegría so she took me in. She and Mila are very kind. Like family.'

Pearl reflected on this. 'And your own family,' she said. 'Do they know what's happened yet?'

'I don't have any,' he said. 'Dad died when I was young and I lost Mum two years ago. Cancer.'

'I'm sorry.'

'It's OK,' he said quickly. 'I'm over it – though I still miss her. She was very special, but when she died there was nothing left to keep me in Norwich. That's where we lived. I'd just got a place to do an MA in Creative Writing there, but I then decided to see if I could transfer to Kent. It's a great university here in Canterbury.'

Pearl nodded at this. 'Yes. My son studied History of Art at the University of Kent before switching to Graphic Art at Canterbury Christ Church.'

James took this in, then continued. 'Blake came and did a talk at Kent Uni last summer. I've always been a fan of his writing and . . . I actually got to talk to him. I think he may have been flattered by my fawning.' He smiled then went on. 'Anyway, he told me about the new book he was working on and said he was look-ing for someone to help him. A personal assistant. He admitted he couldn't pay much until it was pub-lished, but said I could "live in" at Alegría and save on rent.' He shrugged. 'It sounded too good to be true – and in a way it was, because "living in" meant I got to deal with everything *but* Blake's writing – correspond-ence, housework, and keeping his bar and fridge stocked too.'

'So . . . not much free time?'

He managed a smile. 'Friday afternoons off. But, like I said before, when Blake was actually writing, he really didn't want or need me around too much because he'd disappear into a world of his own.'

'In that revolving studio?'

James smiled again. 'That was so Blake.' He shook his head slowly and explained. 'He told me he'd got used to writing outdoors, in the sun, in California. And when he came back to England he hated being locked away in an office. He grumbled about the lack of daylight and someone told him about a writing shed that George Bernard Shaw had built, just a little wooden hut that could be moved around so it faced the sun? It captured Blake's imagination and he decided to build his own but, of course, being Blake, he wanted it bigger and better – and powered by electrics.'

'How does it work?' asked Pearl, intrigued.

'A simple switch on his desk. He'd just press it to keep him in sunlight all day.'

'And . . . you say he wrote in longhand?'

James nodded. 'That's right. His eyesight wasn't what it used to be, so he hated working on a laptop screen.'

Pearl took this in. 'And I suppose you had the job of typing up all his longhand text?'

'No. I offered, but Blake would never let anyone see his work until he was completely happy with it. He'd been talking about getting a dictation programme so that he could narrate what he'd written in longhand straight on to a laptop, and then use that as another drafting process – another edit, if you like.'

The waiter returned with two light Mexican beers served in tall glasses with salted rims on which lime slices were perched.

'When we got to the house yesterday,' Pearl began, 'you went straight upstairs.'

James nodded. 'I heard something. You heard it too, right?' He paused to sip his beer. 'I thought it was Blake getting ready so I went upstairs to check – but his room was empty. The window had come off its latch and it was banging against the frame.'

Pearl nodded. 'And then?'

James shrugged. 'I closed it and went to check the bathroom and then the guest bedrooms.'

'How many are there?'

'Blake had the master bedroom overlooking the sea and then there are five others.'

'Including yours?' Pearl asked.

James shook his head. 'No, mine's on the ground floor in a kind of . . . granny annexe. Just a bedsitting room, a kitchenette and my own shower room, but it's quite enough for me.'

'And then you came straight downstairs after checking all the other rooms . . .'

'And found you weren't there,' he said. 'So I went into the dining room and then saw you through the window – at the door to Blake's studio – and I followed you.'

'Did you expect to find Blake in there, writing?'

He shrugged. 'Well, he wasn't in the house.'

'And you heard the music?'

'Music?' He looked confused for a moment, then: 'Oh. You . . . mean the record playing?' He nodded. 'Yes. I heard it as I got closer to the studio.'

Pearl thought for a moment then asked: 'Did Blake often play music when he was writing?'

'Nothing with lyrics,' said James. 'He used to say that any recognisable song made him think about the next lyric coming – and he'd lose his thread.' He managed a smile.

'But it was opera that was playing that day,' said Pearl. 'The Humming Chorus from *Madam Butterfly*.'

James shrugged. 'Humming, right? No lyrics?'

Pearl said nothing but remained deep in thought as she noticed a large grey vessel approaching the harbour mouth. It passed by the quay and James's gaze followed Pearl's to the boat. 'Police?'

'No,' said Pearl. 'It's a border control vessel,' she explained, watching as the sixty-foot-long cutter powered through the harbour, kicking up white foam in a bow-wave at its prow. 'It's part of the UK Border Force,' she explained. 'There are several boats and their main task was always to hunt down drug smugglers, but now they're also being used to intercept anyone trying to enter the country by sea. Migrants and refugees.' She sipped her beer and looked back at James, realising he was something of a refugee himself. 'So what will you do now?' she asked.

James shrugged. 'I've been allowed to move back into the house,' he explained. 'But the police have ordered me to stay put for further questioning.'

Pearl nodded. 'Standard procedure,' she said. 'They have a full-blown murder investigation on their hands.'

James considered her, toying with the label on his beer. 'And you're a private detective?'

'I have a small agency,' she said. 'How did you know?'

'Cathy told me last night. She said that between you and the police, whoever murdered Blake was bound to be caught.'

'And I'm sure that will be the case.'

'How can you be so sure?'

'Because Blake was murdered so viciously.'

James frowned. 'I . . . don't understand?'

'At every crime scene,' Pearl began, 'something is either left or taken away by the murderer. But they always leave their mark.'

'Forensic clues, you mean?'

Pearl nodded. 'Yes. But in this instance, the person who murdered Blake left clear evidence of something very important – how much they despised him. Because of that, I don't believe they'll be able to hide for long.'

James held her gaze, then knocked back some more of his beer before setting the bottle on the table. As he did so a phone rang. He reached down and unzipped a waterproof bag attached to his waist and took out his mobile phone. 'Excuse me,' he said before reading the text he had just received. He smiled. 'It's from Lucy Walker. The reporter who was at your restaurant the other evening? She asked for my number that night and . . . now it looks like she wants to meet up.' His smile faded and he seemed thoughtful for a moment before he added, 'I . . . guess she just wants to talk about

Blake's murder.' He pushed a hand through his fair hair. Pearl saw his disappointment and said: 'That might not be the only reason.'

At this, James looked up. 'Really?'

Pearl nodded. 'Really.'

On Pearl's knowing smile, James looked back at his phone and made a sudden decision. 'Then I'd better reply.'

He returned Pearl's smile and finished the last of his beer.

Later that evening, as the light faded beyond the windows of Seaspray Cottage, Pearl took off her reading glasses, pinched the bridge of her nose, then put her glasses on once more. She switched on her desk lamp before re-examining an image she had brought up on her laptop. It was the photograph McGuire had shown her earlier that day on his phone – a publicity shot of Blake Cain seated in his office with the oriental dagger clearly visible among paperwork on his green leather desktop. Pearl focused in on the blade, then on Blake himself, smiling confidently, unaware of the fate that awaited him a few more years down the line.

Searching the writer's website, Pearl went on to read about B. J. Cain's brilliant career and the many nominations he'd received for various awards. There were also glowing reviews of his books, but no hint of his blighted relationships, or the earlier family tragedies he had experienced as Barry Collins – only a précis of what appeared to be a life filled with adventure, fame and a meteoric rise to success. Pearl then reflected on what Wibke had told her that morning, and she managed to find an interview in an old colour supplement which mentioned Blake's time as a young man crewing on the yachts of millionaires in the south of France. A photo from the mid-1990s showed him in cut-off jeans on the deck of a vessel, looking tanned and handsome, a bottle of red wine grasped in his hand. Pearl smiled to herself. At least he had enjoyed his youth and, as Wibke had mentioned, met people who had helped him on his way to success.

Pearl brought up a website for Cathy McTurk and studied the biography section, which explained that she had been brought up in a village in West Sussex, a colonel's daughter, educated at a good private school. The main photo showed Cathy's kind features staring out from the page, surrounded by her book covers, which featured various landmarks against which attractive couples were wrapped in torrid embraces: the Rialto Bridge, the Taj Mahal, Ayers Rock . . . Next Pearl tracked down the website for Vesta Korbyn – the Queen of Gothic Noir; the web page was dominated by an image of Vesta herself, staring intently from the screen as a series of animated creatures orbited her book titles: bats, crows and rodents. Pearl cleared the page, wondering for a moment how three such diverse writers could possibly have formed part of what appeared to have been a powerful emotional triangle – though whether that triangle had been powered by sexual chemistry, and nothing more, Pearl had yet to discover.

She noted the time on her screen: 23.58. McGuire had not been in touch since lunchtime but she wasn't surprised with a murder case on his hands – and Bosley looking over his shoulder. She moved to switch off her desk lamp, then hesitated and decided to punch two more names into her search engine. They duly appeared on a German business directory. The first reference included a photograph of Laurent Ruppert looking even more debonair than in real life. A number of companies and charities were listed beneath his name along with the words *Firmenchef* and *Charity-Treuhänder* which, in the absence of Dolly, Pearl got her search engine to translate for her as company director and charity trustee. Wibke Ruppert's entry was shorter and listed her profession as *Beamte* – or civil servant. Pearl was about to switch off her desk lamp for the final time when something caught her eye among Wibke's educational qualifications – an Arts and Humanities degree gained at the University of Nice. The date was 1996 – only a year after the photograph had been taken of Blake Cain aboard the yacht on the French Riviera.

Chapter Twelve

Although Pearl was neither particularly religious nor a regular churchgoer, she had attended St Alfred's Sunday School as a child and learned her Scriptures there while absorbing the local church into the fabric of her life. Situated in the middle of Whitstable's High Street, St Alfred's had remained, for over 150 years, at the heart of its community – both geographically and in relation to those it served. It held a special position in what had been principally, for centuries, a fishing town, so that when members of its parish had inevitably been lost at sea, St Alfred's clergy had always offered solace and a suitable memorial service.

Passing through the church's tall oak doors on the evening of Whit Fest's candlelit concert, Pearl found the church's narthex strangely devoid of the usual social interaction and chatter that took place during the daily lunches and fundraising events that were regularly held there. Instead, the area seemed to be a solemn anteroom for the purpose of reflecting on Blake Cain's tragic demise. In due course, everyone was allowed to file through into the church, with Pearl taking up an aisle seat at the rear, a vantage point from which she was able to see most of those who were attending. The bench ends of the pews were numbered, harking back to a time when every parishioner had been allotted a seat, as the church had capacity for several hundred people, though its large gallery, which housed an impressive pipe organ, remained empty this evening. Looking around the stained-glass windows, she viewed the biblical scenes that were so familiar from her childhood – images of Christ preaching from a fishing boat on the Sea of Galilee, as though doing so to St Alfred's congregation. Pearl had attended weddings of friends and relatives in this church as well as funerals – including that of her father, and the oyster fisherman whose murder two summers ago had first brought her into contact with McGuire. Now St Alfred's was about to mark the death of another – Blake Cain.

Though in winter a smell of damp usually hung in the air, the church's squared ragstone block walls now seemed to trap the heat from the lit candles for the concert, and it wasn't long before members of the audience began to use Heather Fox's festival programme to fan themselves. Dolly had already seated herself between Laurent and Wibke Ruppert, with Heather Fox and her father, Colin, nearby at the front of the church. Cathy McTurk and Mila Anton sat together in a row further back, close to James Moore and the young journalist, Lucy Walker. Councillor Peter Radcliffe made a dramatic late entrance, requesting those already seated to move up so that he could take a central position on a pew.

Other familiar figures were present, including the landlord of the Old Neptune pub, Darrell Walton, and Brian Hatchard, the president of the local Chamber of Commerce, underscoring the community aspect of tonight's event. After a few moments, St Alfred's vicar, the Reverend Prudence Lawson, appeared from the direction of the vestry. Though she was a petite woman with pixie-cropped grey hair, she had a commanding presence, and clearly acknowledged the solemnity of the occasion by donning a surplice and cassock. She lowered her head for a moment, as if preparing herself for the event, then looked up and spread her arms wide.

'Welcome to St Alfred's,' she said, in a voice powerful enough to reach everyone present without the use of a microphone. 'Our candlelit concert this evening was intended to be a celebration of the collective talents of our choir and the children of our local church school. A joyous event to mark the relationship between two towns – Borken and Whitstable.' She threw a respectful glance towards Wibke and Laurent Ruppert and then continued. 'Seventy years ago we were separated by conflict, but today our countries are joined firmly in peace, and that is surely a victory for us all.' Heads began to nod in agreement. 'Peace is always possible if we commit to it,' Rev Pru said firmly. 'Nevertheless,' she continued, 'evil is always among us, and so tonight I ask that before we begin our wonderful concert, we bow our heads for a few moments in prayer to give thanks for the life of a talented member of our community, struck down last night in his own home. We are grateful for the life and work of Blake Cain. We pray for his soul, for his family and loved ones, and we trust that whoever was responsible for his murder will, in due course, be found.'

Rev Pru fell silent and heads bowed in sombre reflection, but Pearl alone glanced back towards the gallery as she felt someone's eyes upon her. High above her, she saw McGuire seated at the gallery rail.

Getting up quietly from her seat, Pearl slipped away towards the rear of the church and silently mounted a spiral staircase to the gallery. Taking a seat beside McGuire, she noted he was dressed smartly in a dark suit and crisp white shirt. His blond hair was slightly damp and smelled of a citrus shampoo. He leaned close to her. 'Looks like a full house,' he whispered, staring down at the packed church below.

'A brutal murder like this affects our whole community,' said Pearl, pausing for a moment as she reflected once more on what Marty had mentioned to her at the Whit Fest launch party just a few days ago: 'Like ripples in a lake after a stone has been tossed in.' She looked at McGuire. 'Have you got the time of death yet?'

'An estimate,' said McGuire. 'The pathologist's report says death couldn't have occurred much before five p.m.'

'Because of livor mortis?'

McGuire nodded and Pearl began to muse as Rev Pru introduced details of the evening's concert.

'Once blood stopped circulating in the body,' said Pearl, 'and fell to its lowest point . . .'

'Blake's corpse would have taken on a discoloration,' said McGuire.

'Particularly around the face as he had been leaning forward?'

'That's right.'

'And that hadn't happened when I found him.'

'Or when the emergency services arrived . . .' McGuire broke off, took a notebook from his pocket and flipped through it. '. . . at 6.40.'

Pearl nodded slowly. 'Method . . . Motive . . .' She paused for a moment before adding: 'We never did get as far as discussing "Opportunity", did we?'

McGuire shook his head. 'But there's plenty of that because no one closely connected to Cain, or the event, has an alibi for the time of death – though Mila Anton and James Moore can account for each other being in Canterbury that day. James Moore was caught on CCTV leaving the Beaney Library and Museum just after 3.30 and they were both seen on CCTV in the Abbott's Mill area at around 4.27 – that's close to Mila Anton's home.'

'Tight,' said Pearl. 'But still enough time for James,

or Mila, or both of them, to get back to Whitstable from Canterbury, and murder Blake within the time frame you have. I know I've suggested a possible motive for Mila but . . .' She considered something for a moment before asking, 'Why would James Moore want to murder the man who was paying his wages and putting a roof over his head? He told me his mother died of cancer two years ago in Norwich, and that's true because I checked out the death certificate online last night. Surely he'd be killing off the goose who was laying his own golden egg?'

'You said yourself Cain was demanding. Maybe the kid had had enough of him and . . . flipped?'

'An impulse killing?'

McGuire held Pearl's look, while below them the church choir began to sing. Pearl glanced down at her programme and saw that the piece they were performing was from Fauré's *Requiem*. She listened to the angelic melody before whispering to McGuire: 'What else have you got?'

'As yet, very little. Forensics say the killer was very careful to leave no evidence.' Pearl looked away as she took this in and McGuire noted her thoughtful reaction.

'What is it?'

'Well . . . wouldn't a lack of forensic clues seem to indicate premeditation rather than impulse? Think about it – the murderer would have needed to prepare well and leave sufficient time to clean up afterwards.'

McGuire shrugged. 'And?'

'And if it was a premeditated crime, surely the murderer would have been more likely to have brought a weapon of their own, rather than making use of one at the crime scene?'

McGuire considered this. 'It's still possible the murder wasn't premeditated and the dagger was picked up from Cain's desk in the heat of the moment, maybe during an altercation, with the killer still having enough time to clear up? They managed to do a thorough job of that,' he added. 'Apart from the blood on the floor.'

Pearl frowned at this. 'There didn't seem to be much of it considering the force of the stabbing. That dagger had gone straight through Blake's windpipe and out the other side.'

'True,' said McGuire. 'But apparently there are no major blood vessels between the trachea and the back of the neck, and the blade emerged at the side of the spinal column, missing two big arteries – the jugular and carotid.'

'Which accounts for the slow dripping, but no great flow?'

McGuire nodded. 'That also helped Forensics with the time of death, because once the heart stops and blood's no longer pumped around the body, the actual flow stops fairly soon.'

Pearl took a moment to process this, then: 'What about fingerprints on the weapon?'

McGuire shook his head.

'The record deck?' Pearl asked.

McGuire shook his head again. 'So far, nothing that could help us. But, as far as forensic evidence goes, as soon as you and Moore entered the studio, the scene was contaminated.'

'Yes,' she agreed flatly. 'But at that point I had no idea I was going to find Blake Cain's body.' She looked at McGuire. 'I saw the studio from the French windows and then I heard the music. So beautiful. Just like this.' She closed her eyes for a moment as the church choir continued in the background, but McGuire kept his eyes on Pearl, aware that it had been weeks since he had been this close to her; but now, ironically, he was stuck in a church with her – and almost two hundred other people. He drew closer to her but saw her expression suddenly cloud. 'What is it?' he asked.

Pearl opened her eyes. 'This piece, it's so . . . calming, peaceful. Just like the music that was playing on the day of the murder.'

McGuire nodded slowly then said thoughtfully, almost to himself: 'I guess he must have needed a change of mood.' As he looked down at the congregation below, Pearl asked, confused. 'What do you mean?'

'Cain,' said McGuire. 'With the music? According to his ex-wife, he didn't like to listen to classical music when he was working. He preferred something more contemporary.'

'Such as?'

'Jazz. Avant-garde. Progressive. Miles Davis. Coltrane . . .'

'Cathy McTurk told you this?'

McGuire nodded. 'She said she could never work with his choice of jazz playing. It made her feel "stressed", but it had the opposite effect on Cain.'

'And the record that was playing that day . . .'

'A very old version of *Madam Butterfly*,' said McGuire, noting Pearl keenly computing this. 'Why? What are you thinking?'

'The timing,' she said. 'The Humming Chorus came to an end just after I found the body. Nothing else played so it must have been the final track?'

McGuire flipped through his notebook once more before finding a certain page. He went on, relaying information from his notes: 'That track is actually the final part of Act Two of the opera. It lasts for two minutes fifty-five seconds and the record side was thirty-one minutes and twenty-six seconds long in total.'

'OK,' said Pearl. 'We drew up outside the house at 6.25 that evening. I heard the music as soon as I opened the French windows to the garden. It was that particular track playing because I heard it. And it ended just as I found Blake's body. That was just after 6.30.'

'Your call to emergency services was timed at 6.34,' said McGuire, checking his notebook again. 'The ambulance arrived at precisely 6.41.'

Pearl nodded. 'Which means that the Humming Chorus track probably began a while after James and I arrived at the house, in order for it to end shortly after I found the body around six minutes later – which means

the record itself must have been put on . . . around 6.02.
Does that makes sense?'

McGuire nodded to acknowledge this. 'Yes. But
remember, Cain could have been killed as early as five p.m.'

'And if he was murdered at that time,' mused Pearl,
'he couldn't possibly have put the record on himself – or
it wouldn't have still been playing.' McGuire looked at
her and Pearl asked quickly: 'Did any of Blake's neighbours hear music that afternoon?'

'Not on the day he was murdered, but on other
occasions – yes. One neighbour had even complained.
But curiously no one heard, or saw, a thing on the day of
the murder.'

Pearl considered this and applause rang out suddenly
in the church as the choir came to the end of their piece.
McGuire stole a look at Pearl as she joined in with the
applause. It felt good to be with her again – even while
discussing the details of a vicious murder – and he was
about to tell her as much when she stopped clapping and
leaned forward as she noticed something below.

'Look,' she said. 'Down there . . .'

McGuire followed Pearl's gaze to see Vesta Korbyn
sitting alone towards the rear of the church. She was
dressed in a deep purple suit and a black cloche hat, to
the side of which a long black feather was attached.
Picking up a copy of the festival programme, Vesta
appeared to read a section then closed her eyes – not in
grief, thought Pearl, but in what seemed to be a sense of
calm, and possibly even relief . . .

'Pearl,' whispered McGuire. She turned to him, brought out of her reverie. 'Is there somewhere nearby that you and I can go where we won't be seen or overheard?'

His eyes searched hers for an answer. Finally Pearl smiled. 'I know just the place.'

In centuries past, Whitstable's old alleys had offered escape routes to smugglers. Moments after leaving the church, Pearl led McGuire into Skinner's Alley and past Slaughterman's Cottage – so named because it had once been the abattoir of an old butcher. Cutting through a few more back streets, they soon found themselves on a long pedestrian and cycle path, which lay largely hidden by high privet hedges on either side.

'Where are we?' McGuire asked.

'Stream Walk,' smiled Pearl. 'It's named after the Gorrell – a stream that rises from a source near a local village green called Duncan Down, and it then flows downhill into town and all the way to the harbour. But it does so unseen for the most part because the waterway was closed over many years ago – imprisoned, if you like, beneath the concrete of this footpath. You'd never know but for this . . .' She pointed to a faded serpentine blue wave that had been painted a few years ago by some local community volunteers on to the concrete path. 'That's the only clue that it actually flows here, right beneath our feet. So it's a bit like this case . . .' She looked up at McGuire. 'A stream of events leading to Blake

Cain's death, though the murderer has been very careful to cover their tracks. Nonetheless, as with this blue paint here, there are still clues for us to make sense of, like the message that was called in to the station, alerting you to a murder linked to the festival. And the music that was playing in the studio that day – opera, when Blake Cain was really a jazz fan. And why the rope tied around his legs like that?'

McGuire offered no response but instead took advantage of the first private moment they had shared together for some time, and stepped forward to hold her in his arms. As he kissed her hard, he felt her melt beneath him, her lips responding to his. Straight after, his hand gently framed her face as his eyes searched hers.

'I've missed you,' he whispered.

Pearl buried her face against his shoulder, hearing his heart pounding against her cheek as he continued. 'Why're we always having to meet like this – in secret?'

Looking up again at him, Pearl was about to reply when she heard the sound of footsteps approaching. An elderly couple appeared from around a bend in the footpath, arm in arm, as much in mutual support as affection. A plump Jack Russell terrier took up the rear, waddling to keep pace with his owners. The couple nodded towards Pearl and McGuire as the terrier panted, tongue lolling to one side.

'Lovely evening,' said the old lady.

'Yes,' said Pearl. 'Isn't it just?'

As the couple passed on, Pearl looked back at

McGuire. His face moved closer to hers once more, then stopped as his phone began to ring. 'Damn!' he looked at the caller ID and answered brusquely. 'What is it?' He listened carefully as Pearl looked on. 'Are you sure?' he asked into the phone. Silence again as he took in more details. Pearl waited until he finished his call before asking: 'Well?'

He turned to face her. 'Witness account has just been taken from a local builder. He claims he was driving his van on the old access road at the rear of Blake Cain's property on the afternoon of the murder and saw a woman in a white dress on the lawn just after six p.m.'

'Is he sure?'

'No,' McGuire said. 'He "thinks" it was Cain's house – he remembers seeing a structure in the middle of the lawn . . .'

'Well then—'

But McGuire broke in to finish his original sentence: 'The garden next door has a large pergola on the centre of its lawn.'

Pearl took this in as McGuire continued. 'But Bosley says Cain's neighbours can't give any reason as to why a woman would have been seen in their garden on the day of the murder. They were at home, watching sport all afternoon on TV, but they were also facing a picture window on to their lawn.'

Pearl considered this. 'Lucy Walker was wearing a white dress on the night of the party. But why would she wear something so conspicuous if she was about to murder Blake Cain? And why on earth would she *want* to murder him?'

'I don't know,' McGuire said slowly. 'And I'm not sure this witness account would hold up in court. The driver says he was blinded by a light just before he saw the figure.'

Pearl remembered something. 'The CDs in the trees,' she said. 'There was a breeze that afternoon and they were turning and catching the sunlight.'

'So the whole thing could have been an optical illusion?'

Pearl shrugged and conceded: 'Perhaps.'

McGuire looked torn. 'Look, I have to get back to the station, Pearl. Can we talk tomorrow?'

She nodded. 'Go back the way we came.'

'And you?'

'I'll follow this path to the harbour.' She smiled. 'Go on.'

McGuire leaned in and kissed her once more. She looked up at him. 'Tomorrow,' she whispered.

As McGuire turned away from her and headed back along Stream Walk in the direction of town, Pearl hitched her bag over her shoulder and was setting off in the opposite direction when her own mobile sounded. For a second, she expected to see the caller ID display McGuire's name, but it showed another instead.

'Pearl?'

'What is it, Marty?'

'Listen, I'm at Covent Garden right now, meeting a

new wholesaler, but I want you to meet me at the shop first thing tomorrow morning, OK?'

'Why?'

'Because I've got a good idea who did this murder.'

Chapter Thirteen

Marty Smith was always in Cornucopia by eight o'clock each morning and Pearl met him there shortly after, in the knowledge that his staff would not arrive for at least another hour. She found him in his store room, busily checking items on a list attached to his clipboard: supplies of exotic fruit, including some tropical durian, which Pearl knew tasted like heaven and smelled like hell.

'What was it you wanted to tell me?' she asked impatiently.

Marty looked both ways in his empty store room but, just in case there was a chance he might still be overheard, he took Pearl's arm and steered her to one side before whispering pointedly: 'The Germans.'

Pearl frowned. 'What about them?'

Marty raised his index finger to his right cheekbone

and dragged down the suntanned skin beneath his eye. 'Watch 'em like a hawk.'

Pearl shrugged, confused. 'Why?'

'Well, why d'you think?' said Marty. 'Because they've got it in for us.'

'About what?'

'Brexit, of course,' said Marty. 'We voted for it, didn't we?'

'*I* didn't,' said Pearl. 'And neither did Mum—'

'Well most of us did,' said Marty, cutting in. 'And the Germans aren't happy about it. They're not happy at all. I know because I talked to them at your party. But I only remembered last night. No one likes being rejected.' He gave her a knowing look but Pearl looked down at his hand still on her arm, and freed herself from his grasp.

'Marty, if you've brought me here just to go on about Brexit, you're wasting your time – and mine – because I can't, for one minute, see what on earth that could possibly have to do with Blake Cain's murder.'

Marty threw down his clipboard and raised his hands in the air. 'Whoa!' he exclaimed. 'And you're meant to be a detective? Do I have to spell it out for you? This festival, Whit Fest, is about our town – us – and our achievements. Your oysters. My asparagus. But now it's been ruined – by someone bumping off one of its biggest stars. Just think,' he said. 'Who would want to spoil things for us like that?'

Pearl looked askance at Marty. 'You're seriously

suggesting that Wibke and Laurent could possibly have murdered—'

Marty interrupted quickly. 'They're on the Borken committee, right? They're German. And we don't exactly have much in common, do we?' He leaned in to her and whispered, 'We don't even like the same colour asparagus.'

'Marty!'

'I'm serious, Pearl. We bombed Borken in the last war. Maybe they hold a grudge. If it was me, I would.'

'Yes,' said Pearl, 'I'm sure you would. But fortunately not everyone is like you. And Wibke Ruppert happens to be one of Blake Cain's devoted fans. So why on earth would she, or her brother, want to kill him?'

Marty held Pearl's look as he took this in, blinking a few times, which at least demonstrated to Pearl that some of his brain cells were reacting to her question. Unfortunately they failed to come up with an answer. Instead, Marty picked up his clipboard once more and plucked his pen from behind his ear before commenting: 'Dismiss it, if you will, but *I* reckon I'm on to something.'

Grateful to escape the confines of Marty's exotic vegetable store and his smelly durian and xenophobic suspicions, Pearl welcomed the distraction of a busy lunchtime service at The Whitstable Pearl. But, in the late afternoon, as she walked home along the beach, she reminded herself that a good detective should never dismiss any information out of hand, which is what she feared McGuire might do with the new witness account of a 'woman in white' having been seen crossing the lawn at Alegría on the afternoon of Blake Cain's murder.

Back home at Seaspray Cottage, she took a cool shower and rooted in her wardrobe for an outfit to wear for the evening's poetry event at Cathy McTurk's house, and began to reflect on what had seemed, on first hearing, to be an utterly ridiculous suggestion from Marty Smith. Slipping into a loose pale blue shift dress, she tied back her damp hair, then sat at her laptop and brought up Wibke Ruppert's name on her laptop as she considered once more how Wibke's period of study at the University of Nice had coincided with the time during which Blake Cain had been working in the south of France. Could it really be that Wibke had met Blake long before the Whit Fest launch event at The Whitstable Pearl? If so, was it possible she might have been yet another woman disappointed in love by Blake Cain? It hardly seemed possible to Pearl, since Wibke appeared so infatuated with the writer – but the thought prompted Pearl to wonder just how far Laurent Ruppert might go to protect his beloved sister . . .

Half an hour later, Pearl found herself staring up at the grand Edwardian exterior of Cathy McTurk's home. The house stood at the northern end of Northwood Road, close to the gatehouse entrance of Whitstable Castle which, in turn, was just a stone's throw from Alegría. Pearl admired the large front garden filled with foxgloves and towering hollyhocks. The elegant windows were framed by beautiful drapes featuring kingfishers, and the front door was painted a bright blue shade to match – a far cry from the chilling exterior of Vesta Korbyn's home with its rat-shaped doorknocker. Not for the first time, it struck Pearl how difficult it must be to live in a small town like Whitstable, alongside a former partner or spouse, especially after a relationship had ended acrimoniously. At the same time, she realised that Cathy and her former husband, Tom Maitley, had managed to preserve a good relationship, and Maitley's own home was no more than a few moments' walk away on Tankerton Road, separated from Alegría by little more than the castle itself.

Pearl rang Cathy's doorbell; after a few moments a young woman, dressed in faded blue jeans and a loose kaftan, came to the front door.

'Hi. I'm Anna,' she smiled, explaining: 'I'm afraid you've missed the first session of readings, but there'll be some more straight after the break.'

She led the way through Cathy McTurk's hallway to the rear of the house, where an enormous orangery formed almost an entire extension. The huge space had been built off the kitchen and dining area, a bright south-facing structure with a lantern roof that allowed maximum sunlight to enter. For a moment, Pearl allowed herself to imagine this space filled with the children Cathy and Blake Cain had once fostered. Now it housed miniature lemon trees, exotic palms, and poetry lovers, most of whom were gathered around Mila Anton, who was dressed in a stunning African robe and scarlet turban. On seeing Pearl, Cathy hurried across to welcome her, ushering her over to where a long table was filled with wine and food. 'It's so good of you to come,' she said. 'Though you've missed Heather and her father. They've only just left – to take Wibke and Laurent off for supper.'

Pearl nodded as she took this in. 'I'm afraid I couldn't get here earlier; I was at the restaurant,' she explained.

'Of course,' said Cathy. 'Let me get you a glass of wine.' She smiled and handed a glass of Pinot Grigio to Pearl, which she sipped before looking down at the programme in her hand.

Cathy spoke again. 'I'm sure you're wondering how we can possibly go through with this after Blake's murder?' As Pearl looked up at her, Cathy raised her eyebrows. 'Life goes on,' she said. 'As does this festival. Mila has put so much energy into this event, it's only right that it should continue. You've missed some of the earlier readings, but James and Mila are yet to come.'

'James?' asked Pearl.

'Yes. He mentioned you'd said something to inspire him – with his poetry? Whatever it was, it must have worked. He put his name forward to Mila for a reading.' She summoned a smile now. 'Thank you,' she said.

'For?'

'Encouraging him,' said Cathy. 'Young people are the future, so it's up to us to help them as much as we can.'

Pearl took a sip of her wine and glanced around the orangery once more as Cathy explained: 'Such happy times we've had here,' she whispered, almost to herself. Then, misreading Pearl's thoughts, she stiffened as she went on. 'If you were expecting to see Vesta, you'll be disappointed. I know that a festival event should be open to all, but . . . I did make it clear to Heather that Vesta Korbyn would not be welcome. She must have got the message because she's at least had the decency not to show up.' She looked back at Pearl and explained: 'You really don't need to be a detective to work out that I strongly dislike the woman. It's no secret. Blake and I were over, but that didn't mean to say I had to approve of any woman he might have taken up with.'

She turned away and filled the glass in her hand with more wine. 'I'm a good judge of character, and I know there's something phoney about Vesta Korbyn. I've yet to put my finger on exactly what it is.' She sipped her wine. 'All that . . . overt sexuality in her books? Maybe in reality she's frigid.' She shrugged. 'It's true she threw herself unashamedly at Blake – but I'm sure that was only to raise her own profile. Everything's for effect with Vesta, the whole image. The costumes? The hearse? The house of horror? Blake would have seen through all of that, I'm sure. And I'm equally sure he would have been highly amused by it all too – until he got bored with her, of course. He had a short attention span, so boredom was always a problem for him. He got bored with me, bored with the children. He even got bored with his own work – and when that happened, so did his readers.' She fixed Pearl with a look; when she failed to receive a reply, she glanced away, as if trying to hide the fact that, in spite of all she had just said, she was, nevertheless, grieving for the man she once loved – and perhaps still loved. In fact, Pearl now began to wonder if the passionate relationship between Cathy McTurk and Blake Cain could ever truthfully have been described as 'over'. Perhaps their love had endured even though their marriage had ended. Before Pearl had a chance to comment on this, she saw James Moore heading across to them, and offered a smile for him. 'I've just heard that you'll be reading something this evening?'

'That's right.' He looked between Cathy and Pearl and managed a nervous smile. 'I . . . thought I'd write something to support the festival,' he said. 'And Mila, of course,' he added quickly. 'She told me on Friday how this event is acting like a showcase for her group. So I hope I do it justice.'

Cathy McTurk laid a gentle hand on his shoulder. 'You will, James.' She gave him a reassuring look. 'Now go and get yourself a glass of wine and just relax.'

James nodded and moved off to the other readers standing with Mila by the open conservatory doors. Cathy stared after him, a smile now fading on her lips as she said: 'Poor boy's a bag of nerves – as we all are when we try something new. But that's what so wonderful about being young, don't you think? Wanting to do something in spite of your nerves? In spite of a fear of failure?'

Looking across the conservatory, Pearl noticed Lucy Walker, dressed in a white shirt and jeans, with her reporter's notebook in hand, now joining the group of poetry readers, as Cathy continued. 'I felt just like that with Blake – like a teenager all over again. But I managed to overcome my nerves . . . and all my fears too. Perhaps I should have taken heed of them, but in truth I could do nothing else.' She looked back at Pearl. 'I was drawn irresistibly to him, and I think for some years he felt exactly the same. He loved me as much as he was able to love anyone.'

She went to sip her wine as Pearl commented: 'You mean his capacity for love was limited.' Cathy hesitated for a moment, the glass still at her lips, as Pearl went on: 'Wibke happened to mention Blake's childhood yesterday. It sounded as though he didn't have the best start in life.'

'That's right,' Cathy agreed. 'I think he tried to escape from it all – from his roots. But he was bound by them, nonetheless. As we all are.' She looked across at Mila, who caught her gaze and offered a smile before she continued talking to her group of poets. 'If I've learned anything, especially from Mila, it's that we can never really escape our heritage – perhaps even our destiny. We can only . . . distract ourselves from it for a while.'

Pearl went on. 'It was kind of you take James in last night after he'd been questioned by the police.'

'Why wouldn't I?' asked Cathy. 'He's a young man without a family who devoted himself to his job.

Unfortunately, Blake had him running around after him the whole time like a blue-arsed fly.'

'Apart from when he was writing,' said Pearl. 'His autobiography?'

Cathy gave a derisive snort. 'Blake may well have been pretending to write, but I suspect it was all rather a joke on his part.'

'A joke?'

'I've told you,' said Cathy, with more than a hint of impatience. 'He was *bored* with writing. And his career was over.' She paused. 'I'd always rather thought that Blake had been born out of time because he would have fitted in so well with that whole breed of testosterone-fuelled writers who were utterly convinced of their own genius – Mailer, Miller, Hemingway . . . They were literary stars, but those days have long gone. Blake hated the idea of having to promote his own books – he'd got used to having a publicity machine to do it for him, but in the end that machine ground to a halt with his dwindling sales – not to mention the fact that he could be so bloody difficult.' She paused and heaved a sigh. 'I really believe he had written all he had to write,' she said finally.

Pearl frowned. 'But the other evening, in the restaurant . . .'

'Sheer theatre on Blake's part. Trying to stir things up and create a bit of hype. And perhaps he was trying to make us all sweat a little?'

'Us?' asked Pearl.

'Those of us he might have wanted to punish,' said Cathy. 'Or simply make money out of. I wouldn't have bothered too much about anything he had to write about me, but what little family life we had together, with the children we fostered, with Mila . . .' She looked pained as she glanced across the room. 'I would have fought him in order to keep that private. I even sought Tom's advice about that, just to be sure, but . . . I honestly don't believe that Blake had any publisher lined up. He didn't even have an agent any more to negotiate a deal, so I'd be very surprised indeed if any manuscript ever comes to light – at Alegría, or anywhere else.' She paused before adding: 'By the way, Blake's name for the house was another joke on his part – Alegría is Spanish for joy, but it's also the brand name of his favourite Cuban cigars.'

At that moment, a hush fell in the room. Cathy put a finger to her lips as she whispered to Pearl: 'We must be quiet now. It's Mila next.'

Pearl saw that Mila Anton was standing in the centre of the room. She allowed a few moments' silence before speaking.

'Those of you who attend our poetry sessions know that not all our poets are comfortable about reciting their own work. In those instances, I will always read for them, but tonight I want to read the work of Mavernie Cunningham, a Whitstable poet who cannot be with us this evening. I feel very honoured to recite, in her place, this piece which has resonated for me since I was first introduced to it. It's called simply – "Hair".' Taking a deep breath, Mila then fixed her gaze straight ahead as she held a sheet of paper in her left hand, while her right moved to the blood-red silk turban wrapped around her head. She unclipped it, allowing it to unwind slowly – a scarlet river of fabric flowing to the floor. Shaking her head, she now freed a magnificent mane of tight curly black hair, which fell to her shoulders, framing her beautiful face. Slowly she began to recite.

'*This is the hair. The hair of the Maroons. Once pulled and dragged through streets, through mud, through mire. On a misty morning, warm and fragranced, on the fine road to Spanish Town.*' Mila paused to look across at Cathy and her voice softened as she continued. '*Yours stands reflected back to me. Runs fair and ringleted, oval and straight. It cascades over your shoulders so soft and sensuous, like the Golden Fleece itself.*' Looking straight ahead now, Mila went on: '*But no healing balm from this head. No cares, no comfort, no succour, no prayers. It rests like freshly hewn hay on the shoulders of Mars. Red silk and brocade drapes like a blood shroud tousled and resplendent. Helix, nappy, spiralled and kinky, Cotton, wool, spongey. Shrinking hair straight hair. Ellipsed, rare, original, out of time. Unkempt, sored, scalp soured. Brush it with kerosene and paste it with cornmeal. To find relief.*'

Mila allowed another moment, then lowered her head as a respectful silence fell before applause rang out. Pearl noted Cathy's proud expression as Mila looked up once more and stared across the room, her face suddenly lit with the beacon of a special smile – one of gratitude, of appreciation; a sign of an inseparable bond between the women.

'Thank you,' said Mila finally. Then she looked back at all those assembled and continued more brightly. 'And now I'd like to introduce a new poet to our group. Someone else who is also finding his own . . . Way with Words.' She smiled. 'James Moore.'

Gathering up the red silk of her turban, Mila stood aside as James came forward. But in contrast to Mila's confident performance, the sheet of white paper in his own hand began to flutter for a moment, betraying the young man's nerves. He took a moment to compose himself, clearing his throat before he began to read in a soft voice.

'*Like a snowdrop in midwinter, She waited, patiently, To break through cold earth, To raise her head to flower. She knew her time would come, When she would blossom, Beneath his gaze, And he would see her, In all her beauty, A blank canvas on which a future could be drawn. Frozen in time, she waited. Waited for him, To complete the picture. A heart worn upon her sleeve. And I waited too. Perhaps too long, Never knowing if I would be worthy. Time moves on. Winter shows no mercy. The snowdrop dies, Though its beauty lives on.*'

He looked up from the sheet of paper and a round of polite applause rippled around the room, led principally by Mila and Cathy. Pearl now saw that the object of James's gaze was, in fact, Lucy Walker, who stood smiling proudly at him for a moment before she too began applauding. In that instant, the look that passed between those two young people took Pearl back more than twenty years, to when she had first met Charlie's father, Carl, a young Australian who had been passing through a small town, working in a local bar until he'd saved enough money to head off to the Far East. An artist, just like his son. A man who didn't want to be tied down – just like McGuire. Pearl could have made the decision to go with Carl but, with a police training course ahead of her, she had failed to. Then a pregnancy test changed everything . . . altered the course of her life. Nevertheless, as she looked across at two young people, she remembered another hot summer, like this, when love had still seemed far simpler – unthreatened by all the obstacles which constantly came between Pearl and McGuire. What Pearl had heard in the words of James Moore's poem was, in fact, a reminder of how truly special first love can be – a blank canvas upon which the futures of two young people really could be drawn.

An hour later, Pearl was back home, sitting once more at her desk, her cats dozing at her feet, as she listened to a soundtrack of the Humming Chorus on her laptop with her landline telephone receiver to her ear as she waited for a call to connect. Finally, it did so.

'Nathan,' she said quickly. 'Have you got a moment?'

'Sure,' came Nathan's reply. 'Any possible reason you might have to distract me from finishing my Paris piece will be more than welcome. What is it?'

'*Madam Butterfly*,' said Pearl. 'You know the story well.'

'Don't we all?'

'Well, I know the famous arias, like 'One Fine Day', but I'm sure you could tell me more about the opera itself?'

Nathan paused for a moment before explaining. 'In many ways it's a story of abuse,' he said starkly. 'A poignant tale of innocent young love crushed between two distinct cultures.' He took a deep breath and went on. 'It opens in Nagasaki, Japan, when Lieutenant Pinkerton of the US Navy is buying a house which happens to come with a bride – a young geisha called Cio-Cio-San – the Butterfly of the opera. And when I say "young", I mean young – a teenager. The whole deal is just a . . . convenient business arrangement for Pinkerton because, according to Japanese law at that time, a marriage could be declared void if the husband was absent for more than a month. Pinkerton doesn't take the marriage too seriously, but his young bride does, and she's denounced by the Japanese high priest for converting to Christianity in order to marry this American. Her family and friends turn against her for doing this, but poor Butterfly is naïve and deeply in love. Fast forward three years and my fellow countryman, Pinkerton, is long gone, leaving Butterfly, her young son and a loyal servant all living in poverty. In spite of what's obvious to everyone else, the girl is still convinced that her husband will return – and at last, he does . . . but *with* a new American wife.'

He paused, allowing Pearl to remember: 'And . . . Cio-Cio-San, Butterfly, is so heartbroken that she commits suicide . . .'

'That's right.'

'How?'

'Hara-kiri, darling. Japanese ritual suicide. Fortunately offstage.'

'And the Humming Chorus?'

'A kind of musical interlude while Cio-Cio-San, her son and the servant, Suzuki, are keeping an all-night vigil, waiting for Pinkerton to arrive. It's . . . the calm before the storm, if you like.'

'Yes,' said Pearl, softly. 'That's just how it felt before I found the body.' She fell silent.

'Are you OK?' asked Nathan, concerned.

The Humming Chorus had come to an end on Pearl's laptop, but she was sure she had just heard another sound beyond her window.

Nathan spoke urgently on the line. 'Pearl? Are you still there?'

'I'm fine,' she quickly whispered. 'Good luck with your article. And thanks.'

Ending the call, she now got up from her desk and switched off the desk lamp. Standing close to the wall beside her window, she listened hard and was finally rewarded as she heard what sounded like soft footsteps outside – almost like those of a child. Perhaps, she thought, it *was* a child, having come into the garden to rescue a kite or ball – or perhaps a pair of young lovers were using Pearl's bench to steal a kiss . . .

She moved to the kitchen. The light was off and she peered out of the window. The trees in her garden were still, the tide yet to return. Pearl waited a few more moments then quickly opened the kitchen door and stepped outside. Her sea garden was in full flower, the blossom heavy wherever she looked, but it wasn't sweet honeysuckle or fresh lavender that she could smell resting on the evening air. It was the pungent scent of patchouli.

Chapter Fourteen

The following morning, Pearl was spoiling her cats, Pilchard and Sprat, with some leftover salmon from The Whitstable Pearl, her mobile phone propped against her ear as she asked: 'So what did Vesta Korbyn have to say about why Blake Cain happened to be with her on the morning of the day he was murdered?'

McGuire, walking briskly along a corridor in Canterbury Police Station, replied into his mobile phone: 'She said he'd spent the night with her.'

'Really?'

'There was no reason to disbelieve her,' said McGuire. 'Bosley checked it out.'

Pearl frowned. 'Checked what out?'

'The facts.' He paused for a moment to look out of a corridor window at the steady stream of traffic clogged on the major Canterbury route of Longport, feeling grateful he wasn't trapped in it. He was desperate for a coffee to sharpen his wits but equally keen to talk to Pearl. He continued to her: 'James Moore confirmed to Bosley that he didn't see Cain after they returned from your launch party around 11 p.m. on the night before he was murdered. Korbyn said she'd picked Cain up in her car on Marine Parade and taken him back home with her.'

'Have you checked phone records?' asked Pearl. 'Presumably there must have been a phone call between Blake and Vesta to arrange this?'

'Not according to Korbyn. She said she'd passed a note to him at The Whitstable Pearl.'

'Sneaky.' Pearl took a moment to absorb this.

McGuire asked: 'And what makes you so sure Korbyn paid you a visit last night?'

'Her signature perfume,' said Pearl. 'Though I'm not sure why she would want to visit me – unless it was to scare me off?'

McGuire looked away from the corridor window and smiled to himself: 'I'd like to see her try.'

Pearl fell silent on the line. McGuire asked. 'What's troubling you, Pearl?'

'Everything,' she admitted. 'If Blake Cain wasn't a fan of opera, then surely the piece of music that was playing that afternoon had been specially selected – a kind of soundtrack . . . to the murder?'

McGuire frowned. 'But why?'

'I don't know – yet – or why the murderer should

possibly have rung the police with a cryptic message signposting a murder.'

'Like Bosley said, that could have just been a hoax call . . .'

'And maybe Bosley's wrong,' said Pearl starkly, having heard the name of McGuire's new DS too many times for comfort during the call. 'You know as well as I do that serial killers often play games with the police.'

'This isn't a serial killer.'

'We hope. But why was that particular piece of music playing that day, and why did you receive that message – if the killer *wasn't* laying down clues for you?'

'Clues to the identity of the murderer?'

'Or why Blake was murdered.'

'Look,' said McGuire. 'There's no real evidence that the music and the message are connected . . .'

'But think about it,' said Pearl impatiently. 'An arts "fest" in Whitstable. A literary event featuring three writers. A triangle – just like in the opera, *Madam Butterfly*. In that, the American, Pinkerton, marries a young Japanese girl, breaks her heart . . . and she commits suicide – hara-kiri – using a knife.'

'Not a paper knife, I'm betting.'

'Though the murder weapon had an oriental design, didn't it? A lion?'

'The knife was nothing special. Bosley checked it out—'

'It was special enough to silence Blake Cain,' said Pearl fiercely. 'For ever.'

McGuire held his tongue and Pearl continued. 'Look closely into Vesta Korbyn.'

'Why?'

'Something Cathy McTurk said last night. She thinks there's something "phoney" about her.'

McGuire shrugged to himself. 'She would say that, wouldn't she?'

'Not necessarily,' Pearl argued. 'There are many things a woman could say about a rival, but Cathy told me that in particular. And it's true Vesta Korbyn's something of an enigma, but behind the public image she may well be hiding something.'

McGuire frowned to himself. 'Anything else?' He began to continue on along the corridor.

'Yes,' said Pearl. 'Have you found the manuscript yet? Blake's precious autobiography?'

'Not yet.'

'Well, don't waste too much time on it.'

McGuire stopped in his tracks. 'But it could well be the motive for his murder. You said that yourself.'

'I've changed my mind.'

McGuire heard another phone ringing at the end of the line. 'Pearl?'

'I have to go,' she said. '*Don't* let Bosley take over this case.'

'Pearl!'

But all he heard was a click on the line. The doors before him swung open and two of the DCs on his murder team nodded to him as they passed by. McGuire watched them move on along the corridor, then pocketed his mobile phone and headed out through the swing doors himself – needing a coffee more than ever.

Back at Seaspray Cottage, Pearl had just picked up her ringing landline receiver to find Dolly on the other end of the line.

'Just in case you wonder where I am,' she said. 'I'm at the harbour with Laurent.'

'Oh?'

'Yes. I've been showing him the area down at the east quay where I painted *Undertow*. Then I brought him over to the Harbour Village market and he was just taking some photos of the *Greta* when we discovered there are three spaces left on her sailing trip this afternoon, so we've decided to take them.'

'Three?'

'We just called Wibke, and she's coming along too. Laurent thinks it will be a good distraction for her. Heaven knows the woman hasn't been quite herself since the murder.'

'OK,' said Pearl softly. 'Well, enjoy the trip. And I hope it does Wibke some good.'

'Me too,' said Dolly. 'Laurent says she's been moping around Beacon House the whole time, talking about what might've been.'

Pearl frowned. 'What does she mean by that?'

'Missing out on meeting Blake Cain, I suppose. She won't do that now someone's plunged a dagger in the man's throat.' Dolly sighed. 'Any word from the Flat Foot about finding the murderer?'

'DCI McGuire is conducting his inquiries,' said Pearl pointedly.

'Well, tell him to get a move on – and stay out of it,' warned Dolly, ending the call abruptly so that Pearl had no chance to argue. A moment later the phone rang again. Pearl felt sure it had to be Dolly having forgotten something, so she picked up the receiver and replied smartly: 'What is it now?'

'Could I come and talk to you?' said Lucy Walker.

Half an hour later, the pretty fair-haired journalist was sitting in the garden of Seaspray Cottage as Pearl handed her a glass of homemade elderflower cordial.

'Thanks,' said Lucy. She wore a pale pink T-shirt, faded blue jeans, and a friendly smile.

'I know how busy you must be, so I promise I won't keep you. It's just . . . you found the body, with James. And last night, after the poetry event, he happened to mention to me that you'd been kind to him – that you'd talked, since the murder?'

Pearl nodded. 'We ran into each other on the beach.' She smiled. 'He's into paddle boarding. Have you tried it?'

Lucy shook her head. "Fraid not. I'm ashamed to say I'm a really poor swimmer.'

'Well,' said Pearl, 'I wouldn't let that stop you, because I've heard that good paddle boarders don't even get wet.'

She began fishing now. 'James seems like a really nice young guy, don't you think?'

Lucy Walker looked up to see Pearl's smile and dropped her guard as she admitted: 'Yes, I do – not that I know him too well. But he moved here from Norwich where I've got some friends at uni, so we got talking for a while at your launch event – and last night.' She paused, then said ruefully: 'I'm not sure what he's going to do now, once this is all over. He doesn't seem to have anyone here in Kent.'

'Except for the friends he's made,' said Pearl. 'Cathy, Mila . . .' She paused for a moment, before adding: 'You?'

'Hardly,' said Lucy. 'It's early days and . . . I don't actually have much time for a boyfriend because my job keeps me pretty busy.'

'All the same,' said Pearl, 'sometimes you know when meeting a person might change your life for ever.'

'Yes,' said Lucy, nodding slowly. 'I think I know what you mean.' She paused for a moment, then frowned before she looked down at her notebook, then up at Pearl as she took on a more efficient tone. 'But, to be honest, I'm not really looking for a relationship right now. I want to concentrate on my work.'

'I understand,' said Pearl, recalling that those were the very same words she had used more than twenty years ago to Charlie's father, just before the course of her own life was to change for ever. She nodded and gave an understanding smile. 'So, what was it you wanted to talk to me about?'

'The other night,' Lucy began, 'when I was asking you about your detective agency, you mentioned that clues to a murder are like . . . ingredients for a meal? You have to put them together in the right way, you said, and that's exactly what I've been trying to do.' Lucy set down her glass. 'I think I may have something.'

'Go on,' said Pearl.

Lucy picked up her reporter's notebook. 'Well, James told me that you and he found the body with some music playing on the record player in the studio?'

Pearl nodded. 'That's right. The Humming Chorus from *Madam Butterfly*.'

Lucy flicked through her notebook. 'I've been trying to find a connection between the music and the actual murder – and I think I've found one.' As she looked up, Pearl could see a fire in Lucy's blue eyes.

'And . . . why are you talking to me and not the police?'

Lucy scoffed. 'I'm not sure they'd take me too seriously, would they? A cub reporter on a local paper? But you . . .' She broke off. 'Well, I . . . just hoped you'd hear me out.'

Lucy's gaze met Pearl's and in that instant Pearl recognised something in herself. She nodded. Lucy quickly took a smartphone from her bag and began to search for some information on it. 'Blake Cain was murdered with—'

'A paper knife,' said Pearl.

Lucy qualified: 'Not exactly. To be precise, it was a dagger he had been *using* as a paper knife.'

'And had bought in a local antique shop many years ago,' said Pearl. 'As Cathy McTurk told the police.'

Lucy brought up an image on her smartphone screen and handed it across to Pearl, who recognised the same publicity photograph she had first been shown by McGuire.

'I've seen this photo,' Pearl said. 'It's on Blake's website.'

'But have you taken a good look at the knife?'

Pearl frowned. 'What do you mean?'

Lucy enlarged the image on her phone. 'I'm sure the police are looking into this too, but I've been doing my own research. I think the design is actually Chinese. But the size of the dagger corresponds to that of a Japanese *tanto*.' Lucy paused for a moment and then continued, this time very clearly, as if she was trying to clarify things for herself, as well as Pearl. 'A *tanto* is a knife that was used in ritual suicides in Japan.'

Pearl looked back at Lucy. 'Hara-kiri, you mean? I always thought that was done using a sword.'

'That's true,' said Lucy, 'in the case of Samurai warriors. But I found an old article which explained that hara-kiri is actually a spoken, slang term, and the ritual was always referred to as *seppuku* in writing. The more modern Japanese word for suicide is *jisatsu*. And in some of the martial arts magazines I've been referencing, I've read that the term has also been linked with the suicide of Samurai wives. They sometimes used drowning as a method of ritual suicide in order to escape dishonour, but they also used a knife, a *tanto*, to cut the arteries of the neck with a single stroke – so that they could die quickly in order to avoid capture.'

Pearl looked confused before admitting: 'I . . . don't understand . . .'

'The opera that was playing in Blake's studio on the afternoon of the murder was *Madam Butterfly*, at the end of which the Japanese bride commits suicide.'

Pearl looked sharply at her. 'You're . . . not suggesting that Blake committed suicide?'

'No,' said Lucy. 'But I think the two things are connected – the opera and the knife? Look,' she brought up another page on her phone. 'Before committing a ritual honour suicide, a Japanese woman would often bind her legs together so that her body would be found in a . . . dignified pose. There are texts about how invading soldiers entered homes to find the woman seated alone, facing away from the door, and it was only as they approached her that they realised she had ended her life in this way. Look . . .' Lucy brought up another image on her phone and handed it to Pearl. It showed an ancient painting of the wife of a Samurai lord, dressed in a thick kimono, her legs bent at the knees and bound at the thighs with rope.

'There has to be a connection with Blake's murder, don't you think?' said Lucy, keenly. 'If not, why did the murderer tie Blake's legs together – and not his arms?' Pearl continued to look at the image on the smartphone, suddenly transported back to the afternoon in Blake

Cain's studio when she had come upon his dead body, his legs trussed at the thighs.

'You researched all this yourself?' asked Pearl.

Lucy nodded. 'Like you said: put the clues in the right order? That's what I've been trying to do.'

Pearl considered the girl's expectant expression and handed back the smartphone.

'You're a clever girl, Lucy Walker.'

The young reporter's face broke into a broad smile. 'Thanks.'

'Have you told anyone else?'

Lucy shook her head.

'What about James?'

'No one but you,' she said. 'I only pieced that last piece of information together, about the Samurai wives, this morning before calling you.'

'Good,' said Pearl. 'You're going to make a great investigative journalist.'

The girl beamed and pocketed her phone as Pearl continued to muse on Lucy's findings. 'But if you're right, it looks very much as though Blake Cain was murdered to underscore a woman's "dishonour" . . .'

Lucy looked at her. 'To be honest, I tried to get James to tell me what he knows about Blake Cain but . . . I think he's still being totally loyal and won't really say anything negative about him, but it's pretty much public knowledge that Blake was not only a sexist dinosaur but a misogynist too. I'm sure there are plenty of women he's behaved despicably to – in one way or another – and that goes for his former wife as well.' She picked up her glass and finished her cordial.

Pearl asked. 'You've come up with a potentially crucial piece of information.'

'I know,' Lucy smiled. 'Are you going to tell the police?'

Pearl nodded. 'I'm obliged to.'

Lucy took this in. 'I understand.'

'But, before I do,' said Pearl, 'I want to talk to someone else.'

Chapter Fifteen

As soon as Pearl arrived at Tom Maitley's house on Tankerton Road, it occurred to her that he must have been rattling around the vast double-fronted property for some years since his divorce, living in the hope that someone might join him – or perhaps even rejoin him – there, since he had never moved very far away from his former wife.

He led the way for Pearl into a large open-plan dining room, dominated by a long oblong table around which Pearl imagined a salon of interesting guests had once sat during his marriage to Cathy – though it now looked to be only a dumping ground for legal paperwork.

'Thank you for agreeing to see me,' said Pearl.

'It's OK,' Tom said flatly. 'Can I get you anything?' he added. 'Tea? Coffee?'

'Just a few moments of your time, please.'

Tom gestured for Pearl to take a seat while he cleared a space among a pile of legal tomes and reference books. 'Presumably this *is* about Blake's murder,' he said.

Pearl nodded.

'OK,' said Maitley. 'What can I do for you?'

Pearl took a moment to organise her thoughts before she explained: 'I know from having spoken to you that you have Cathy's best interests at heart. And so I think I should warn you that she may well soon come under police scrutiny . . . once they learn about some new evidence concerning Blake's murder.'

Tom frowned at this. 'What evidence?'

'It relates to the murder weapon and the circumstances of his death.'

For a moment, Tom Maitley seemed to be reflecting on Pearl's careful choice of words. 'I hope you're not suggesting that the police suspect Cathy in any way?' he said finally. 'Because I'm telling you now, she would never hurt a soul – not even Blake Cain.' Pearl saw his lips tighten at the mention of Blake's name. He took a moment to settle himself, though his hands remained clenched on the table before him.

Pearl spoke softly. 'I know Cathy loved him – and Blake let her down.'

Maitley looked away from Pearl's gaze, a muscle tightening in his jaw. When he looked back at her, he nodded stiffly. 'Yes,' he said. 'He did let her down. But that's what so often happens when marriages are based on romance.' Noting Pearl's confused look, he stared at her defiantly as he went on: 'You realise the whole idea of . . . romantic love is a relatively modern concept? It's not based on companionship or even lust but . . . a series of perpetual emotional highs and lows. It's a form of madness – so hardly a good basis for a long-term functional relationship.' His face set unapologetically as he added: 'No doubt you'll think that's sour grapes on my part – for losing Cathy to Blake? *I'd* say that looking at life, unclouded by useless infatuation, offers me a fair degree of clarity.' He waited for her response but Pearl thought very carefully before offering it.

'It must have been very difficult for you to see Cathy hurt by Blake.'

Tom frowned as he admitted: 'It was difficult to see her hurt, full stop. And she was. Firstly, by her inability to have children, and then . . . to fear losing her foster family because Blake became so jealous of sharing her love. He really was nothing less than a monster. He craved attention and devoured it at the same time, so nothing was ever enough for him. And yes, he could be the epitome of charm, wit, humour – even intellect at times – and he could certainly write, but beneath all that was a cavernous vacuum that could never be filled – certainly not by Cathy's love.' He looked down at his clenched hands as though gathering his thoughts.

Pearl asked: 'And he was jealous of her success?'

Tom looked back quickly as though stung by the question. 'Of course. He was jealous of anyone else's success – but *especially* Cathy's. The only reason she began writing in the first place was to help keep things together financially.' He pushed his hand through his dark, receding hair, almost in exasperation, as he explained: 'Look, Blake was never around and he'd stopped producing good work. I tried to help, but Cathy would never accept any financial support from me after our divorce. She took full responsibility for our marriage ending – even though Blake pursued her mercilessly – and she wouldn't take a penny from me. She has her pride. But she also had Mila to think of – and so she began writing, and she succeeded with it. She became a respected author in her own right, but I honestly believe she would have been just as happy keeping house and fostering more children *if* Blake had remained on track. Any other man would have been proud of what she managed to achieve – but not Blake.'

'He accused her of stealing his research?'

'Yes!' he snapped. 'But that was all nonsense. Cathy did *all* Blake's research for him, and he'd got her doing some work on the history of the Australian Gold Rush. She did so – she spent months on it – only for Blake to sit on it all. He did nothing with it, so, finally Cathy used it herself – her *own* research – to write her first novel, and it sold. For that, Blake never forgave her. He taunted her with spiteful barbs – and she took it all – the putdowns about her work. But, even in spite of those, they might still have been married today if he hadn't handed the final humiliation to her, by . . . taking up with other women right under her nose.'

'So, he . . . dishonoured his wife?'

Looking directly at Pearl, Tom Maitley said finally: 'Yes. Blake "dishonoured" Cathy. And if you'd like to know if I care one jot about finding out who thrust that knife into his throat and put a final stop to his continual demands for fame and acclaim, I don't. In fact, to be perfectly honest, I'm glad I'll never see Blake Cain's face ever again.'

The look he gave now to Pearl acted as a punctuation mark to the conversation. She got slowly to her feet and thanked him for his time. Moving to the door, she had almost reached it when Tom spoke again. 'I know for a fact that Cathy didn't murder Blake.' As though answering the question already posed in Pearl's mind, he went on: 'She isn't capable of murder,' he said, his voice filled with certainty.

As soon as Pearl was out of Tom Maitley's house, she took a deep breath, aware that she needed some physical space in order to clear her mind and shake off the long-held bitter hatred she had just witnessed from him – hatred which clearly remained even after Blake Cain's death.

She decided to head straight down towards the harbour so she could walk home along the beach. Having switched off her phone before the meeting with Maitley, she now switched it back on again and checked to see if McGuire had left any messages for her. Infuriatingly, there was nothing, and yet she felt emboldened by the fact that she was now in possession of the important information Lucy Walker had pieced together about the murder weapon – and which the police, and she herself, had missed. Pearl brought up McGuire's name on her phone's contact list, intent on telling him all that she had learned about the ancient ritual suicide methods used by Samurai wives. It seemed clear to her now that the opera that had been playing that day in Blake's studio was indeed part of the bigger picture – a tableau created by the murderer, pointing directly to the motive.

Pearl only wished that she herself had done more research on the dagger, especially since she had been the first person to discover the body. Perhaps McGuire had been right in warning her that she was in danger of splitting herself in two by trying to run the restaurant and her agency at the same time, and not for the first time she questioned if she could ever give her best to either while she did so. Lucy's research findings were important but Pearl had missed them by looking in the wrong places for clues. In her usual way, she had been seeking to build up a picture of Blake Cain from the people to whom he was most closely connected – but in doing so she had found only confusion.

In spite of all McGuire had told her about Bosley, it was still unsettling for Pearl to think of him working so closely with another woman – and such an attractive one at that. Although part of her felt justified in working alone – or even in tandem with Lucy Walker – to uncover more clues, Pearl knew she could never withhold crucial evidence from McGuire's investigation. She pressed the call option on her phone and, after a few rings, heard McGuire's efficient voicemail message sounding on the end of the line. 'Call me as soon as you get this,' she said quickly. 'It's important.' She rang off, frustrated further by the fact that he wasn't even responding to his calls but, a moment later, her mobile rang and she answered quickly, certain that it had to be McGuire. She soon found she was wrong.

'Pearl . . .?'

'Wibke . . .' Pearl recognised the voice on the end of the line, though it sounded faint. 'Are you on the *Greta*?' Pearl was now at the harbour entrance and craned her head to try to gain a view of the boat's distinctive brown sails at sea.

'I didn't go,' said Wibke. 'I'm . . .' The line broke up, then returned as Pearl heard the words: '. . . Beacon House.' A pause, then: 'I should never have gone.'

In spite of the bad reception, Pearl registered concern in the woman's voice. 'Wibke?'

The voice on the line returned. '. . . called Heather but she's not answering . . . Laurent . . . still out with Dolly . . . Do you have . . . moment?'

'You're breaking up . . .'

'I'm what?'

'The phone reception isn't good,' Pearl explained. 'Where are you?'

'Can you hear me?'

Pearl spoke clearly, asking: 'Is everything all right?'

Silence. Then: 'I'm . . . not sure . . . Perhaps . . . a ghost I saw . . . in a white dress . . . like a dream . . . I wondered perhaps if she . . .' Her next words were lost again.

'Who?' asked Pearl. 'Who did you see? The reporter, Lucy Walker?'

'No . . . her hair . . . it was dark. It's like . . .' The line broke up once more.

'Wibke, I can't hear properly. What did you just say?' Pearl waited in frustration for a response.

'Like . . . she's willing.'

'*Who's* willing?'

'I promised, Pearl . . . the photo . . .'

Wibke's voice faded once more and Pearl made a final decision. 'Don't worry. I'll meet you at Beacon House right now. You can explain.'

'*Danke!*'

It took only minutes for Pearl to head back on foot, away from the harbour entrance, and towards Tower Hill, passing the busy tea gardens on the slopes where a long queue had formed at a little thatched tea cabin that served homemade sponge and sandwiches. It was situated on the upper level of the slopes above Colin Fox's bungalow, and families sat on the tea gardens' lawn, enjoying the view and the sun.

Pearl took out her phone in order to try Wibke again, but soon registered that her mobile signal was weak, as it was so often along this stretch of coast, so she stuffed the phone back in her pocket and tried to make sense of what she had been able to glean from the call. It seemed Wibke had seen something that had distressed her. A 'ghost'. In a white dress. Not Lucy Walker but a woman with dark hair. Pearl heard Wibke's words echoing in her head: 'She's willing.' But they made no sense to her. Eager to know more, she quickened her pace, and headed across the top of the grassy slopes to a well-worn path which descended to the rear of Beacon House and the stretch of brightly coloured beach huts which extended eastwards almost as far as the neighbouring coastal town of Herne Bay.

As she did so, she looked out to sea, and from this high vantage point she could now clearly see that the Thames barge, *Greta*, was already moored safely in the harbour. Perhaps Dolly and Laurent might even still be aboard, having enjoyed an afternoon's sail out to the Red Sands Fort. But why had Wibke not taken up her place on the trip as planned? A group of noisy children ran past on the promenade below, calling out in pursuit of an ice-cream vendor on a tricycle bearing the name Lickett & Smyle. Parking up, the vendor sounded a familiar bell, and figures began to head towards him from the beach. For a moment, Pearl considered joining them in order to buy an ice cream to take to Wibke, having remembered how she had enjoyed the raspberry sorbet at The Whitstable Pearl. Although the party at the restaurant had taken place only a few nights ago, it now seemed part of a different period of time altogether

– one that had innocently preceded Blake Cain's horrific murder. Staring down at the crowd of holidaymakers surrounding the ice-cream vendor's tricycle, Pearl changed her mind and continued on instead to the rear of Beacon House. Heading into the shade of some tall sycamores, a breeze blew in from the sea and a chill ran through Pearl, not from the cool air but because of what she now saw straight ahead.

A woman's shoe lay upturned on the path, flat, stylish, a number visible on its polished sole – 39. Pearl bent down to pick it up then saw a second shoe, not lying on the path this time, but still attached to a woman's foot. Pushing back the branches of a hedge, Pearl found Wibke lying near a coarse bush, her face pointing upwards, as though she was staring towards the white clouds that were rolling in from the sea, though Pearl knew her bulbous eyes could have seen nothing through the blood that filled them. Wibke's mouth was fixed open in a clown-like grin as a thin trail of blood trickled down from its corner to where a garrotte of green string lay almost buried in the flesh of her neck, suddenly reminding Pearl of the old washing line in Dolly's garden around which the bark of a pear tree had grown . . . She quickly dismissed the image from her mind, and was just getting to her feet when the sound of church bells began travelling on the air from St Alfred's Church. It was precisely 4.31 p.m. – but too late to save Wibke Ruppert.

Chapter Sixteen

It was dusk on the day that followed Wibke Ruppert's murder, and Pearl and McGuire made for shadowy figures on the Street of Stones. Looking back towards Beacon House, Pearl could see crime-scene tape fluttering in the evening breeze; a white forensic tent was still visible on the pathway on which she had discovered Wibke's body. She looked away from it and down at the golden spear of shingle beneath her feet. It pointed, as ever, in the direction of the horizon, as though it might be indicating an important clue that had gone, as yet, unnoticed. As McGuire slipped his arm around her shoulder, she looked up at him and said: 'You're getting careless. Bosley could be spying on us.'

'And you're getting cold,' said McGuire. He tipped her face towards him and his eyes scanned hers. 'You did well not to lose it with her during the interview yesterday.'

'That was a challenge,' Pearl admitted. 'But I realise I could be arrested – and even charged – on suspicion of murder.'

'You found both bodies, Pearl.'

'But I didn't murder Blake or Wibke. And I explained everything to you about Lucy Walker's evidence.'

McGuire continued to hold her look. 'Eventually.'

Pearl heaved a weary sigh. 'Look, once I'd met with Lucy, I called you and left a message,' she said in her defence. 'Is it my fault you didn't get back to me?'

McGuire shook his head slowly. 'No. It's mine. I was caught up in a meeting and I should have called you, but I didn't. Nevertheless, what Lucy Walker gave up to you was information, not "evidence".'

Pearl met his gaze. 'It was good work on her part,' she insisted. 'Your investigation missed that Samurai connection – and so did I.'

McGuire nodded to acknowledge this, then took a deep breath of sea air as he looked away to the waves gently lapping up on to the shingle beneath their feet.

'All right,' he conceded. 'If Blake Cain's murder *was* choreographed in that way, with the phone message, the music, the weapon, the method for murder, including the binding of his legs, how exactly does that fit with Wibke Ruppert being strangled?' He looked back at Pearl for an answer.

'It doesn't,' Pearl admitted in frustration. 'I agree the

method used for her murder doesn't follow the pattern of the first.'

'Which means we could be looking at two murderers.'

Pearl paused to give this some thought. 'Or the second murder was purely opportunistic,' she said finally. 'As I said in my statement to Bosley, when Wibke called me, it was a bad line, but I could still tell she sounded anxious. Something had happened to upset her. She'd seen someone.'

'A woman in a white dress,' said McGuire.

'Yes,' Pearl frowned. 'But a woman with dark hair.'

'Mila Anton?' asked McGuire.

'Or . . . Heather Fox or . . . Vesta Korbyn?' She sighed in exasperation. 'If only the reception hadn't been so bad, but I just couldn't understand what it was she was trying to tell me. All I could make out were the words "she's willing" – at least, that's what it sounded like.' She paused for a moment. 'Were you able to track Wibke's movements yesterday afternoon from her phone?'

McGuire frowned. 'It would have been easier if she'd been using a smartphone. She'd only brought an old mobile with her from Germany, and from that we managed to get an approximate location using triangulation between the phone signal and local mobile towers. Seems she was never more than around 300 metres from Beacon House.'

Pearl mused on this. 'So, she could actually have been at Alegría,' she said. 'Have you managed to question James yet?'

'Terri has.'

'Terri?' Pearl repeated knowingly.

'DS Bosley,' said McGuire. 'James Moore said he was out paddle boarding and didn't get home till gone six p.m.'

'Anyone to back that up?'

'A waitress at a café on the east quay said she served him a beer at 4.52 – that checks out with the time on a till receipt – and she remembers he was wearing surf shoes and had damp hair.'

Pearl took this in. 'What about everyone else?'

McGuire shrugged. 'Mila Anton and Cathy McTurk said they were together at McTurk's house in Northwood Road. Maitley was working alone in his home. No one to confirm that.'

'And Vesta?'

'At home in Ham Shades Lane, working on a new book. Alone.' McGuire looked at Pearl. 'Lucy Walker was chasing a story for her paper in Canterbury – no corroboration. And Heather and Colin Fox were together at Fairview until 6.20, when Heather Fox left the house to meet a local councillor about some funding.'

'So, both Cathy and Mila, and Heather and Colin Fox give themselves alibis . . . and the others—'

'Have none,' said McGuire.

'At least we can be sure of the time of death,' Pearl added. 'Wibke's call is logged in my phone at 4.16 . . .'

'And you found her dead at exactly 4.30.'

'That's right. I'd just stumbled on her body when the

church bells rang out the half-hour. What about the weapon?' she asked. 'The green string?'

'Standard garden twine,' said McGuire. 'Nothing special.'

'Certainly nothing as elaborate as an Oriental dagger,' she said. 'Again it points to opportunism with this murder, the killer having perhaps overheard what she had to say to me on the phone?'

'Or knowing what she was about to tell you,' said McGuire darkly, '*if* you'd managed to get to her in time.'

Before Pearl could respond, a cool gust of sea air blew in from the north, and with it came a sudden rush of waves at their feet.

'Careful,' she warned. 'The tide comes in so fast here at this point, before you know it you can be cut off and at the mercy of the currents – even a local like me.' She looked down again; sure enough, the golden arrow of shingle beneath her feet was blurred by the incoming tide.

An hour after leaving McGuire on the Street, Pearl stood with Dolly in the conservatory of her home on Harbour Street, looking out towards Laurent Ruppert. He was sitting outside at the garden table, staring into space as he gently stroked Dolly's black and white tomcat, Mojo, on the chair beside him.

'It's so good of you to have taken Laurent in,' Pearl whispered. 'Should I go and talk to him?'

Dolly winced at Pearl's suggestion. 'I wouldn't if I

were you,' she said softly. 'He said he'd like some time alone and . . . Mojo seems to be keeping him company. Cats have an uncanny instinct for knowing when we need comfort.' She looked at Pearl and confided, 'I heard the poor man sobbing earlier.' Turning away from the window she sighed. 'We had such a glorious day together on the *Greta*. If *only* Wibke had come with us . . .'

Pearl frowned. 'I thought she was going to?'

'So did Laurent and I – but she dropped out, at the very last minute. Said she had something to do.'

'Like what?'

Dolly shrugged. 'We'll never know, although, at the time, Laurent seemed to think that she might have said that just as a polite excuse for her not to . . . impose on us?' She looked at Pearl. 'What a stupid thing to think. Laurent and I are just good friends. We talk about art and he's been helping me with my *Deutsch*.'

Pearl nodded and considered something. 'It's also possible Wibke may have been telling the truth – and that she *did* have something to do?'

Dolly frowned. 'Such as?'

'If I knew that,' sighed Pearl, 'I'd be further along with this case.'

'It's a police case,' Dolly reminded her firmly.

'I know,' agreed Pearl, 'but considering I came across both bodies – forgive me for being curious?' She sat down, took a deep breath and organised her thoughts. 'I've replayed that last telephone conversation with

Wibke over and over in my head, together with everything I saw after I left Tom Maitley.' She paused. 'After
leaving his house on Tankerton Road, I walked down
towards the harbour, but before I'd actually entered at
the south quay, Wibke called on my mobile. The reception was so bad I couldn't make out what she was trying
to tell me so I said I would meet her.'

'And where was she when she called you?'

'That's just it, I don't know. She said something about
Beacon House and then, "I should never have gone
there", and then started telling me about some . . .
woman in white – a ghost?'

'Ghost?' echoed Dolly, confused.

'Yes. I'm sure that's what she said. The mention of a
white dress made me think of the reporter, Lucy Walker.
But Wibke said this woman had dark hair. Then she
said something about, "she's willing".'

'Who's willing?'

'That's what I asked,' said Pearl. 'But the line was so
bad I gave up; I told Wibke I'd meet her at Beacon
House so she could explain.'

'And if she wasn't already there, she couldn't have
been too far away to have agreed?'

Pearl nodded. 'That's right. We all know there's often
bad or intermittent phone reception on the slopes.'

Dolly nodded. 'What then?'

'I walked as fast as I could to Marine Parade, and
then headed across the top of the slopes to the path
leading down to Beacon House.' She paused. 'I didn't

get very far before . . . I found poor Wibke.' She took another deep breath then looked up at Dolly who said ruefully, 'If only the *Greta* had docked a little earlier.'

Pearl looked at Dolly, who explained: 'Laurent could have been back and perhaps Wibke would still be with us.'

At this, Pearl remembered something. 'I saw the *Greta* in the harbour from the slopes.'

Dolly nodded. 'Yes, we docked promptly at four and Laurent and I came ashore. He wanted to try out the Harbour Garden Restaurant on the quay. But I had to get back because I had the Fells to meet and greet – David and Liz, remember? Regular guests at my Attic?'

Pearl gave a nod. 'So . . . did Laurent come back here with you?' she asked tentatively.

As Dolly shook her head, Pearl realised something. 'So Laurent doesn't actually have an alibi for the time of Wibke's death?'

Dolly looked quickly at her daughter and whispered sternly: 'You're not suggesting he could possibly have murdered her?'

Pearl said nothing. Dolly frowned and continued: 'Now look here, you may well argue that there's nothing to prevent a brother murdering his own sister – but *not* Laurent. For goodness' sake, you *saw* them together, Pearl. They were so close, they almost finished each other's sentences.'

'Yes,' said Pearl. 'Like twins.'

'And if there's one thing I am, it's a good judge of

JULIE WASSMER

character, and I know for a fact that Laurent is a kind and honourable man who's in a deep state of shock and grief about losing his sister. If I learn that the Flat Foot is about to put him in the frame for this terrible murder, I will do *all* I can to bring a case of wrongful arrest, do you hear?'

In that moment, the fire in Dolly's dark eyes betrayed to Pearl her mother's characteristic determination to fight against any possible injustice – but it also conveyed her true feelings for the man sitting, bereft, in her garden.

Much later that evening, Nathan Roscoe looked up from working at a laptop in his stylish cottage on Island Wall and said to Pearl: 'I must admit, I only got to exchange a few words with the woman in The Horsebridge bar that evening, after you left with Blake Cain's assistant, but she seemed nice enough – just like her brother. A charming and innocuous pair,' he said. 'Like Tweedledum and Tweedledee?'

'Sadly, no longer,' said Pearl.

Nathan considered her and said: 'That phone message to the police really *has* become rather prophetic, hasn't it? This *is* a veritable Murder Fest.'

'Yes. I think you're right,' Pearl replied. 'And though I would never condone any murder, I can almost understand why some people might have wanted Blake Cain out of the way – for good. After all, he was arrogant, selfish, inconsiderate, and by all accounts he treated the women in his life appallingly. But poor

Wibke was so innocent – guileless – and probably the one person who remained in complete awe or admiration of him – apart from James Moore, of course. Wibke was so sad at his death, so disappointed that she would never get to meet him properly.' She paused. 'I suppose it's possible that she could have gone to Alegría that afternoon because, from her phone signal, the police know that she remained within a few hundred metres of Beacon House that afternoon.'

'Then she would also have been close to Heather's home,' said Nathan.

Pearl agreed. 'That's right,' she said thoughtfully. 'But if you think about it, there are actually four properties lying within equal distance of Alegría – Cathy McTurk's home on Northwood Road, Tom Maitley's house on Tankerton Road, Colin Fox's cottage, Fairview – and Beacon House.'

'Yes,' Nathan nodded. 'Of course. Though I can't for one minute imagine why anyone would possibly want to throttle to death a middle-aged woman from a German twinning association. Can you?'

Before Pearl could offer a suitable response, her mobile phone rang. The caller's number was unfamiliar, so Pearl excused herself to Nathan and answered it to find it was Mila Anton on the line. Her tone was low but forceful in intent. 'It's terrible news about the German woman,' she said. 'But I'd like to speak to you about something. Do you think we could meet in Canterbury tomorrow?'

'Where?'

'I'll be home in the afternoon and . . . I'd be very grateful if you didn't tell anyone you're coming?'

Pearl shared a look with Nathan then made a decision. 'Of course. Let me have your address, Mila.'

Chapter Seventeen

Pearl had arranged to meet Mila Anton at 2.30 p.m., but arrived in Canterbury in plenty of time so she could make a quick stop at a familiar store. The vintage clothes shop, Revivals, was a favourite haunt of Pearl's – a veritable Aladdin's cave of fashion items ranging from dresses, jewellery and corsetry to top hats and tails, as well as relics from Carnaby Street's 'Swinging 60s', all vying for attention among hacking jackets and deer-stalkers. Entering the shop never ceased to remind Pearl of the afternoons she had spent as a child, dressing up in Dolly's clothes, teetering around in her mother's stiletto heels that had long been exchanged for more comfy pumps. As a teenager, Pearl had again raided Dolly's wardrobes, this time for items that might have regained some fashionable status, including bell-bottomed trousers and floral summer frocks until, finally, Pearl had discovered her own distinctive style, reflecting her love of all things vintage.

The shop was always a popular haunt but seemed unusually empty for the time of day. In the summer months, it was so often filled with tourists, photographing themselves as they tried on various items, but today, Pearl appeared to be the sole customer. 'Can I help?' asked the owner, a stylish middle-aged woman with an engaging manner and friendly smile.

'I was just wondering if you might have a fifties vintage dress?' asked Pearl. 'White, with perhaps some shell buttons down its front? I happened to see one just like that recently.'

'Well,' said the woman, 'the beauty of a vintage dress is that it's likely to be a one-off – a bit like those who appreciate them?' She winked as she recognised a kindred spirit in Pearl. 'No shell buttons,' she continued. 'But I do have a very special white dress that would suit you down to a "T".' She led the way to the rear of the store and knew exactly where she would find the dress she'd been describing. 'Here,' she said. Grabbing a hanger from a high rail, she took down a garment and let it lie across her forearm for Pearl to inspect. 'Isn't this just the most beautiful thing you've ever seen?'

Against the sunlight, the white satin bodice was almost blinding. It sank into delicate steep points from which intricate lacework fell. 'All antique French silk, that is,' said the owner. 'You'll never see anything that fine made these days.'

Pearl recognised this was true. The skirt of the dress was a network of silk lace that plunged almost to the floor. 'Yes,' Pearl agreed. 'It's incredibly beautiful but . . . it's not quite what I had in mind,' she admitted. As the owner looked at her, Pearl continued: 'This is a wedding dress, isn't it?'

The woman nodded. 'That's right,' she said. 'And you'll look beautiful in it.' Pearl returned the woman's smile and glanced back to admire the dress, almost tempted before she confided: 'I'm afraid I shan't be walking up any aisles soon.'

Outside the shop, Pearl stared directly across to the other side of the street, where a group of Japanese girls, carrying numerous shopping bags, were milling outside a store selling fancy-dress costumes. They appeared to be tourists enjoying a sunny afternoon on the main shopping thoroughfare of an old English city that was most famous for the murder of a rebel archbishop and the bawdy tales of Geoffrey Chaucer. Pointing to a variety of party wigs in the window, the girls giggled before finally stumping up courage to enter the store, no doubt to try some of them on. As they disappeared inside, Pearl found herself reflecting on what Lucy Walker had told her about the tragic fate of the Samurai wives who had chosen a path of ritual suicide rather than face dishonour – and wondered why Mila Anton had summoned her today . . .

*

Ten minutes later, Mila was welcoming Pearl into an apartment near the old Abbott's Mill in Canterbury. The block was a redevelopment that overlooked the famous old water mill on the River Stour, which ran through the heart of the city. Outside Mila's open window, the sound of rushing water drifted in, along with the voices of children playing in a riverside orchard through which theatre-goers were taking a short cut to a matinee performance at the Marlowe Theatre.

'Thank you for coming,' said Mila, gesturing for Pearl to take a seat on a generous sofa that was covered with a velvet throw and scattered with large batik cushions. Above it hung a framed poster advertising a festival featuring Caribbean music. Mila was dressed in a long multi-coloured kaftan, her scarlet turban back in place, taming her beautiful black hair.

'Can I get you anything?' she asked. 'Iced tea? Coffee?'

'I'm fine.'

Mila paused for a moment then nodded and sat down opposite Pearl, casting a look towards the open window as she whispered, almost to herself: 'This is such a difficult time.'

'I'm sure,' said Pearl, softly.

Mila looked back at Pearl and qualified: 'But not for the reasons you might think. Grief at Blake's death? Anger at his murder?' She paused. 'It's true that at one time Blake was . . . like a father to me. But he was never my father. Cathy always made that plain and supported me, not only by fostering me when I was a child, but by helping me to find my real heritage. That wasn't easy,' she went on. 'My father . . . didn't want a relationship with me. And my mother and I . . .' She frowned. 'Things didn't work out,' she said concisely. 'But roots go much deeper,' she added. 'I'm no longer the fuzzy-headed brown child belonging to no one. I am me. Mila. And so now I have a sense of belonging, wherever I go. Yes, I have conflicting emotions about Blake's murder. I know I should be grateful to him for having taken me into his home at a time when I most needed one. But I'm also aware of how much he resented me – and my place in Cathy's heart.'

Pearl allowed herself a moment to take this in. 'Resented you?' she asked. 'But . . . you were only a child.'

'I know,' said Mila. 'But in many ways so was Blake.' She got to her feet and wandered across to the open window where she looked out at the river below as she went on: 'There was, of course, no need for his resentment, or jealousy, because Cathy's heart was big enough to include us all. What she taught me was that love is not a finite resource. It doesn't run out when you give it freely to others. It simply replenishes. The more you give, the more there *is* to give. But unfortunately, Blake never learned that lesson – no matter how much Cathy tried to demonstrate it.' She looked back at Pearl and returned to her seat. 'He was a jealous man – jealous not only of the love she gave to others, but of the love she received from her many friends, and all the children she cared for.'

'You,' said Pearl.

Mila nodded. 'But I was one of several. Blake never understood how Cathy remained without enemies. Even Tom forgave her for leaving him and blamed Blake entirely for their marriage breaking down.' She paused. 'Cathy is a rare human being,' she said finally. 'Beautiful, caring, intelligent, special . . .'

'But . . . not without flaws?' asked Pearl.

Mila looked up quickly, as though instinctively needing to challenge this, but Pearl clarified. 'After all, she fell for Blake.'

Mila's expression clouded now before she nodded finally as she accepted this. 'It's true there was a great passion between them both – like a raging wildfire.'

'And wildfires are destructive,' said Pearl.

Mila nodded. 'Yes. They can be fatal.' She looked down for a moment, as though appraising something, then she met Pearl's gaze once more. 'Look, I'd be very grateful if you didn't tell Cathy what I'm about to tell you. She's been humiliated enough as it is by Blake – by his affairs, his tantrums about her success, his threats to sue her over her first book, and even his attention-seeking performance the other evening at your restaurant when he tried to convince everyone he had damaging secrets to reveal in his autobiography?'

'And . . . you don't believe he had?'

'Nothing could possibly damage Cathy,' Mila insisted. 'Though I am sure there may well have been more secrets to hurt her.'

'More?'

Mila met Pearl's gaze. 'Concerning Vesta Korbyn, for one. But that was almost to be expected. Blake was always an opportunist and Vesta is a self-publicist. I think they were just using one another. It was so obvious . . .' She looked at Pearl, her dark eyes simmering with rage. 'But I also know for a fact that Blake betrayed Cathy with someone else. Someone she trusts to this day.' Mila's beautiful dark eyes now seemed full of sorrow. 'Cathy must never know this,' she said. 'As I just told you, she was humiliated enough by Blake's behaviour and I never wanted her to take part in this festival . . . but I couldn't tell her why. I'd . . . really appreciate it if you kept it that way?' She fell silent and her eyes lowered.

'Who was it?' Pearl asked. 'Who betrayed Cathy?'

Finally, Mila looked up again at Pearl. After a long silence, she replied darkly, 'Heather Fox.'

Chapter Eighteen

It was late afternoon as Colin Fox led the way for Pearl into his well-maintained back garden, his shirtsleeves rolled up to his elbows as he explained: 'I'm afraid Heather's not here.' Then he put on some gardening gloves and returned to carefully plucking weeds from terracotta pots containing seedlings. 'Neither of us slept very well after hearing the news about poor Wibke.' He paused for a moment, as he reflected on this. 'I know Heather's taken it particularly badly, so I told her some fresh air might do her good.' He looked at Pearl then pointed to his plants. 'I also wanted to get on with this,' he added. 'So I'd be grateful if you didn't tell her you saw me out here? She hates me gardening and worries I'll overdo it but . . . well, to be honest it's the only thing that keeps me going – watching new life grow.' As he turned to secure some young sweet peas climbing up a wall of vertical lines of green twine, Pearl sensed he was using these activities as a displacement tactic to hide his true emotions.

'She shouldn't be long now,' he said. 'I have a doctor's appointment to get to this afternoon and Heather always insists on taking me. Life doesn't offer much else these days.' Finally, he turned to face Pearl and she saw his defeated look as he took off his gardening gloves and reached inside his trouser pocket for a tissue before blowing his nose.

'I'm . . . really sorry about Wibke,' said Pearl. 'She was a lovely lady and I know how close you were.'

Hearing this, Colin Fox's façade finally crumbled. He used another tissue to wipe his eyes. 'Yes.' He looked broken as he continued: 'I never thought I'd outlive my dear friend.' His sorrow transformed to anger as he asked: 'What kind of monster have we got here among us?' He looked back at Pearl as if for an answer but, before she could offer one, a sudden loud cry caused them to look up towards the roof of the cottage.

'It's just the herring gulls,' Colin said testily. 'They're nesting on a chimney.' He was still looking up as he explained: 'They lost one of the fledglings to a fox the other night, so they're being particularly noisy at the moment. And aggressive. I don't have to tell you they can be dangerous when they're protecting their young.'

Pearl gave a nod. 'Yes,' she said. 'Perhaps we all are.' Colin looked back at Pearl who added: 'You must really feel for Heather right now? I mean, she's worked so hard on getting this festival together – and for very little reward.'

'Little financial reward,' said Colin stoically. 'But money isn't everything.' He moved to a small basin outside his potting shed and washed his hands. 'What was it you wanted to talk to her about?'

'She . . . happened to mention to me that she once worked with Blake Cain in London – a few years ago?'

Colin dried his hands on an old towel. 'I don't know about that,' he said. 'I didn't see too much of her in those days. She was working far too hard.'

'Until she came back for a long break?' Pearl asked.

Colin nodded. 'That's right. She'd been living on her nerves. And no one can do that for ever. It wasn't good for her health. To be honest, I don't know how anyone copes with the frantic pace of life these days. In my time, you worked from nine to five with breaks for lunch and tea – and a good summer holiday to look forward to. But Heather always seemed to be on the go, with people bothering her on her mobile phone and e-mails to respond to twenty-four hours a day. Everything has to be done so quickly now; it's easy to fall out of the natural rhythm of life and . . . never have time to even look up at a blue sky.' He did exactly that for a moment before looking back at Pearl. 'Life goes fast enough as it is. You never get back lost time.'

He rolled down his shirtsleeves as Pearl asked: 'So, Heather stopped working in London and came home – here to Whitstable?'

Colin turned to face Pearl but another voice responded.

'That's right.'

Heather Fox was standing behind Pearl, having entered the garden from a side gate, rather than the house. Pearl wondered how long she had been standing there and how much she had overheard of the conversation with her father. She took off the wide-brimmed sun hat she wore. 'If you must know,' she began, 'I'd taken on too much. I was young and . . . I didn't know what I was getting into. You could say I just got out of my depth.'

Colin Fox's eyes locked with his daughter's. 'But she's OK now,' he said to Pearl.

'Yes,' said Heather. 'I learned my lesson. An important lesson.' She paused and summoned a faint smile for Pearl. 'And now I have to take Dad to a doctor's appointment. Are you ready, Dad?'

Colin gave a nod and picked up a light cotton jacket that was resting on the back of a garden chair. As he and his daughter led the way for Pearl out of Fairview's garden, Pearl looked up thoughtfully, one last time, at the herring gulls' nest on the roof of Colin's property.

Almost an hour later, McGuire was on the phone to Pearl. 'Look, it's a really difficult time right now.'

'And when will be a good time?' she asked pointedly. 'I've been waiting for you to call me.'

'I know. And I'm sorry,' he said in frustration. 'But we've had a bit of a breakthrough here.'

'Oh?'

'Bosley re-interviewed the local builder . . .'

'The one who "thought" he might have seen a woman in white on the lawn of Alegría?'

'That's right,' said McGuire as he raked his fingers through his blond hair. 'Only now he's sure.'

'Why now?'

'Because Bosley managed to jog his memory. She took him back to the house and got him to retrace his journey in the van at exactly the same time of day.'

'And what time was that?'

'Around 6.03.'

'How can he be so sure?'

'Because he was heading back to relieve a labourer who was working for him that day. Bosley interviewed him too. He claims he was due to work until six that evening – so he had his eye on the time – and his boss arrived five minutes late, but in time to pay him for the day.'

Pearl took a moment to process this information. McGuire spoke again. 'You said you had something to tell me?'

'Heather Fox,' said Pearl. 'I think she worked with Blake Cain a few years ago. But would you be able to check this out for me?'

A pause followed before McGuire said: 'I'll try, Pearl. But I'm in the middle of something else right now and my DCs are all out following it up.'

'Following what up?'

'Another line of inquiry from Bosley. I can't say any more at the moment. I'm sorry.'

'OK,' said Pearl, trying not to feel too sidelined by DS Terri Bosley. 'I'll let you know what I discover.'

'Pearl . . .' McGuire's voice sounded quickly on the line. But Pearl had already ended the call.

It was 5.30 on that same afternoon before Pearl set off in her car for Marine Parade. Instead of continuing to drive on the long coastal road itself, she turned off into a side street where she parked her Fiat before striding off on the narrow access road which ran along the back of the expensive sea-facing homes. Counting out the properties, she paused at the rear of Alegría, intent on trying to view for herself what McGuire's witness had seen when he claimed a woman in a white dress had crossed Blake Cain's lawn on the afternoon of his murder.

Though a security fence was in place, it was easy enough for Pearl to see that it was perfectly possible for the driver of any regular builder's van to glance across it into Blake Cain's garden. Up high in the branches of the tall oak trees, silver CDs still turned, shining in the breeze, reminding Pearl of the afternoon she had discovered Blake's body slumped at his desk as though he had merely been taking a rest from his work. Now, in the absence of any manuscript, it appeared the author had not been working at all – merely pretending to write an autobiography that threatened to rock the worlds of several people who had once been close to him. Cathy and Vesta were two of those people. Perhaps Mila and Tom Maitley also had reason to fear its effect on Cathy, but it was only now that Pearl added Heather Fox to that list. She had been honest about having worked with Blake Cain in London, but had Mila Anton been honest with Pearl when she had told her that Heather and Blake had been lovers? If so, could Heather also have had reason to fear revelations from the pen of Blake Cain?

As Pearl reflected on this, a bicycle bell sounded sharply behind her as a cyclist, dressed in Lycra vest and shorts, powered quickly by on the access road. Pearl waited until he had disappeared into the distance, then approached a door in the security fence leading into Alegría's rear garden and tried its metal latch. As she suspected, she found it was securely locked; she was just beginning to move off, when she heard a sound and turned to see the door suddenly opening. A figure stood on the other side of the fence.

'Pearl . . .' said James Moore, clearly surprised to see her. 'I . . . heard someone trying this latch. You gave me a bit of a fright.'

'I'm sorry.' Pearl smiled. 'Creeping around in back alleyways is a bit of an occupational habit.'

James returned her smile. 'Come in.'

Pearl entered the garden as James closed the door firmly behind them. 'I just made some coffee,' he said. 'Will you join me?'

Pearl nodded and the young man led the way to a small, flat-roofed extension to the main house.

'Your "granny annexe"?' she asked.

James nodded. 'Though I'm not sure for how much longer.' He seemed to brood on this for a moment, then gestured for her to enter. Pearl stepped inside the annexe to find herself in a small kitchenette filled with the smell of freshly made coffee.

'Milk? Sugar?' asked James.

Pearl nodded and the young man filled a second cup from a cafetiere before indicating the way through an open door that led into a small bedsitting room. It was sparsely furnished with a small table on which stood a desk lamp and laptop. A few packed bags and holdalls lay strewn across the floor. He explained: 'I don't have too many belongings but thought I might as well start getting my stuff together. Here . . .' He offered Pearl a chair at the table and set down her coffee near to his laptop before sitting down himself on the bed. As Pearl smiled at him, she noted a framed photo behind him on a shelf.

'Your mum?' she asked.

James nodded and picked up the photo to hand it to her. It showed a pretty young woman in her early twenties against a rural backdrop.

'I think it's my favourite photograph of her because she looks so happy,' said James. 'It was taken at a village fete near Banbury where she grew up. She said she'd been made Queen for the Day and got to . . . "spin the drum" for the Tombola and hand out all the fete prizes. Must've been quite a big thing for her.'

Pearl smiled down at the image and remembered an old nursery rhyme. 'Ride a cock horse to Banbury Cross.' She looked back at James and realised: 'She's probably younger in this photo than you are now.'

James looked surprised for a moment and checked the photograph. 'Yes,' he said. 'You're probably right. Odd to think your parents were ever younger than you, isn't it?'

Pearl sipped her coffee and agreed. 'Yes. And I'm sure my son thinks the same.'

James smiled at Pearl. 'What's his name?'

'Charlie. He's just twenty-one and away doing an animation course in Dorset right now. He takes after his grandmother for creativity.'

'Cooking's creative.'

'It can be,' said Pearl. She smiled. 'Here's a secret: I don't actually use recipes.'

James looked suitably surprised. Pearl went on: 'I like to find my own way with a dish.'

'Improvise, you mean?'

Pearl nodded. 'That way you always discover something new – even if it doesn't work out.' She handed back the framed photograph and watched James replace it carefully on the shelf. Then he looked back and asked: 'I'm guessing you're here to talk to me about something other than cooking?'

'To be honest, I was just snooping,' Pearl confessed. 'A witness has told the police that he saw a woman in a white dress crossing the lawn here at Alegría on the afternoon of Blake's murder.'

James frowned. 'Is this witness absolutely sure?'

'There seems to have been some doubt at first,' said Pearl. 'But he's certain now.'

James glanced out of the window towards the lawn and looked confused. 'Well . . . How did the woman get in? The garden fence is too high to climb, and the door in the fence is always kept locked.'

He looked back at Pearl who gave a shrug. 'I don't know the answer to that,' she admitted. 'But it's possible Blake could have been expecting a visitor that afternoon and let that person in himself – or even left the rear door unlocked for them to enter?' She paused for a moment before adding: 'He had spent the night with Vesta Korbyn – at her home.'

James nodded slowly. 'So that's where he went. The police asked me about his movements that night . . .' He looked up at Pearl with a new train of thought.

'Do you think this woman could have been Vesta?'

'I honestly don't know, James. She doesn't seem to have an alibi for the time of the murder but then neither does Heather Fox.' She paused again. 'And Mila only has one because you corroborated it.'

He looked up quickly. 'I did meet with her in Canterbury that afternoon,' he insisted.

'I know,' said Pearl quickly. 'You were caught together on some CCTV footage near her home just before 4.30 p.m. But it's still possible she could then have driven back here to Alegría. There was just enough time . . .'

'You don't think Mila could possibly have killed Blake. That's absurd.'

Pearl finished her coffee and asked: 'Is it?'

'Well, what possible reason could she have had to murder Blake?'

Pearl paused before she replied: 'To protect Cathy from any revelations in his book.'

James considered this for a moment. 'No, it's impossible. I don't believe for one minute she could possibly harm anyone.'

'Interesting,' said Pearl. 'That's exactly what Tom Maitley said about Cathy.' Pearl smiled. 'Nice to have such glowing testimonials.'

'But it's the truth,' James assured her. 'Besides, *I* could just have easily got back from Canterbury in the same time.'

'Not by train, you couldn't. And you'd be cutting it fine by bus and you don't have a car.'

James thought quickly. 'I could have got a cab.'

'Yes. I'm sure the police are looking into that,' said Pearl. 'But, alternatively . . .' she paused for a moment before continuing. 'You could have returned here with Mila.' She held his gaze. James remained unperturbed.

'But I didn't,' he said determinedly.

Pearl was about to respond when a sudden flash of light reflected on the walls of James's bedsitting room. Outside the window, the CDs were spinning in the tall oaks on the breeze, catching the sunlight as they revolved.

'Who was it that put those discs in the trees?' asked Pearl, curious.

James followed her gaze to them. 'Blake, I think. He told me the noise of the crows had disturbed him when he was writing.'

Pearl watched them for a moment then finished her coffee and got to her feet. 'What will you do when you leave here?'

The young man shrugged. 'I don't know,' he said helplessly. 'Cathy's been very kind. She says I could stay there for a while and help her with her next book but . . .' He broke off.

'What?'

'Well, I . . . don't want her to feel obliged to help me just because I worked for Blake.' He looked conflicted. 'She doesn't owe me anything.'

'Who says she does?' asked Pearl. 'Maybe she's just grateful for your help. She's seen how hard you worked for Blake.'

James looked down, as though embarrassed. Pearl went on. 'And Lucy?' As he glanced quickly back at Pearl, she offered him a knowing smile. 'That was a lovely poem you recited the other evening.'

James blushed. 'Was it obvious?'

'Obvious?'

'That it was about her?'

Pearl paused before offering up her response. 'Well, let's just say that if I was in Lucy's shoes I'd be very flattered that someone felt inspired to write such a beautiful poem about me.'

At this James's face lit up with a bright smile; so

bright, in fact, that Pearl stopped herself from reminding him that Lucy Walker was the owner of a white dress and had no alibi for the timing of the two murders.

'Thanks for the coffee, James.'

He smiled. 'Any time.'

On returning home to Seaspray Cottage, Pearl tossed her shoulder bag on to an armchair and quickly investigated her answerphone, but she found no messages from McGuire. She heaved a sigh and stepped into the kitchen, opening her refrigerator to feed the cats who were performing intricate slaloms around her legs. The fridge was usually packed with plenty of food – ingredients for dishes she would cook for Charlie and then use as an excuse to go and visit him in Canterbury. She knew she fretted far too much about whether he ate enough, or properly, as Dolly always reminded her, but then Dolly was a terrible cook. For that reason Pearl never allowed her mother to do anything beyond the basics in the kitchen at The Whitstable Pearl, and instead used Dolly's skills mainly for 'front of house' duties – and her homemade ceramics for serving up Pearl's oysters.

Dolly ate to live while Pearl lived to eat, and food was the medium by which Pearl expressed love. It therefore always irked her that McGuire disliked the one item for which her restaurant, and her home town, was famous – its local oysters. Nevertheless, Pilchard and Sprat at her feet were grateful for the poached wild salmon she had just set before them and Pearl now determined that, whatever the result of this murder case, as soon as Charlie came home she would spoil him with one of his favourite dishes – seafood lasagne or her own classic stargazy pie, for which she always used herrings rather than pilchards or sardines. Reminded of the herring-gulls' nest on the roof of Colin Fox's home, Pearl mused for a moment on what he had told her about the bird's aggressive protection of its young. Heather Fox had flown the family nest, only to return, a fledgling after all. And with that thought, and in the absence of McGuire's help, Pearl sat down at her laptop and decided to find out all she could about Heather's career path over the last ten years.

Her laptop screen had barely sprung into life when the doorbell sounded. In spite of the interruption of her research, Pearl smiled, certain that the caller had to be McGuire, finally in possession of some important information for her, or an update about his new line of inquiry. Pearl opened the door expectantly but saw not McGuire on her doorstep, but a woman with dark hair, wearing a white shift dress.

'I need to tell you the truth,' said Heather Fox.

Chapter Nineteen

Heather Fox confessed: 'I'm not very good at keeping secrets.'

She was standing facing Pearl's living-room window, gazing out at a great plain of estuary mud lying exposed by the outgoing tide. After a moment, she turned back towards Pearl. 'I should have told the police – but I didn't.'

'About?'

Heather paused for some time before answering Pearl's question. 'My relationship with Blake,' she said. 'It had been over for a long time but . . . some things still remain.'

'Like what?' asked Pearl.

Heather struggled with herself for a moment before replying. 'Guilt.' She slumped down, defeated, on Pearl's sofa.

'You mean . . . because Blake was still married to Cathy?' Pearl crossed the room to Heather who shook her head slowly. 'No. *Legally* they were still married – but I knew the relationship was over. That's what had given me hope.'

'Hope that you could make things work?'

Heather nodded. 'Oh, I know it sounds stupid now, but it was true back then. I honestly don't think I would have succumbed to Blake otherwise.'

Pearl moved to her drinks tray, poured a small glass of brandy and offered it to her. 'Here.'

Heather hesitated for a moment, then took the glass, and a hefty sip of the dark liquid. As Pearl sat beside her on the sofa, Heather admitted: 'I haven't had that many relationships. I was always caught up with work. But then . . .'

Pearl completed her sentence. 'Blake became your work?'

Heather nodded. 'I had the job of promoting some events for one of his books. I fell for him. And I fell hard.' She paused to take another sip of brandy then took a deep breath. 'I read somewhere that most women are prepared to end an unhappy marriage, even if it means being alone, but men are more likely to stay in a failing marriage . . . until they find another partner?' She looked at Pearl. 'I think that's what Blake was doing at that time – searching for an alternative.' She stared deeply into the glass in her hand and swirled the brandy, as if in the hope that it might present her with answers. She went on. 'Cathy's career was taking off, her books were selling, she was doing so well – and Blake hated it. Before that, she'd been at home, at his beck and call, doing all his research, pandering to his every need, taking care of the home and the children they had fostered together.'

'Mila Anton,' said Pearl.

Heather nodded. 'Yes, Mila was at home then. She was just a young teenager but she had bonded so well with Cathy, who was helping her to find her Caribbean roots and . . . it was all just too much for Blake. He felt neglected, unloved, and maybe it reminded him of his rotten childhood when he'd been sidelined by everyone else's problems.'

'He . . . confided in you about that?'

Heather nodded. 'But it's all there in his first two novels, which is what made them so powerful. Writing those books must have been cathartic for him, but then he simply kept repeating the formula and finally ran out of steam. I had the job of promoting his fifth book but to be honest it was a hard sell and . . . I began to feel sorry for him. Blake played on my sympathies.'

'And you said you fell for him.'

Heather nodded. 'I truly did. And I honestly believe that, in his own way, he fell for me too. I *was* the "alternative" he'd been looking for – young and attentive to his needs. But I was also very naïve and, I realise now, I lacked what's called "emotional intelligence". Blake was talking about a life for us together, somewhere different, somewhere the sun always shone.'

'California?'

'No,' said Heather. 'He said he'd been there, done that, and he wanted to return and retire to the south of France. To Nice – where he'd been as a young man, working on board yachts. He said he would buy one and we'd just drift off together.' She gave a sad smile.

'What else?'

Heather shrugged. 'He said he'd been happy there, that he'd found people who had been kind to him, had helped him – encouraged him to be who he was and to do what he wanted.' She paused for a moment. 'I think he felt that a new beginning and a new relationship in a new country would be just what he needed. He'd convinced himself of this and he convinced me too.' The sad smile on her lips suddenly faded.

'What happened?'

Heather looked back at Pearl, her lips tight shut, before she finally admitted: 'I ruined everything . . . by getting pregnant.' She stared again at the drink in her hand but this time gulped the brandy down before explaining. 'It's true it wasn't planned – an accident – but, once I knew, I really wanted to keep the baby. Why wouldn't I? We had been making so many plans for the future but . . .' Her expression darkened. 'Blake was insistent that a child wasn't part of it.' She frowned. 'At the time I thought perhaps . . . that he was scared of hurting Cathy. She'd wanted children of her own so much . . .' She broke off for a moment before continuing: 'But there again, perhaps he just knew he could never be a good father? So he gave me an ultimatum: told me we would be finished if I went through with the pregnancy . . .' She trailed off again, leaving Pearl to verbalise the one thought in her mind in that moment: 'And you had an abortion?'

Heather nodded. 'And there's not a day goes by that I don't regret it.' She turned to Pearl, heartache written on her pretty features. 'He left me anyway,' she said. 'I felt such a fool. I . . . came home . . . to Dad. I needed to reassess what I wanted from life.' She opened her handbag and took out a handkerchief with which she dabbed her eyes.

'And why come and tell me all this now?' asked Pearl gently.

Heather turned to her. 'Because you're a detective, and I know you're helping the police with their inquiries. Sooner or later, you were bound to find out. In fact, when I saw you with Dad earlier I . . . thought you might even have broached it with him.'

'Does he know?'

Heather shook her head. 'No. I've never told him, but that doesn't mean he hasn't suspected something. He was always against me working in London. He often asked me why I would want to be a small fish in a big pond when I could be a big fish here in my home town.' She replaced the handkerchief in her bag and looked back at Pearl. 'We all have guilty secrets,' she said. 'Sometimes it's best to share them.' She took a deep breath and steadied herself. Pearl took a moment to properly absorb what she had just heard, then asked: 'Did Blake ever tell Cathy about your relationship?'

'No. Not that I know of. I'm absolutely certain she didn't find out. If she had, she would never have agreed to do this festival event, surely? But Blake once mentioned that he thought Mila had overheard him on the phone to me. I just assumed at the time he might have been overreacting – he was drinking too much and could become paranoid. But nothing ever happened. Nothing was ever said.'

Pearl took this in. 'And when Blake announced the other evening that he was working on an autobiography . . .'

'I honestly didn't know anything about that,' said Heather. 'I'd discussed the Take Three Writers event with him, and also with Cathy and Vesta, and I'd explained to each of them, separately, that they could give a reading from one of their books. But I never dreamed, for one moment, that Blake was planning on reading from a memoir.'

'But, once you knew, you must have been anxious . . . concerned about this book? You'd been part of Blake's life and his plans for a "new beginning" in a "new country" . . . ?'

'Yes, but . . .' Heather stopped, troubled, then shook her head as though dismissing her next thought. 'I can't believe that Blake would ever have written about our relationship . . . about the abortion . . . in a book.'

'Why not?'

'Because . . . it was a terrible episode – for both of us. What possible good could have come from making this public?'

Pearl saw the passion with which Heather asked this, but, before she could respond, Heather went on: 'Look, I made the most terrible mistake – and I paid for it. I'm sure even Blake knew that nothing could be gained from making this public – in an autobiography, or any other way.' She spoke slowly as she explained: 'I was young. I'd been so impressed with Blake – and then . . . I came to realise how little there really was to him, compared to my father. Dad's worked hard all his life. He looked after Mum when she was ill and brought me up single-handedly after she died. He still found time for all his voluntary work with charities, and with the twinning association. While Blake was amusing, attractive, witty, sexy, ultimately he was shallow. And utterly unreliable. Dad was right. I belong here in Whitstable.' She turned to face Pearl. 'And I don't know how much longer I'll have my father with me, but I intend to make him as happy as I possibly can. I owe him that.' She stared down into the empty glass in her hand, then gave it to Pearl, before getting to her feet to leave.

After Heather had left Seaspray Cottage, Pearl reflected for some time on what she had just heard. She stepped into the kitchen to wash Heather's brandy glass, then moved to the window and looked out at the view. Outside, a young family passed by on the beach: two small boys were kicking a football on the pebbles while their parents followed on behind, carrying a heavy beach bag and windbreak. As the figures disappeared on towards the Old Neptune pub, a solitary seagull swooped low in the sky. Pearl remembered her earlier conversation with Colin Fox, and her thoughts returned to an image of a blinding light in the trees. James had told her that Blake had put CDs in his trees to deter birds. Not seagulls. But another kind of bird . . .

Turning back to the living room, Pearl sat down at her laptop and punched in the word 'crow'. Numerous links appeared on her screen, together with a multitude of different facts about the birds. Pearl learned how crows usually build nests in tall evergreens – like the evergreen oaks in the garden at Alegría. An ornithological site explained that the birds are also an extremely intelligent species, known for their problem-solving skills. Although they can be solitary creatures, they will often forage in groups and band together to chase predators in a form of behaviour called 'mobbing'. Pearl also learned that crows were members of the genus *Corvus*, which led her to another interesting fact relating to the bird's name: a modern English variant of the French name for 'raven' or 'little crow' was Korbyn . . .

Pearl looked away from her laptop screen, now reminded of something she had known for many years, but which she had only just recalled – the collective noun for a group of crows is a 'murder'.

Chapter Twenty

I t was dark before Pearl found herself at the old ivy-clad house on Ham Shades Lane. She took a deep breath, raised her right hand and reached up towards the black cast-iron rat before rapping the knocker against the front door. A few moments later, the same door opened to reveal Vesta Korbyn. She wore a long purple crushed velvet dress, cinched tight around the waist, and with a black laced bodice. The contours of her body were serpentine, long limbs accentuated by the batwing sleeves of her dress and the high black stiletto boots she wore. Her jet-black hair, parted in the middle, fell like curtains either side of her face, framing her striking features. Her green eyes were accentuated by heavy eyeshadow and a streak of silver shimmered on her brow bone to match the single silver streak in her raven hair. Pearl suddenly realised that the woman's image wasn't fabricated at all. This was no costume drama. It was Vesta Korbyn's true identity.

'What do you want?' the writer asked icily.

'To talk to you?'

Vesta stared directly at Pearl for some time, as though testing her resolve, then she opened the door wider for her to enter. As she did so, she asked waspishly: 'What happened? Did I leave another earring behind?'

'No,' said Pearl. 'But your perfume is unmistakeable.'

At this, Vesta gave a slow smile. 'Patchouli,' she said. 'An old favourite of mine. It's from the dead nettle family of plants. Thrives in hot weather – but never in sunlight.' She gestured for Pearl to follow her through a long hallway. 'Do you know, the Pharaoh Tutankhamun is said to have been buried with ten gallons of patchouli oil inside his tomb?'

She turned back to face Pearl before opening a door to a large room at the rear of the house. Pearl stepped inside to find it dimly lit. High up around the walls, imprisoned in glass cases, various stuffed animals and birds peered down at her. Name plates identified a huge South American spider, known as *Pamphobeteus antinous*, locked in permanent battle with a black scorpion, while in another case two yellow-and-black-striped cobras reared up, poised to strike. In a third case, the amber eyes of an alert young fox seemed to follow Pearl around the room, but her own gaze became focused on another creature – a bird above the door. With its black waxy plumage and menacing curved beak, it was far larger in every way than the crows Pearl had researched earlier on her computer. Vesta smiled coldly at Pearl's reaction and began to recite in a soft low tone: *'While I nodded, nearly napping, suddenly there came a tapping, As of someone gently rapping, rapping at my chamber door . . .'*

Pearl instantly recognised Edgar Allan Poe's narrative poem and whispered the next line, as if to remind herself: *'"Tis some visitor," I muttered, "tapping at my chamber door – Only this and nothing more."'*

Vesta looked at Pearl in admiration. 'Well done, Ms Nolan, I see are a fan of "The Raven"? Ever since I first read that poem, it spoke to me – as do the creatures themselves.' She looked up at the bird preserved for ever in the glass case above her door. *'Corvus corax*, devourer of carrion, mammals, birds, eggs and insects—'

Pearl broke in. 'And a member of the crow family.'

Vesta was clearly impressed. 'You're on fire. And do you also know that when one crow dies, the group, known as the murder, will surround the dead bird – not to mourn, but to gather together to find out who, or what, killed their member?' Her eyes searched Pearl's. 'Just like you're doing now. That's right, isn't it? You're here tonight . . . to find a killer?' Vesta tilted her head, birdlike, to one side.

'Yes. I am,' said Pearl, determinedly.

After a pause, Vesta replied: 'Then let's not waste time.'

Vesta Korbyn moved to a cabinet and used a long match to light a candelabra. It illuminated two chairs

– set between a games table on which a wooden board rested. Taking a step closer, Pearl saw the board showed an alphabet of letters, spread in two wide semi-circles, with a straight line showing the numbers 0 to 9 beneath them. In the flickering candlelight, Pearl also saw the words, 'Yes' and 'No', in the upper corners of the board, with lunar symbols beside them. Two other stars were set in each of the lower corners – with the word 'Goodbye' between them.

Vesta eyed Pearl. 'Do you know what this is?'

'A Ouija board?'

'Very good!' Vesta smiled. 'Otherwise known as a talking board.' She sat down in one of the chairs and allowed her long fingers to hover respectfully above the board as she went on: 'This one is over a hundred years old, made when talking boards had been devised merely as . . . parlour games to solve problems, answer questions, disclose the secrets we want to know. That's what the makers boasted at the time. It was only years later that spiritualists began to use them – to help the dead . . . contact the living.' She looked at Pearl. 'You're here tonight for answers, aren't you?' She raised her arched eyebrows and reached out her hand as she gestured for Pearl to take the other seat. Finally Pearl did so, asking: 'Why did you come to me the other evening?'

'Why else?' said Vesta casually, 'but to confess.'

As Pearl looked questioningly at her, Vesta explained: 'The concept has always appealed to me – unburdening the soul, lightening the load we all carry by leaving it with another; a stranger seated in the shadows, always willing to forgive.' She lost a faraway look in her eyes as she continued solidly: 'But I was born a Presbyterian, not a Catholic. So I decided to choose you. A kindred spirit. Another woman. To whom I could unburden myself.' She paused, thoughtful. 'Do you have a secret, Pearl Nolan? Something you carry with you but never share, even with those you are closest to?' She fixed Pearl with her emerald gaze, willing her to answer.

'Don't we all?' said Pearl.

Vesta shrugged. 'I don't know,' she said. 'I'm not like most people. I've never made friends in my life. I've always been an outsider. In fact, I've excelled at it. I've made a living from it – the strange woman from Ham Shades Lane; the Queen of Goth.' She smiled unexpectedly. 'How nice to have become a "queen" of anything.' But her curious smile faded as she went on. 'I did indeed come to you the other evening. Though I lacked the courage to rap upon your own "chamber door".' She shrugged. 'But here you are anyway.' She looked across at Pearl and her green eyes seemed to dance in the candlelight as she laid down a challenge to Pearl. 'Do you dare to discover the truth?'

'You mean . . .' Pearl began, 'am I scared to sit at this table with you and allow you to spell out the answer you want me to see on that board? No,' she said firmly. 'I'm not scared of charlatanism.'

Vesta gave a slow smile. 'I'm afraid you don't understand.' Reaching across the table, she picked up a small heart-shaped piece of wood. Holding it up between her long fingers, she explained: 'This *planchette* can only be moved by spirits. I could sit here alone tonight and ask the board for answers, but it's always more powerful to do so with others.'

Pearl frowned with suspicion. 'Why?'

'Because there will be twice as much energy for us to connect with a spirit.'

'You really believe that?'

'Oh yes,' said Vesta. 'Though any answers given to us tonight may not be the ones we wish to hear. Spirits can be playful. They can even pretend to be someone we know – a lost relative; someone needing our help?' Her face set before she went on: 'But they can also be malevolent. So I don't blame you if you are too scared to try . . .' She held Pearl's gaze for a moment more before Pearl looked down at the board between them and made a final decision. 'What do we have to do?'

Vesta gave a satisfied smile and began to explain. 'One of us will be "leader" – and *only* the leader can ask questions of the board. The other will remain silent and simply press the *planchette.*'

'I'll ask the questions,' Pearl said firmly.

Vesta nodded. 'So be it. Now we must both focus our energy on the board, and remember at all times: that if we should make contact with a spirit who tries to draw the shape of a circle on the board, or the infinity symbol, 8, then you, as leader, *must* immediately put an end to the session by saying "Goodbye".'

'Why?' asked Pearl, suspicious.

Vesta lowered her voice as though others were listening. 'Because this is a known way for malevolent spirits to reveal themselves. Keep hold of the *planchette* at all times or you could open a portal through which an evil spirit or demon might escape and enter this room.'

In the next moment, she placed her forefinger on the *planchette*. Pearl reluctantly did the same. Vesta closed her eyes for a moment and breathed deeply before nodding for the session to begin. Pearl took another moment before framing her first question. 'We need to know who killed one of our group. Can you tell us?'

A pause before the *planchette* moved slowly to the word 'Yes'.

Vesta held Pearl's look and nodded to her to ask another question.

'Who killed Blake Cain?' Pearl looked down at the *planchette* and waited for movement. This time – nothing. The sound of a fox shrieking from the nearby fields suddenly filled the silence. Pearl reconsidered her question and decided to rephrase it. 'Who was it that murdered the man . . . *known* as Blake Cain?'

Before she could even draw breath, the *planchette* moved rapidly beneath her finger. 'Take note!' said Vesta urgently, and Pearl did so as the *planchette* appeared to fly around the board, pointing to various letters in turn: W O M A N I N W H I T E. Then it stopped and Pearl looked again at Vesta, who continued to stare intently at the board as she whispered urgently: 'A woman in white.' She signalled again to Pearl who braced herself before asking: 'What is the name of this woman?'

A pause before the *planchette* moved very slowly to the word 'No'. Pearl tried once more. 'We *need* to know. Please give her name to us.' The *planchette* again moved to 'No', then returned to the centre of the board. Pearl frowned, and continued. 'All right,' she said, 'who killed Wibke Ruppert?'

The *planchette* failed to move. Pearl asked again. 'Wibke Ruppert. Tell us who killed her.'

Nothing.

'The spirit's gone,' said Vesta flatly. She took a breath but, no sooner had she begun to lift her finger from the *planchette* than Pearl felt it moving slowly towards the figure 8.

'No!' said Vesta. 'Say goodbye!' she ordered. 'Now!'

Pearl did so – but the *planchette* moved faster, continuing to draw several circles on the board before it finally flew to the floor. Vesta paused to gain her breath, then looked at Pearl, who yelled: 'This *is* a parlour game! You did this just to distract me!'

Vesta heaved a sigh. '*You* asked the questions. *You* were given your answer.'

Pearl shook her head determinedly. 'A woman in white? That's no answer at all. A local witness gave an account to the police about that and there's every possibility that word has travelled around town – *and* to you.' She held Vesta's gaze with an accusing look but the writer gave a slow smile. 'I know what you're thinking,' she said. 'But it's a very long time since I wore white.'

'Is it?' Pearl asked, suspicious. 'You said you wanted to "confess"?'

'And I do,' said Vesta. 'So in the absence of a . . . priest or a policeman – will *you* hear my confession?' She got slowly to her feet and moved to a drinks tray. Hesitating for a moment, she took the glass stopper from a decanter of ruby-red liquid and poured a goblet of wine which she offered to Pearl, who refused it. Vesta shrugged, unconcerned, and took a deep draught herself. Her left hand gently stroked her long hair.

'You will have noticed, I am dark,' she said. Looking up at the bird above her door she continued: 'My hair is raven black. But as a child I was as fair as an angel in a Renaissance painting. One of Raphael's cupids. A cherub?' She gave an incongruous smile. 'And I loved all things pretty . . .' She broke off, then: 'One of my earliest memories was of making daisy chains . . .' Her eyes took on a faraway look before her expression darkened. 'But then came the time when I was told to put away . . . childish things . . . girlish things. It was time to grow up. A time to be myself. The only problem was, I did not know who I really was.' She took another sip from the goblet in her hand. 'So I set out on a path, the one that was there before me, but soon realised I would never reach my destination. I was lost. Perhaps lost even before I had ever embarked on that journey . . .'

'What journey?' asked Pearl confused.

'Why, the journey of life, of course.' said Vesta. She stopped suddenly and stared up towards the raven in the glass case. *'Deep into that darkness peering, long I stood there wondering, fearing, Doubting, dreaming dreams no mortal ever dared to dream before . . .'* She reflected on the words before continuing. 'I joined a group of like-minded people and in time I finally began to see the light – like dawn breaking within a forest of trees. I left behind who I had been, and I became what I am now: Vesta Korbyn. I made money, found a new home, a new life, a new identity; but still I wasn't properly whole – complete – until I took one more step. All things are possible when you have enough money. And, as Vesta . . . I even fell in love.'

'With Blake Cain?' asked Pearl.

Vesta smiled wistfully. 'He really was a wonderful writer but his failing was as a human being.' Her expression set. 'I trusted him and so I confessed to him – not to a stranger in the shadows of a confession box, but to the man I loved.' A moment more and her smile had become fixed. 'I . . . didn't dream that he would betray me.'

'Blake . . . betrayed you?' said Pearl. 'With another woman?'

Vesta spoke in a low whisper. 'With his book.'

Pearl frowned at this. 'How?'

'By telling the truth.'

'You mean . . . he was going to write about your relationship?'

Vesta smiled. 'If only. I was proud of that. Of what we had, or what I thought we had. But in the end, I was to learn, we had nothing. I was just . . . another story for him. But *what* a story. One of transformation. Angel to Queen of Gothic Noir!'

'I don't understand . . .'

'Then let me explain,' said Vesta. Her fingers moved to the outer corners of her eyes as she peeled off thick black eyelashes, leaving behind only a white trail of dried adhesive on her charcoal-shaded eyelids. Reaching into her sleeve for a handkerchief, she now smeared off her dark red lipstick, revealing a pale face of androgynous features. Then her hand moved to her hairline and, with one swift movement, she ripped the thick mane of raven-black hair from her head. Beneath it lay only a blonde crop, receding at the temples. A ghost of herself, she now opened her mouth and began to recite once more from memory: '"*Though thy crest be shorn and shaven, thou,*" I said, "*art sure no craven, Ghastly grim and ancient Raven wandering from the Nightly shore . . .*"' She fell silent for a moment before she turned to Pearl. '*Now* do you understand?' she asked, her voice lowering further. 'My real name . . . is a stranger's name.'

Pearl suddenly realised. 'A man's name . . .'

Vesta's cropped head lowered. 'If I had never confided to Blake, he might never have known. All things are possible with money . . . but confession comes with a price . . .'

'And you were about to pay that price – with his book,' said Pearl.

Vesta closed her eyes.

'But . . . you spent the night before his death with him.'

'To implore him to keep silent,' said Vesta. 'He drank himself to sleep.'

'And . . . in the morning I arrived to return your earring . . .'

'I had begged him,' said Vesta, 'to respect my secret, but he toyed with me like a cat with a bird. He had a particular talent for cruelty, but I couldn't allow him to humiliate me after the years of humiliation I had already suffered. How could I let him . . . expose me?'

'And he had threatened to do that at the event?' asked Pearl.

Vesta's hands clenched and unclenched before she turned and picked up an object from the table. Pearl saw it was a stiletto dagger, as beautiful as it was deadly. The blade caught the light of the chandelier under Vesta's trembling grip, then, with the deft sleight of hand of an artful magician, she vanished it inside a batwing sleeve.

Unnerved, Pearl got up from her seat. 'You went to Alegría . . .'

Vesta nodded. 'I knew it was James's day off. Blake had told me that the boy was going to Canterbury so he was looking forward to spending the afternoon in his studio, writing. I came by the old lane, at the rear of the house, and found the gate unlocked. I'd been worried in

JULIE WASSMER

case the studio window would be facing the fence but, as it was late afternoon, it had already turned west to follow the sun, so I was able to cross the lawn without Blake seeing me. The studio doors were open and I came in behind him. I saw he was looking down at his desk and it suddenly occurred to me that, for once in my life, everything was being made so easy . . . so I must be doing the right thing.' She gave a strange smile and continued. 'I felt for the handle of the dagger.' Pearl saw Vesta reaching for the stiletto blade in her sleeve, long fingers circling around the hilt. 'I took it in my hand. I raised it up and, as I took a step forward, to where Blake sat, the words of the poem came back to me: *And the Raven, never flitting, still is sitting, still is sitting* . . .' Suddenly she broke off as though confused: 'I saw blood,' she said. 'A circle of red dripping down from the dagger blade that was sticking out from the back of Blake's neck . . .'

'You mean,' said Pearl, 'he was . . . already dead?'

Vesta nodded slowly. *'And his eyes have all the seeming . . . of a demon's that is dreaming* . . .' She paused. 'He *was* dead. And I was free. Free as a bird.' She took a deep breath. 'A wave of emotion came over me – relief, gratitude, release. I took a gulp of air and breathed in the stale smell of Blake's cigar smoke for the very last time; and then I ran from that studio – that . . . symbol of his vanity – all the way home, here, as fast as I could.'

'But your clothes . . .'

'I took them off . . . put them all straight in the washing machine as soon as I got back. And then I

252

showered and got ready for the event. I didn't have long and my hands were still shaking as I put on my make-up . . . I could still hear the music that had been playing in the studio.'

'*Madam Butterfly.*'

Vesta nodded. 'I knew it was just a matter of time before Blake's body was found. And I prayed I hadn't been seen or—'

'You would have been arrested for a murder you didn't commit . . .' Pearl looked back at her. 'But the white dress,' she said. 'You put that in the washing machine?'

Vesta shook her head. 'No. There was no white dress. I couldn't risk being recognised so I had worn black – a T-shirt, jeans . . .'

Pearl took a moment to register this. 'You . . . weren't dressed in white?'

Vesta shook her cropped head. 'I just told you . . .'

'But . . . did you see anyone else that day at Alegría?'

'No,' Vesta frowned at this. 'I've just *told* you,' she said impatiently. 'I came to you the other evening because I know it's only a matter of time before the police discover—'

A bell suddenly rang, followed by urgent banging on the front door. Vesta looked down at the stiletto dagger in her hand and dropped it as if it were a hot poker, then she looked around helplessly and – with trembling hands – grabbed the wig of long black hair still lying on the table. Before she had a chance to put it back on, it slipped from her hand. Voices sounded from the rear of the house followed by heavy footsteps. The door opened roughly. DS Terri Bosley appeared first and McGuire followed, with two detective constables at his side. His gaze met Pearl's but he nodded to Bosley who then spoke: 'Vesta Korbyn, I am arresting you on suspicion of murder . . .'

Pearl protested. 'No . . .' But as she went to take a step forward, McGuire's hand moved fast to her arm. He gave her a warning look and DS Bosley continued with the police caution as Vesta Korbyn, standing beneath the raven imprisoned in the glass case above the door, hung her shorn head low.

Chapter Twenty-One

'I got a phone call this morning from that young reporter,' said Cathy McTurk as she stood at the marble fireplace in her comfortable sitting room.

'Lucy Walker?' asked Pearl.

Cathy nodded. 'She said the police have issued a statement about having arrested Vesta in connection with Blake's murder. Is this true?'

As she turned to face Pearl for an answer, Mila and Tom Maitley did the same.

'Yes,' said Pearl. 'I was there at the time.'

Cathy issued a small sigh while Mila shared a look with Tom before asking: 'And . . . the rumour, about her being a transsexual?'

Pearl hesitated. Having been summoned that morning on the pretext of Cathy having something to explain, Pearl realised now that it was Cathy who wanted an explanation – as well as added information about Vesta Korbyn's arrest. Resenting the fact that she was now under pressure to answer these questions, Pearl nevertheless replied: 'It's no rumour.'

Cathy appeared liberated by this news and paced across the room as she exclaimed: 'I *knew* there was something she was hiding.'

'And if she lied about her gender,' said Tom, 'a jury should see that it's quite possible she's lied about everything else – including the murders.'

Pearl turned to meet his gaze. 'Vesta didn't lie about her gender,' she said determinedly. 'Her reassignment treatment and surgery took place some years ago. It was a private matter and something she didn't need to divulge – to anyone.'

Cathy frowned at this. 'But . . . Blake was threatening to broadcast it in this book. Is that it?'

'I believe so,' said Pearl finally.

Cathy failed to hide her frustration. 'So she had motive enough to kill him. Surely in those circumstances, she should have been more honest with the police?'

Before Pearl had a chance to answer, Mila crossed the room to her, a pained expression on her face. 'It really is reason enough for Vesta to want him dead?' Her look was more questioning than confrontational. Aware of all that Vesta had divulged the night before, about her visit to Alegría on the afternoon of Blake's murder, Pearl heaved a sigh and admitted, truthfully: 'Perhaps.'

Cathy nodded. 'Well, the police must think so,' she said firmly. 'Or they wouldn't have arrested her.'

'She's been arrested but not charged,' said Pearl. 'For that they'll need more evidence.'

Cathy frowned, and exchanged a look with Tom as she absorbed this. 'I see.' Then she paused for a moment and glanced across at Mila before summoning a weak smile for Pearl. 'Well,' she said finally. 'Thank you for coming,' she continued. 'As a family, I felt we at least had a right to know.' She moved closer to Mila and took her hand, though in that moment Pearl felt it was difficult to tell which of the two women was more reassured by the gesture. Tom Maitley moved across to Pearl and said simply, 'I'll see you out.'

Maitley led the way out of the room while Pearl reflected on the description Cathy McTurk had just given of them as a 'family'. Perhaps, thought Pearl, Cathy honestly saw them operating within this dynamic – or perhaps she had simply never got used to Blake Cain being outside it, even after their divorce. Tom Maitley walked ahead of Pearl through a bright hallway decorated with flowers and paintings, then he stopped and turned to her as he demanded darkly: 'Can I ask what you were doing at Vesta Korbyn's house last night?'

They had just reached the front door and his hand rested on the latch, as though he had assumed for himself the role of gatekeeper. Pearl hesitated before she replied: 'I . . . was following a line of inquiry.'

Tom considered her for a moment. 'Wouldn't that be best left to the police?' For the very first time since they had met, Maitley fixed Pearl with an unflinching gaze, then he leaned forward to open the door for her. Without another word, Pearl left.

Fifteen minutes later, on returning to Seaspray Cottage, Pearl found her phone was ringing. She answered it to find it was Nathan, keen to discuss the latest turn of events. 'You've got to admit,' he said. 'That's *some* turn-up for the books. Vesta Korbyn – a transsexual?'

'News travels fast,' said Pearl. Setting down her bag she checked her answerphone but found, to her disappointment, no messages left by McGuire.

'To be honest,' Nathan continued, 'I was never much attracted to works of the Queen of Gothic Noir, but I'm now so intrigued about how she became her own creation, I'm keen to read *all* her books.'

'Not before you finish that Paris piece, I hope?'

'Almost finished!' said Nathan smugly. 'And it's really not a difficult brief to sell Paris as a travel destination. It's a wonderful city, though I do try to avoid the usual clichés. Always best to look beyond the obvious, don't you think?'

Pearl had fallen silent for a few moments, sufficiently long for Nathan to check: 'Are you still there?'

'Yes. But I was just thinking: there's no relation, is there?'

'Between?'

'The ritual suicide of Cio-Cio-San . . . And Vesta Korbyn's books. Her genre?'

'Gothic noir?' said Nathan. 'None at all, darling. But I'm sure your inspector will get to the bottom of it all, now Korbyn's in custody.'

'Or perhaps not,' said Pearl. 'Like you just said, it's always good to look beyond the obvious.' She picked up her bag again and made a quick decision. 'I'll call you later.' And she ended the call.

Half an hour later, Pearl was in a corridor of Canterbury police station, trying to keep pace with McGuire. His expression was stony as he told her firmly: 'You shouldn't have come here. There's procedure to follow . . .'

'I know,' she said. 'But I had no choice. I don't believe Vesta killed Blake Cain.'

'And you don't have to,' said McGuire.

Two detective constables appeared in the corridor, acknowledging McGuire with a polite nod as he waited for them to pass by. Having watched them head down the staircase, McGuire turned again to Pearl and explained: 'Vesta Korbyn has been arrested because of evidence following Bosley's line of inquiry.'

'What line of inquiry?'

McGuire hesitated before he decided to explain. 'Financial. Blake Cain's will left everything to Cathy McTurk – not that there was much to leave.'

Pearl took this in as he continued. 'Bosley had been going through his accounts. Cain was property rich, cash poor – and heavily in debt. But several large transfers had been made to him recently.' He paused for a moment. 'By Vesta Korbyn.'

Pearl looked away to assimilate this. 'So . . . she was being blackmailed by Cain – because of his book?'

McGuire held her look. Pearl went on: 'But there *is* no book. No one's read it. No one's even seen it. You certainly haven't found it . . .'

'That's true,' said McGuire quickly. 'But even if it had never existed, Cain could have lied to Vesta and convinced her that it did—'

'And extorted money from her on a bluff,' said Pearl.

'Judging from the evidence that Bosley's managed to turn up, it seems reasonable he did just that.'

Pearl suddenly realised: 'You . . . didn't tell me any of this . . .'

McGuire protested: 'I couldn't, Pearl. Things were moving so fast with the investigation, I didn't have time . . . and I couldn't risk news of an imminent arrest getting back to Vesta – or anyone else, for that matter.'

'Including me,' said Pearl, stung.

McGuire failed to hide a guilty look and pushed his blond hair from his forehead.

'What were you doing there, Pearl?'

'Does it matter?'

Torn, McGuire glanced around then tried to explain. 'You know I've got Welch on my case, and Bosley looking over my shoulder. I can't afford for anything to go wrong with this investigation.'

'I know,' said Pearl helplessly. 'That's why I'm here. Right now. But you're still not listening to me. You're listening to Bosley instead.'

'She's Deputy SIO on this case—'

'I know,' said Pearl, breaking in. 'But you need to look beyond the obvious. Vesta may have confessed to being a transsexual, but she hasn't confessed to murder, because she's *not* the woman in white.'

'That's what she told you,' said McGuire. 'But remember. Method. Motive. Opportunity. She had all three. Or do you now think none of that's important?' His eyes desperately searched hers for some under-standing. 'I *have* to do things by the book, Pearl. I have no choice. So, please, let me get on with my job – because the sooner this is over, the sooner you and I can be together again. And I *swear* I'll make things up to you.'

His hand moved gently to her face. Pearl closed her eyes, willing him to kiss her, but instead she heard the sound of double doors bursting open as two young PCs entered the corridor, laughing. At the sight of McGuire, they were silenced, and carried on to disappear down the corridor. Pearl turned quickly in the direction from which they had appeared, and walked briskly away as McGuire watched her go.

'If I'd only known what this festival would bring,' said Heather Fox ruefully, later that same afternoon. She was sitting at Dolly's garden table beside her father, who gently laid his hand on hers. 'It's not your fault,' Colin said softly. Across the same table, Laurent Ruppert nodded slowly. 'Evil is always among us,' he said softly, his gaze moving wider to take in Dolly and Pearl as he went on: 'Your vicar, the Reverend Prudence, was right when she said that at the church concert.' He closed his eyes as if to hold back a weight of emotion. Pearl felt for him. 'I'm so very sorry, Laurent.'

'So am I,' he said, before opening his eyes once more. 'My sister was a quiet, gentle soul. I know many siblings do not get on but . . . she really was my best friend.' A heavy silence fell which no one quite knew how to fill.

Laurent's sadness transformed into a panicked anxiety. 'I have so much to do,' he said quickly. 'I have to get back . . . to Borken, and notify everyone properly. The police here they . . . won't release Wibke's body for some time. I can't even bury her.' He looked helplessly at Pearl then said, 'You have all been so good – especially you, Dolly.' He took her hand and squeezed it tightly. 'But . . . now I feel caught up in a wave of terrible events. Like your painting, Dolly. An undertow?'

'And Vesta has been arrested too,' said Heather. 'I'm . . . totally dazed by it all . . . But I suppose things will move more quickly now?'

'Now?' asked Pearl.

Colin spoke up. 'Now we know she's not what she appeared to be.'

'She's a woman,' said Pearl. 'But I'm still not sure she's a murderer.'

'Pearl . . .' Dolly began, keen not to upset Laurent

further, but he patted her arm and looked directly at Pearl as he explained: 'I care nothing about this woman,' he said, 'because nothing will ever be the same for me. Not without Wibke. The only thing I am sure of is that justice will be done – and our friendships must endure, especially those between our two towns.' He paused before going on. 'I have lost my dear sister, and Borken has lost Wibke, but Whitstable also lost Blake Cain. It is a twin tragedy – so, one we share. I aim to write the special piece my sister wanted to write. It must serve as a fitting tribute to her.'

Dolly nodded slowly. 'Yes,' she said. 'A twin town tragedy. Perhaps that will even make a good title for your piece, Laurent? *Eine . . .*' Her face crumpled for a moment as she tried to attempt the phrase in German. '. . . *Zwillingsdorf Tragödie*?'

Laurent turned to her and offered her a sympathetic smile. '*Nein, meine Liebste*, Dolly.' He explained: 'We use the term *Partnerstadt* for twin town. The German word for twin is *Zwilling*.'

Dolly shook her head. 'I'm sorry, Laurent, my German is so bad . . .'

'At least you try,' he said, smiling sadly. Dolly glanced back at Pearl but found her daughter transfixed as she gazed at Dolly's old pear tree with the washing line embedded within it.

'What is it, Pearl?' she asked, concerned.

Pearl, still rapt in thought, said: 'I'm . . . not sure. But there was something Wibke said to me on the phone that last day . . .' She tried to recall. 'The reception was poor. But what you just said, Laurent, made me think—'

Laurent frowned. 'What?' he asked. 'What did I say?'

Pearl got quickly to her feet. 'I need some more information,' she said determinedly. 'And then I need to put everything in order, but first, I need to make an urgent call.'

Chapter Twenty-Two

I t had just gone six p.m. McGuire knew this because he had just checked his watch as he sat in the incident room at Canterbury police station. For some time he had been observing DS Terri Bosley making the most of her role as Deputy Senior Investigating Officer while briefing the team of DCs about Vesta Korbyn's arrest. So far, Korbyn had been in custody for nineteen hours and could be held, without charge, for only a further five hours unless application was made to a court to hold her for longer due to the serious nature of the crime. Thus far, she had not responded to questioning, other than through the solicitor she had appointed. McGuire kept finding himself thinking about what Pearl had told him earlier that day – Korbyn had confessed to being a transsexual, but that didn't make her a murderer.

He had to admit that he had little experience of transsexuals – though he remembered he had once had to arrange police protection for a group of drag queens in the run-up to a trial concerning sexual harassment by a Soho club owner. He had simply been doing his job and following procedure, but he didn't like bullying in whatever form it came, and so he had celebrated with a few large tequilas on news of a guilty verdict. Right now, he couldn't help feeling sorry for the woman he had interviewed earlier. Separated from her make-up, hairpiece and identity, she looked nothing like the beautiful creature on her website photos.

Bosley was still going on, but giving a self-admiring smile as she did so, confident in the knowledge that she was holding the attention of most of the male DCs present. They fancied her. Even the married ones. Comments from fellow officers left McGuire in no doubt of that, though Bosley left him cold. The woman was on a mission – to promotion – and nothing was going to stand in her way. Least of all DCI Mike McGuire.

At that moment, his mobile vibrated in his pocket. He took it out and registered the caller's name. Pearl. Ordinarily, he might have let it go straight to voicemail, especially during a briefing like this, but he'd heard enough of Bosley for one morning, and knew Pearl wouldn't be calling him so soon after this morning's confrontation if it wasn't something important. He listened carefully to what she had to say then replied:

'Are you sure?'

Across the room, Bosley's eyes met his, but McGuire gave his attention to Pearl.

'OK,' he said finally, keeping his response as economical as possible before ending the call. Getting to his feet, he crossed the room and mouthed his apologies to Bosley. 'Something's just come up,' he said. 'I'll call.' Bosley's eyes followed him as he left the room.

'Thanks for meeting me,' said Pearl to the two young people sitting before her at a café table on the east quay of Whitstable harbour. It was some time since her call to McGuire, and the café had long closed, so they were now the only people there to enjoy the sunset. James's hair was still damp from the sea and Lucy sat beside him with her notebook. 'You . . . said you needed some more information?'

Pearl nodded. 'That's right. I haven't been able to piece everything together in the way I need to.'

Lucy smiled. 'Putting the ingredients in the right order, you mean?'

'Exactly.'

'Well,' said Lucy. 'Fire away.'

Pearl smiled warmly at the girl and continued. 'On the day before Blake was murdered, a call went in to Canterbury Police. Just two words – "Murder Fest". A new DS working with DCI McGuire dismissed this as a likely crank call, but it was enough for the police to come and ask if this phrase meant anything to me, and if it could possibly be connected to the festival which was just about to begin here.'

'Whit Fest?' James asked.

'That's right,' said Pearl. 'Once Blake was murdered, it seemed to me to be too coincidental for that message to have been simply a random hoax call. But then I kept wondering to myself: why would anyone want to actually signal a murder to the police? Warning calls are given for things like . . . terrorist attacks, so that the perpetrators can take responsibility for them, but it made no sense for someone to do so ahead of a murder unless—'

Lucy broke in: 'It was a serial killer, wanting to create fear and draw attention to themselves?'

Pearl nodded. 'Precisely – but it's risky for any killer to play a cat-and-mouse game with the police, because each call or message is likely to leave more clues behind, and although there was a second murder, there was no warning given for that.' She paused. 'Why not?'

'Because . . . the murderer had no time to do so?' James suggested.

Pearl nodded. 'Perhaps – which points to what I always suspected, that the murder of Wibke Ruppert was entirely opportunistic. Just before she was killed, Wibke called me. She was disturbed – agitated – because she had seen someone. Somewhere. A woman in a white dress.' She looked at Lucy Walker. 'You wore a white dress to the launch event for Whit Fest.'

The girl scoffed. 'Yes, I did. But I can assure you it wasn't me.'

'No,' said Pearl. 'Wibke said she had dark hair. But I don't believe it was Vesta Korbyn either, and I'm sure DCI McGuire's questioning of Vesta will throw up something entirely different concerning her motives and whereabouts that afternoon.'

Lucy and James exchanged a look before Lucy suggested: 'Could it have been Mila . . .?'

James shook his head forcefully. 'No. I've already told you—'

'Yes,' Pearl broke in. 'You don't believe Mila could have been involved. And I agree,' she said before leaving a long pause. 'I think it was another woman altogether.'

She let the statement sit there for a moment as a large pleasure craft motored past the east quay on its way to the harbour, carrying passengers who sported satisfied expressions on sunburned faces. Then she continued. 'I went to a vintage clothes shop when I was in Canterbury. I was about to question Mila, and it was a long shot, but I was hoping to find a similar dress to yours, Lucy.' She smiled. 'As I mentioned, I'm also a fan of vintage clothes, but I was unlucky that day.' She shrugged. 'However, the owner happened to show me something else – a wedding dress – and weddings are invariably when a woman is most likely to wear white . . .'

'Cathy and Blake were divorced,' said James.

'And Vesta Korbyn was hardly about to marry Blake Cain?' said Lucy confused, adding, 'Though she *has* just been arrested for his murder . . .'

'But not charged,' said Pearl. 'The police can hold her

only for a limited period without doing so, and for that they'll need more evidence. But I don't believe they will find it.'

James frowned. 'So, if Vesta isn't the woman in white, who is?'

To this Pearl left a long pause before replying: 'A ghost.' Seeing the confused reactions of the two young people before her, she explained. 'If you think about it, Blake Cain was as much a . . . reinvention of himself as Vesta Korbyn – and perhaps that's what attracted him to Vesta in the first place. Blake hadn't started out as a successful author – he had been plain Barry Collins, a boy from a troubled family who had escaped his roots, and history, to *become* Blake Cain. It was perhaps ironic that once he was happily married to Cathy, they should have fostered Mila Anton, a girl Cathy had helped to discover her roots and heritage, when Blake had done so much to bury his own? But, as a young man, Barry Collins had also received help. I knew that because I had been told by one of his biggest fans, Wibke Ruppert, who had studied Blake's whole career and background.

'At one point, I began to wonder if Wibke might actually have met him, because she had been studying in Nice at the same time Blake had been crewing on boats on the French Riviera. But then Wibke, too, was murdered, which led me to suspect that perhaps she knew something from that time which she might have given away without realising its importance.'

Pearl shook her head. 'I couldn't think what on earth it might have been, but when a friend happened to use the phrase: "It's always good to look beyond the obvious", I began to do just that. Method. Motive. Opportunity. It's true Vesta had all three in relation to both murders, but now I began to look differently at everything we already had before us that day: a tableau presented at the murder scene, complete with soundtrack; the murder of a man who had reinvented himself to become Blake Cain; clues to a woman's dishonour: a dagger and a method of murder linked to the ritual suicides of Samurai wives? Not forgetting the cryptic warning the police had been given – Murder Fest . . .'

Lucy looked perplexed. 'But . . . I still don't see how this points to anyone in particular? You mentioned a ghost?'

Pearl nodded. 'Yes. It was a ghost that *motivated* these crimes.' She paused for a moment then continued carefully. 'As I mentioned, Wibke had told me in a phone call on the day of her murder how she had seen a woman in white – but the phone reception had been poor, as it so often is in the area around Tankerton Slopes, and I couldn't understand all that she had to say to me on the line.' Pearl paused. 'Apart from telling me she had seen a dark-haired woman in a white dress, she also said, "she's willing" – something that made no sense at all to me – until today.'

Pearl looked from Lucy to James, and held his gaze as she said: 'Your mother was dark – and very pretty.

You have her eyes, James, and at the same age you might have looked like twins if it had not been for your fair colouring.' James frowned at this but Pearl continued. '*Zwilling* is the German word for twin. That's what Wibke Ruppert was trying to tell me that day when she called – that she had seen a dark-haired woman at Alegría who had so closely resembled someone they could have been twins.'

'A ghost?' asked Lucy. Still lost, she now looked at the young man beside her to see if he was any the wiser, but James Moore remained silent as Pearl continued. 'Blake must have been so shocked to see you there that day, in his studio, coming up on him with that dagger in your hand.' She was looking directly at James, who still said nothing as Lucy's face crumpled in confusion. Pearl went on. 'He had grown to trust you so well, hadn't he, James? And for good reason. You had taken good care of him over the last year or so.' She broke off for a moment then continued: 'I don't believe you ever planned to deny murdering him. In fact, I think you *wanted* to be caught. How else could you possibly explain how much Blake Cain had hurt you – as he had hurt so many?'

Still James remained silent. Lucy, desperate for the truth, prompted him. 'James? Say something – please!'

But it was Pearl who spoke again. 'I'm sure it wasn't just the dagger in your hand that shocked Blake that afternoon – it was what you wore - a dark wig. And the same white dress that your mother, Rose Moore, had worn . . . on her wedding day.'

At this, James's gaze faltered. He blinked several times and looked away, but Pearl continued, with a question this time. 'When did she tell you about her relationship with Blake?'

James closed his eyes tight shut then spat the words derisively: 'He wasn't Blake Cain. Like you said, he was just . . . plain Barry Collins.'

'A student at Oxford University?' asked Pearl.

James nodded, then picked up the coaster on the table and began to toy with it. 'She was working in a local pub,' he said softly. 'And he was nothing then – a fish out of water. But she was good to him. And they fell in love.' He broke off for a moment, then: 'That's what she told me, finally . . . but not until she was dying.' He broke off.

Lucy tried to make sense of this. 'Blake was . . . your father?'

As James nodded, Lucy looked fearfully at Pearl, whose look settled her as she continued gently to James. 'Why did she leave it so long to tell you?'

James looked down, fighting back emotion. 'Because she'd always hoped that he'd get in touch. She wrote to him, so many letters, over the years. But she never had the courage to send them.'

'And the dress?' asked Pearl.

James nodded slowly. 'It was . . . the dress she wore when she waited for him – the day he failed to meet her, at Banbury register office.' He threw the coaster back down on to the table. 'He'd got word that day that his book was to be published. And he'd gone to a meeting in London instead. He used a fax machine to tell her it was over – and to say sorry, except he *wasn't* sorry. He never gave her another thought.' He shook his head angrily. 'Mum went to stay with an aunt in Norwich who told her it would be best to think again about having me, unless she came clean about me being his child.' He shook his head again. 'But she didn't. She didn't want to hurt him, so she never told him. She never told a soul. She lived for me but she also lived in the past, like she was . . . frozen in time.'

Pearl spoke softly. 'Like the snowdrop in your poem . . . I thought you had written that about Lucy. But it was really about your mum, wasn't it?'

After a pause, James nodded. 'She never moved on. So, it occurred to me I would take Blake back to that moment and . . . tell him the same story, but from a different viewpoint. My mother's. I'd bought a cheap black wig from a party shop in Canterbury . . .'

'And you already had the dress,' said Pearl.

James nodded. 'She told me how she had kept it. It was important to her. And it became important to me too. On the day she died I . . . put it on. It made me feel . . . closer to her? So I'd talk to her and . . . I think she heard me . . .' He gave a look that begged for understanding, then he nodded quickly. 'And you're right. When Wibke saw me in my room in Mum's dress and the wig, she must have thought she was looking at my twin.' He paused for a moment, his expression set.

'But on the day Blake died, I knew from the look on his face that he was staring at the ghost of my mother – just as I had intended.' He suddenly gave an inappropriate smile, which vanished quickly on Pearl's next question.

'What happened, James?' she asked softly. 'What happened in Blake's studio that day?'

He looked down at his hands as he collected his thoughts. 'I'd already taken the knife from his desk that morning. He had told me all about it – how he'd found it in some antique shop. He thought it was beautiful . . . Like the Japanese *tantos* that were used for ritual suicides.' He frowned, perplexed, as he remembered. 'He had even . . . mimed to me one day about hara-kiri and explained how the Samurai warriors and their families had taken their own lives. He had wanted to write about it. He said he would one day. But he never did.' His expression clouded. 'And he never will. I still had the *tanto* in my hand when I put the record on. *Madam Butterfly* . . . I explained that every time I'd used that knife to open his mail, I had thought about my mother and the letters she'd written to him over the years – all unsent. He never had a clue how he had broken her heart . . .'

James grimaced at the thought then began trying to explain, his speech coming fast, echoing his erratic mental state. 'Then he tried to get up out of his chair, talk his way out of things . . . He told me that he had problems of his own but that he would make it all up to me once his book was published. He said it wasn't easy for him and . . . he'd always loved Cathy and he'd wanted to have a son with her but she couldn't have children. He went on, and *on* . . . but he *never* said *one* word about *my* mother – only about Cathy, Vesta, Heather and . . .' His voice trailed off and he looked at both Lucy and Pearl in turn as he said: 'In the end, all I wanted to do was to shut him up – once and for all.'

Lucy closed her eyes. James swallowed hard and frowned again as he looked back at Pearl. 'I . . . used the rope to tie his legs together afterwards. That was the clue I wanted to leave for the police. Then I cleaned everything, changed my clothes, and put the record on again before I went on to The Horsebridge, where every-one was in a panic, asking where he was.' He looked at Pearl but it was Lucy who spoke next, trying desperately to make sense of what she had just heard. 'You . . . killed Blake Cain for your mother?'

James nodded determinedly. 'I had to. Don't you see?'

Lucy shook her head slowly. 'But . . . how could you have thought for one moment that she would have wanted you to do this – that she would be pleased about you committing murder in her name?'

James simply tilted his head to one side, as if confused by her lack of understanding. 'But he had to pay for what he did to her. Don't you see that?'

'And how *would* anyone know,' said Pearl, 'unless you left clues for them – to come and find you: the man who murdered Blake Cain?' She went on. 'You surely would have wanted the whole world to know the reason you had done this. Why you had . . . executed Blake to avenge your mother. Is that why you made the call to the police the night before the festival launch? Those two words: Murder Fest?'

'Of course,' said James, a nervous smile playing on his lips. 'I went to the call box, put a scarf over the receiver and disguised my voice. It was as easy as that.'

'As easy as murdering Blake Cain?' asked Lucy. 'And then what?' she asked. 'What if the police *hadn't* solved this crime? Would you have handed yourself in? How would the world ever know what Blake Cain had done to you – and your mother?'

He looked away from her searching gaze but Pearl continued: 'Something happened to change your mind, didn't it? For you to want . . . another chance? A girl in a white dress entered your life.' James remained silent but Pearl went on. 'Did meeting Lucy give you cause to think . . . you might have a future after all?'

As Lucy turned to face him, Pearl saw how the look of attraction she had once witnessed between two young people had now turned to one of mutual horror. James recoiled, shaking his head as he grew more agitated, like a spinning top losing its centre of gravity. 'I-I got confused . . . Things weren't working out the way I planned. I hadn't been arrested or charged and . . . I realised I didn't *have* to give myself in. I began to think I might start again, work for Cathy, have a new life? I'd been packing, but I still had the dress and . . . Blake's memoirs. I'd hidden both high up in the trunk of one of the old oak trees. I'd found the spot when I'd strung up the CDs for Blake – to deter the crows.'

'*You* did that,' said Pearl.

James nodded proudly. 'But days after the police had finished searching Alegría, I took the dress and Blake's memoirs down one afternoon. I planned to burn both of them, but . . .' He faltered again, his face creased as though he was now experiencing physical pain. 'It was so hard and I . . . just needed to be close to Mum, one last time, to ask her what I should do? I knew she would tell me.'

'So you put the dress and the wig on,' Pearl whispered.

James's gaze flickered before he gave a quick nod. 'But I'd forgotten to lock the garden door.'

'Yes,' said Pearl. 'You told me that since Blake's death you had always made sure the door in the garden fence was locked. But as you were the one who had murdered him, there was no need for you to be so conscious of security. The door was *unlocked* that day – and Wibke arrived to try to get some photos of Blake's studio, as she had promised her twinning association committee she would. Perhaps, as one of Blake's biggest fans, she had also wanted to make a . . . personal visit, a pilgrimage, one last time. And then?'

James looked lost before turning helplessly to Pearl. 'I was . . . talking to Mum . . . I needed her advice . . . I was asking her what I should do next, when I saw her . . .'

'Wibke,' said Pearl.

James nodded. 'She was standing at the door to my room and when I turned round she saw me. She looked confused, apologised and left, but I knew it wouldn't be long before she told someone else.' He looked at Pearl. 'You,' he said. 'She'd tell you and then you would work out what it was she'd just seen. So I . . . got changed quickly. Right by the garden door there were some gloves and . . . string. I followed her. She was hidden in the trees near Beacon House, but I heard her on the phone to you, just as I expected. It was very quick.' He broke off and Lucy gasped. Pearl took the girl's hand to comfort her while James looked suddenly alienated from them both – as though set adrift by the truth. 'So, now you know,' he said. 'What are you going to do?'

Lucy fought back tears and whispered. 'James, you need help.'

Seeing the look on her face, he began to shake his head. 'Oh no,' he said firmly. 'No, I don't think so. No one will understand, and I'm not going to spend the rest of my life behind bars or . . . in the hospital wing of a prison.' With that thought, he suddenly got to his feet, realising: 'You're the only ones who know.'

'No,' said Pearl firmly. 'I've already talked to DCI McGuire. He's at Alegría now, searching the garden. It won't be long before the police find your mother's dress and—'

'I burned it!' said James defiantly.

'I don't believe that,' Pearl said, gently. 'I don't believe you could ever do that, and neither could you burn her letters . . .' She paused. '*Or* Blake's memoir. You read it, didn't you?'

James's face took on a flat expression as he said, bitterly: 'There wasn't even one mention of my mother. Not even a footnote!' He turned to Pearl and she could see he was holding back a flood of conflicting emotions, but at that moment her phone sounded an incoming text. She glanced down at it, read the words on the screen, then she looked up again at James. 'The police have it, James. All of it.'

'No!' His voice rang out as he tried to make an escape, but Pearl reached over and grabbed his arm. James yelped like an animal in pain, but the sound melded with a seagull's cry as the bird swooped low into the harbour. James tried to shrug himself free. 'Let me go!' he screamed, pushing Pearl away hard but, as he did so, the back of his calf hit the safety chain on the quayside and he suddenly lost his balance, tumbling backwards. Pearl reached out to him once more, and this time he grabbed her outstretched hand, but the force of his fall took Pearl with him over the quay edge – down towards the water below.

A timeless moment followed before the shock of cold water hit. Then, silence. Darkness. Plummeting down like a herring gull deep beneath the waves, lungs bursting. A gasp of muddy estuary waters sent Pearl struggling upwards for air and light, until finally she found both. As she did so, she retched water before searching the sea's surface for James. Calling out his name she heard only silence. Treading water, she glanced up to the quay several metres above her, and saw Lucy Walker staring down, shaking her head helplessly before she took out her mobile phone and dialled for help. Pearl took another precious lungful of air and dived purposefully, deep into the dark water, arms struggling to find anything or anyone. Nothing. But when she surfaced again, it was to see another figure, some distance away from her. As James choked water from his lungs, it struck Pearl in that moment that he looked little more than a child – her own child, Charlie, struggling for his first gasp of life.

'Swim to me!' she heard herself cry, able to see what James couldn't: a vast grey shape powering towards them as it entered the harbour. Only on the engine's drone did James look back to see the vessel's bow wave bearing down. His head jerked quickly back towards Pearl. She saw a mixture of fear, desperation and confusion in his eyes.

'Swim, James!' she yelled to him. And finally the young man did as he was told, breaking into a powerful crawl until he was just a few metres away from Pearl. She reached out to him but he suddenly stopped, and stared up at Lucy Walker who was still looking down from the quay. James shook his head, just once, before he dropped like a stone beneath the water. The massive grey vessel powered on and, in the next instant, darkness returned. Pearl heard only the whining of the border control boat's engine as it separated her, for the very last time, from James Moore.

Chapter Twenty-Three

Eight days later

It was late morning on a summer's day in Whitstable like any other. Pearl was just one person in the stream of locals and visitors flowing along the busy High Street towards the beach. Before reaching it, she stopped, and stood her ground, allowing the human current to move on without her: shrieking teenagers, tourists with cameras, lovers arm in arm, parents shepherding children carrying plastic buckets and spades; all in anticipation of a fresh incoming tide.

Pearl watched them go and turned back instead towards a tall building, with a timber roof shaped like the hull of an upturned boat. Heading into the foyer of The Horsebridge cultural centre, she paused yet again, this time to gaze through the glass door of the art gallery on the centre's lower floor. There she saw a painting on the opposite wall – *Undertow* by Dolly Nolan. The Whit

Fest exhibition would continue for just a few more days, before the painting disappeared, off to the town of Borken in Germany, to its new owner, Laurent Ruppert – a man forever bound to Whitstable by a tragic connection . . .

Pearl took a deep breath and headed on up the stairs and into the bar where, on the balcony, someone sat at a table, face buried in a newspaper. Pearl took a seat opposite Lucy Walker. 'Thank you for asking me here,' she said gently.

Lucy looked up and met Pearl's gaze and offered a sad smile. 'Why wouldn't I?' she asked. 'Are you OK?'

Pearl nodded and managed a smile for the girl, who explained: 'I . . . just wanted to thank you. For everything.' Her brow furrowed as she went on. 'And for trying to save James, though I'm sure it was his own decision to let go.'

Pearl took this in and nodded slowly. 'I think Blake Cain might have made the same decision,' she said softly. 'If truth be known, perhaps he would never have wanted to see his autobiography published – which is why he may have baited so many people on that launch night of the festival.' She leaned forward and poured herself a cup of tea from the pot already on the table.

Lucy watched her keenly. 'You knew it was James, didn't you? That day at the east quay?' She paused for a moment, then: 'How?'

Pearl looked away, knowing that in the last few days she had thought of little else. 'I told you,' she began. 'For some time I'd got caught up in thinking that because Blake's time on the Riviera had coincided with Wibke's university education in Nice, they might very well have met – and even have had a relationship. But that blinded me to something else that Wibke had told me – Blake had studied at Oxford, and though James was from Norwich, I'd seen a photograph of his mother at a Banbury village fete, and I then remembered that Banbury is only half an hour by road, north of Oxford. James had told me that his mother had died two years ago from cancer. I had checked the details on his mother's death certificate so I knew he hadn't lied about that, but after Vesta Korbyn's sudden arrest, I'd become distracted . . . until my own mother's bad German set me back on the right track.'

Lucy frowned. 'What d'you mean?'

'Well,' said Pearl. 'When I heard the word, *Zwilling*, I realised this is what Wibke had been trying to explain to me on the phone just before she was murdered. She had seen a woman, dressed in white, in the garden of the house – not Beacon House, but Alegría. When I asked her if it could have been you, she had said that the woman she had seen was dark-haired. But she wasn't saying, "she's willing", as I had thought. She was distressed and so using her own language, the word, "*Zwilling*", or twin. Coming into the garden at Alegría in order, perhaps, to take a photograph of herself at Blake's studio – a selfie – she had also come upon someone in the annexe, and might well have thought she was looking at

James's dark-haired female twin – not James himself. Wibke was a polite woman, gentle and modest. She made her excuses and left but, as James confessed to us, he followed her, heard her on the phone to me – and murdered her before I had time to reach her.'

Pearl paused as Lucy looked away. 'It doesn't help for you to know that you were the reason James decided not to give himself in, after having played cat and mouse with the police – and me. It was also a terrible irony that it was you, Lucy, who had pointed out to me that Blake's murder had been a ritual execution – to avenge a woman's dishonour: the dishonour of Rose Moore, James's mother.'

Lucy looked down, reflecting for a moment on all she had just heard. Pearl continued gently. 'I realise that a lot of this may take time for you to come to terms with, Lucy. Like a . . . pebble tossed into a still lake, these murders have had an effect upon us all.'

Lucy nodded. 'Yes.' The girl took a deep breath before continuing: 'Yes, you're right, Pearl – which is why I'm going away.'

Pearl looked up quickly and set her cup back down on the table as Lucy explained. 'I'm taking up the offer of a job in London. It's only another local newspaper, but at least I'll be in the capital, and it might just lead to something else.' She managed a sad smile, then: 'I know I could write this story, *my* side of the story, and sell it – perhaps for a lot of money? But I don't want to. I need to concentrate on doing some good work.'

'And you will,' said Pearl. 'I've no doubt about that. I told you, you've got all the makings of a good investigative journalist.' She paused. 'Or even . . . a detective?'

At this, Lucy slowly shook her head. 'I don't think so,' she said firmly. 'If I had, maybe I'd have seen through James – and I didn't. It was you who did that.' She paused then reached behind her chair for a large white paper carrier bag. 'I wanted to give you something before I left.' She smiled now and handed the bag to Pearl.

'What's this?'

'A present,' said Lucy. 'To say thank you. For everything.' She paused. 'Just one condition, Pearl. Open it once I've gone?'

Pearl nodded and met Lucy's gaze. At that moment, she felt there was so much between them that was being left unsaid, but for the first time in a very long while, Pearl was actually lost for words. Lucy got to her feet and Pearl quickly followed. The girl embraced her warmly, her cheek resting for a moment on Pearl's shoulder as she whispered, 'Goodbye.' Then she quickly freed herself and headed out of the bar.

Pearl sat slowly down again, and for a moment allowed herself to remember another evening, not too long ago, when a group of people had gathered in this same place on the very same balcony, for the opening event of a local festival. The evening had ended in tragedy but, looking around The Horsebridge bar, Pearl saw that all the tables were filled – with visitors, holidaymakers and some familiar local faces, including a toupeed Councillor 'Ratty' Radcliffe, holding court before a middle-aged couple who looked as though they would rather be elsewhere. In spite of all the recent tragedies, life was still going on.

With that thought, Pearl now reached for the white paper bag at her feet and parted the lilac-coloured tissue paper she found inside. She saw a fold of white crepe fabric, and some pretty shell buttons . . . Getting to her feet, she moved quickly to the rail of the balcony, and leaned across it to catch sight of Lucy Walker crossing the piazza below. 'Lucy!'

On hearing her name, the girl looked up, and back at Pearl. The bright smile on her face suddenly reminded Pearl of another young woman, twenty years ago, who had set off from Whitstable, equally buoyant, with a dream of her own. Pearl had returned with her own dream unfulfilled, but as she watched Lucy vanishing into a crowd of tourists, she smiled to herself and whispered softly: 'Good luck.'

A few moments later, Pearl stepped out of the air-conditioned hallway of The Horsebridge and on to the warm street. Then she headed directly towards the sea, and soon found herself at the harbour, at a spot on the south quay known as Deadman's Corner. It had gained its name because it was said that all those who drowned in these waters eventually washed up here – including the body of a young man who had recently lost his life in the harbour, though whether by accident, or his own free will, it was impossible to be sure. One thing Pearl knew was that it would be all too easy for a coroner to determine James Moore's death as simply the result of a young man's disturbed mind. To Pearl it was infinitely more complex, since it concerned the deep love a boy held for his mother, and his passionate need to exercise justice in her name. He had done so, with tragic consequences – not just for Blake Cain, but for James himself, and for an innocent woman called Wibke Ruppert. Perhaps, thought Pearl, things could have been so different if Blake Cain had been told, years before, that he was, in fact, a parent himself: the father of a son born to a woman who had held on to a secret for far too long; the secret of her son's true identity, and the enduring love she had harboured for the man who had deserted her when she had needed him most . . .

Across the harbour entrance, Pearl saw a banner for Whit Fest still fluttering in the warm breeze. Soon it would be replaced by one for the town's Oyster Festival, because time could not stand still, and like Khayyam's moving finger, it was writing a new future even now. Pearl paused to remember the fateful day she had crossed a beautiful garden to find Blake Cain murdered, executed at his own desk in a studio he had constructed to keep him facing the light. It had been another day, like this one, on which the sun had shone and music had filled the warm air – a chorus from an opera in which the young son of Cio-Cio-San goes on to live with his father, Lieutenant Pinkerton. James Moore had chosen a different ending for his own life and drowned, like the Samurai women of old who could not live with dishonour. But Pearl only hoped that three spirits might now be reunited in a happier place – Blake Cain, Rose Moore and their son, James.

It was at that moment that Pearl saw McGuire, waiting for her at the end of the harbour's south quay, just as he had promised he would. He was no longer dressed formally but in a pale blue T-shirt, jeans and trainers, looking younger and more vital – as though a heavy load had been lifted from his shoulders. She ran to him and asked breathlessly, 'Did you get them?'

McGuire's hand moved to his back pocket and he took out a paper wallet, which he handed to her. After reading the details on the two tickets inside, Pearl looked back at him. 'Three nights . . . in Paris?' She looked at him askance. 'Are you sure we won't be spied on by Bosley?'

'Definitely not,' McGuire assured her. 'She's in London – on secondment to the Met. I think she might even try for a permanent transfer – *if* she can jump through the necessary hoops.'

'You mean, she may even get your old job?'

'She's welcome to it,' smiled McGuire. 'Meanwhile, you and I leave tonight – at eight.' His strong hand framed Pearl's face as he leaned forward and kissed her, but she quickly pulled away as she suddenly realised: 'Eight o'clock? But I need to pack!'

'Not yet,' he insisted. 'Come on.' He took her hand

firmly in his own, leading her quickly beyond the harbour stalls selling fresh oysters to eat on the hoof.

'Where are we going?'

'Be patient. Wait and see.'

'But . . .'

Pearl broke off as they rounded the next harbour stall and she saw a figure standing on the quay. For a moment, with his fair hair blowing in the breeze, it seemed she was looking at an afterimage of James Moore, but then the young man turned, as though sensing she was approaching, and Charlie's face broke into a smile. Pearl moved quickly to her son and held him tight, lost in the moment, before she broke away and looked up at him. 'How did you get back?'

He nodded towards McGuire. 'Mike picked me up from Canterbury West station. There *are* trains from Poole, you know.' Seeing Pearl's smile fade, he said softly. 'It's OK, Mum, Gran's told me about what happened, and Mike's explained about this trip to Paris.' He smiled. 'I'm glad you're taking it.'

Relieved, Pearl returned her son's smile then suddenly asked: 'Have you eaten?' Charlie shook his head.

'Well, let's get back to the restaurant,' she said.

But McGuire stopped her. 'No,' he said quickly.

Charlie joined in. 'Not today, Mum.'

Instead, McGuire and Charlie pointed across towards the Harbour Garden restaurant on the south quay, where a figure was already seated at a table in the sun, face obscured by the restaurant's large menu. As it lowered, Dolly became visible, her fringe newly coloured a vivid pink.

'I've ordered paella,' she announced. 'It's on today as the special, and it will make . . .' Pearl braced herself, prepared for her mother to refer to McGuire as the 'Flat Foot', or perhaps even to offer a general dig at the police, but instead she went on: 'the perfect family lunch.' She smiled sweetly now, as if on her very best behaviour, and patted the chairs surrounding her. 'Charlie. Pearl.' Then she paused for moment, clearing her throat, before adding, politely: 'Mike?'

Pearl recognised a détente was in place, perhaps instigated by Charlie. She smiled as McGuire motioned for her to take her seat first, but then she stopped in her tracks as she suddenly heard an all-too-familiar sound behind her. Staring quickly back towards the harbour, she saw the strong wake from a passing speedboat washing up hard against the quay. Instantly, a series of images flooded her brain: the grey prow of a border control boat, a young man desperately swimming towards her before shaking his head and sinking beneath the dark water, a black spiral in Dolly's painting . . . But whatever resonance the sound of a speedboat's engine had for Pearl in that moment, she chose to let it go. Freeing herself from the undertow of this case, she resurfaced back into the present and turned her face away from Deadman's Corner and towards what she knew she treasured above all else – life and love.

'Come on,' she said. 'Let's eat.'

Author's note:

The importance of location in the Whitstable Pearl Mysteries

Many authors invent fictional locations for their detectives, but I chose a real place – my adopted home town of Whitstable, where I've lived for the past twenty years.

W. Somerset Maugham wrote about the town in two of his novels, *Of Human Bondage* (1915) and *Cakes and Ale* (1930), but he referred to it as 'Blackstable', and it's been suggested that he did so because he had an unhappy time there. I don't know if that's true, but I do know that, in writing the Whitstable Pearl Mysteries, I wanted to pay tribute to the town I love and to celebrate it by using its own name.

Whitstable is a quirky place with an independent, anti-establishment spirit, which I feel may be due to its old smuggling history. But it's also quintessentially English and full of interesting characters – the perfect location for my books.

Growing up as a child in a very rundown part of the East End of London, the world was opened up to me by reading books in our public library – particularly those of the Golden Age of Detective Fiction, which made use of exotic locations and fine country houses.

My upbringing may have helped me to go on to write the fictional TV world of *EastEnders*, but it was from reading crime novels such as Agatha Christie's *Murder in Mesopotamia*, *Death on the Nile* and *A Caribbean Mystery* that I came to appreciate the importance of location and how readers can be transported to other worlds simply by turning the pages of a book.

For that reason, I remain a fan of writers who make great use of location in their work, notably Donna Leon, whose Commissario Brunetti novels are set in Venice, and the American writer Stephen Dobyns, who brings alive the Saratoga Race Course in his Charlie Bradshaw crime novels.

I love the idea of location becoming almost another character in a novel, and I'm lucky to be able to feature not only a seaside location here in Whitstable, but also beautiful local countryside and the great city of Canterbury just a few miles away.

I know many readers will never be able to visit Whitstable in person, but I hope that reading my books will allow them to feel they can still enjoy a welcome break here on our mysterious coast . . .

Acknowledgements

With each new Whitstable Pearl Mystery, my list of Acknowledgements grows longer because, thankfully, so many kind people come forward each time to help with the creation of a new book.

This time I'd like to thank Roger and Linda Annable, and Karin Else and Reinhard Elsing, for providing me with inspiration for a plot featuring Whitstable's twinning association with Borken.

My thanks also go to Karen Penn Simkins for assistance with research for the location known as Alegría, and Katrina Brown for help with the location known as Beacon House, as well as to Mavernie Cunningham for allowing me to use her poem, 'Hair', part of a collaborative work known as *Dark Light*, by Mavernie Cunningham and Chris Hunt.

I am also grateful to Brian Hitcham for all his technical support and to George Begg and everyone at Samphire restaurant for transforming the latter into The Whitstable Pearl restaurant during the WhitLit Food Festival – complete with a stunning seafood menu – and to my dear friend, Victoria Falconer, for suggesting that idea, and for all the hard work she puts into the WhitLit and WhitLit Food festivals.

A big hug goes to Lisa Cutts for being such a great crime writer and for partnering me for a series of very enjoyable author talks last year; and to Dan Harding and Karen Marwood, my sincere thanks for much-appreciated support and reviews.

I'm also very grateful to George Galloway for his wonderful comments about the series and kind invitations to me to talk about the books on his shows, and I remain forever grateful to Dominic King at BBC Radio Kent for his unfailing support for the series – from the very first book.

Thanks also to Astrid Ruppert and Dagmar Voss for help with German translation, to Dr Coral Jones for medical advice, as well as her fantastic campaigning for the NHS, and to all at Harbour Books in Whitstable.

I owe a huge debt of gratitude to Krystyna Green at Little, Brown and everyone at Michelle Kass Associates for making this series possible – as well as to all my readers for their kind comments and support throughout the year.

Finally, lots of love (and apologies) to my husband

and family, who have seen practically nothing of me all year while I've been writing *Murder Fest*. They can, at least, now see what I was up to – and I hope they don't guess whodunit . . .